"I have no sons."

Something in his tone pulled at her heart, destroying the heat of her anger. Quickly, Roanna tried to tell herself that his lack of sons was none of her concern, that nothing about him was any of her concern.

Emryss straightened slowly and regarded her, his lips a hard line in his face. "I don't need anyone's pity. I have no sons because I have no wife. With little wealth, a small estate and this face, who would have me?"

"As if all women want are money and handsome faces!" she said, for once not stopping to consider her words.

As his lips curved into a smile, the import of what she had said grew clear. Roanna clapped her hand to her lips as the blood rushed to her face. Emryss came toward her, a gleam in his eye....

Dear Reader,

When I first wrote *A Warrior's Heart,* I had no idea that I was creating a couple who would come to be such a part of my writing life. Sure, I loved Emryss DeLanyea, with his one eye and indomitable spirit, and I thought he deserved the stoic, determined Roanna. I enjoyed doling out justice to the evil Cynric and felt sorry for the young woman he impregnated.

Little did I know, however, that I loved the DeLanyeas so much, I couldn't stop writing about them. What would Emryss and Roanna's children be like? Given his heritage, how did Cynric's illegitimate child turn out? What about little Hu, the shepherd boy who worships the ground Emryss walks on?

Fortunately, Tracy Farrell, the senior editor of Harlequin Historical, liked the DeLanyeas, too. Harlequin has now published fourteen Warrior books. Of course, Emryss and Roanna are not the main characters anymore. That role has fallen to their children and foster children, and now those characters are having babies of their own.

Yes, that's right. My Emryss is a grandpa...and it looks good on him!

Frankly, I don't think Tracy Farrell expected so many Warrior books, either, when she gave me the thrill of a lifetime by offering to buy *A Warrior's Heart* in 1991. I'm wondering if she realizes I'm planning to keep writing about the DeLanyeas for as long as I can type....

Best,

Margaret Moore

MARGARET MOORE

A Warrior's Heart

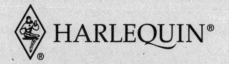

HARLEQUIN®

TORONTO • NEW YORK • LONDON
AMSTERDAM • PARIS • SYDNEY • HAMBURG
STOCKHOLM • ATHENS • TOKYO • MILAN • MADRID
PRAGUE • WARSAW • BUDAPEST • AUCKLAND

ISBN-13: 978-0-373-36155-7
ISBN-10:   0-373-36155-6

A WARRIOR'S HEART

www.eHarlequin.com

Printed in U.S.A.

MARGARET MOORE

Award-winning author Margaret Moore began her career at the tender age of eight, when she and a friend would concoct stories featuring a lovely damsel and a bold, handsome thief who naturally fell in love. Later, Margaret studied English literature at the University of Toronto and graduated with distinction with a bachelor of arts degree. She was also a Leading Wren with the Royal Canadian Naval Reserve.

Margaret sold her first historical romance, *A Warrior's Heart,* to Harlequin Historical in 1991. Since then she has written over twenty books for Harlequin, and her work has been published in fourteen countries around the world. Margaret has also written historical romances for Avon Books and a young adult historical romance for HarperCollins Children's Books. She now writes exclusively for HQN Books.

Margaret has been a *Romantic Times BOOKreviews* finalist for Career Achievement in Medieval Historical Romance, and has won an award for Best Foreign Historical from *Affaire de Coeur.* She's given workshops at Romance Writers of America national conferences, Toronto Romance Writers and the Canadian Authors Association.

When not writing, Margaret updates her blog and Web site at www.margaretmoore.com, which she designed. Margaret lives in Toronto, Ontario, Canada, with her husband of more than twenty-five years. Her two children have grown up understanding that it's part of their mother's job to discuss non-existent people and their problems.

With special thanks to my family and friends
for their support and encouragement,
especially Bill, Steven and Amy.
And to Cheryl Coke Breton,
who persuaded me to read historical romances.

Chapter One

Wales, 1201

"Not changed much, has he?" The tall warrior, kneeling on a rocky outcrop, turned to his foster brother, paying no attention to the rain dampening his leather jerkin and leggings or the cold breeze blowing against his bare arms and head.

Below, a small cortege of mounted shapes in water-soaked cloaks, two creaking, ancient carts and several foot soldiers moved slowly along the muddy road.

The tall one made a short sound of derision as his gaze followed the man at the head of the procession. "Cynric still rides as if he's got a lance up his—"

"Emryss!" his short stocky companion exclaimed, smothering a hoot of laughter.

"God's wounds, Gwil, mail, I was going to say. Like an old woman you are sometimes." He nodded at the small figure covered in a dark cloak who rode a swaybacked nag. "That must be the bride. Rides like a sack of apples, she does. He can't be marrying her for the way she sits a horse, or my sight's worse than I know."

Adjusting the patch over his empty eye socket, Emryss grinned at his foster brother. On another battle-seasoned warrior approaching his thirtieth year, a grin might have looked absurd. But, as Gwilym had good cause to know, a grin from Emryss was more likely a sign of trouble to come.

"She's not got a big dowry, either," Gwilym said, already worrying about what Emryss was really up to. Even Emryss's long-delayed return had not lessened his hatred for the DeLanyeas of Beaufort. Gwilym spoke quickly, hoping to be gone. "The blacksmith's daughter's mother-in-law goes to the market at Beaufort. Rumor is the dowry's pitiful."

"She's beautiful, then?"

"No, that's the wonder of it. Sickly-looking and thin as a stick, they say. But now you've seen for yourself, so let's be gone."

"Not like Cynric to marry one such as that," Emryss said slowly. "What's the rest of the tale, Gwil?"

Gwilym stifled an exasperated sigh as he sat back on his haunches. At least the column below was moving into the woods. "It's the old baron made the match. Her uncle—that's the one beside Cynric, looks like a buzzard—he's in with the court, and they need a friend there."

Emryss pointed at a warrior riding beside the bride. "And who's that, now, the one with the dark hair looking about like he's expecting trouble?"

"Fitzroy. Got to watch him, Emryss. Good fighter."

"Where's he from?"

Gwilym shrugged his shoulders. "Nobody knows. He fights for pay, that's all we heard."

Emryss nodded thoughtfully, then got to his feet as the last soldier disappeared in the trees. "Not surprised Cynric has to hire his soldiers. No doubt the man's wanted for murder or some such thing." Reaching up, he pulled off the patch and stuffed it into his belt. "Well, Gwil, time to let my dear cousin see I'm home."

"You're mad, Emryss." Gwilym stood up hurriedly, trying not to look at the red puckered welt that marred Emryss's face. "Thinking you'll just walk up and give him good day? He hates your entrails, man. He'll have you killed on the spot."

"Oh, I doubt that, not with his future bride to impress. And I thought I'd say the good day in Welsh. He'll like that, I'm sure."

Gwilym shook his head as Emryss mounted slowly, carefully lifting his left leg into place. "Madness. Going to let him see what happened to you already?"

Gwilym could have bitten off his tongue as he saw Emryss's face harden.

"He won't know about the leg. I can manage that. And as for my face, I'm for letting him know I wouldn't let a Saracen kill me. Not while I still had a score to settle with the Beaufort men."

Gwilym nodded and mounted his horse. "Right, then, Emryss. I'm with you."

"They're barbarians, the whole stupid lot," Cynric DeLanyea complained, his voice like the whine of an insect in Lord Raynald Westercott's ear. "I can't understand why the king bothers with this wilderness anyway. All it's good for is raising stinking sheep. And stinking peasants."

Westercott turned his hawklike nose toward Cynric and smiled wanly. He was beginning to grow tired of the younger man's complaints, but he didn't want to risk any antagonism until his dowerless niece was married and mercifully out of his hands at last. "Well, my lord, surely the wool is good for something. Your father doesn't seem to have suffered for being a baron here."

"He finds certain…compensations," Cynric replied, his

smile causing even Westercott, who was not a perceptive man, to feel uneasy. He had heard, of course, that these DeLanyeas spent their money satisfying a number of lusts of the flesh; that was why they were so ruthless in the demands they made of their tenants.

Now they needed any and all support they could muster at the court of the new king, John—so much so that the Baron DeLanyea was willing to marry off his son to get it. Well, at least the baron's foolhardiness had provided a means to be shed of his troublesome niece. The girl was always wandering about his household like some kind of restless spirit, appearing when he least expected her to, and he had despaired of ever finding anyone willing to take her off his hands.

"You spoke, my lord?" Cynric asked when Westercott's self-satisfied sigh interrupted the quiet sound of the rain pattering on the trees.

"I fear the rain is beginning to fall more heavily. Is it far, now, to Beaufort?" Westercott asked. The hour was growing late, as his stomach was beginning to remind him.

"No. We shall be there before nightfall."

Westercott nodded, turning to glance toward the wagons following. He frowned at Roanna, who looked like a wet chicken. God's wounds, he would be a happy man when she was well wed.

"A pity there was no convent near your estate," Cynric said quietly, following his gaze. "It would appear your niece would make a fine nun."

Westercott turned, and saw the distaste evident on the bridegroom's features. He cleared his throat. "The thought did occur to me, but it costs quite a sum. Nevertheless, I was about to make such arrangement when your father…" He coughed. "I thought it much better that Roanna provide a means for us all to benefit, eh, my lord?"

Before Cynric could comment, a crow suddenly flew up in the the gray sky, cawing harshly.

Lady Roanna Westercott clutched her reins and looked about. The foot soldiers, well-armed and clearly nervous, stopped and scanned the trees.

"For God's sake, it's only a bird," Cynric barked, eyeing them all coldly as he twisted in his saddle. His blue eyes narrowed, and his thin lips frowned.

Roanna saw the blatant displeasure in her future husband's features as he looked at her dripping form.

"Not even a band of Welsh thieves would be stupid enough to attack us, you fools."

With the skill born of much practice, Roanna composed her features into a mask of calm placidity. She had heard the men talk of the daring boldness of the Welsh against the Normans, whom they considered invaders even yet. Still, Cynric was a proud, boastful man who would no doubt take it amiss if his future bride contradicted him. She would have to tread very carefully around her betrothed, of that she was certain.

She knew everything about the bargain her uncle had made for her—that the DeLanyeas had accepted a paltry dowry that was virtually an insult to her; that the baron was so mired in trouble with the Normans as well as the Welsh that her uncle would have to call in many debts to bolster support for his new relations; that the DeLanyeas were guilty of heinous crimes against their tenants; that Cynric DeLanyea was notorious for his seduction of women, whether highborn or low; and that the foot soldiers were laying bets that Cynric would not consummate the marriage unless he was almost senseless with drink.

There was nothing she could do now, even if she wanted to. Her uncle had made a contract, and honor demanded that she fulfill it.

The rain began to fall more quickly, and the horse's

hooves made loud sucking noises with each step. Roanna pushed back her soaking hood, but all she could see up ahead was muddy road and dripping trees.

A brief, impatient gesture from her uncle told her that he was thinking of his next meal and paying no attention to whatever Cynric DeLanyea was saying. She hoped they had not much farther to go, or they would all come down with chills from the continual cold rain.

As the wooden cart that contained her meagre dowry and few articles of clothing hit a rock with a loud thud, Roanna glanced over her shoulder. Two brawny cartiers, Normans from the DeLanyeas' estate, jumped down to move the stone. Putting their shoulders to the heavy wagon, they began to push it out of the mud.

Suddenly Cynric reined in tightly. Roanna glanced around and saw Fitzroy draw his sword from his scabbard with one swift motion. Her uncle's fat mare whinnied in protest as he tried to force her backward. The soldiers pulled out their swords, moving closer together.

Craning her neck and trying to stifle the fear welling in her throat, Roanna cautiously nudged her horse toward Fitzroy, who she was sure would be the best fighter.

Then she saw the reason they had stopped.

A lone man sat on a huge black horse, seemingly oblivious to the rain that dripped off his helmet onto the leather jerkin beneath. The helmet covered his head completely, with two narrow slits to see out of. It was old but well-polished and probably stolen. Droplets of rain shone on his bare arms, for he wore no tunic or shirt. His long muscular legs were sheathed in leather and wool. One ankle rested casually on the knee of his other leg, and his dangling foot moved up and down as if beating time to some unheard song.

Roanna let out her pent-up breath slowly. He was easily

outnumbered by Cynric's soldiers. Only a fool would try to rob them single-handedly.

Nevertheless, Cynric pulled out his sword. Instantly something hissed past Roanna. She stiffened as an arrow quivered to stillness in the tree beside her. Gripping her reins, she looked at the trees. Clearly this man was not alone after all.

The man chuckled as he slid from his horse, his broadsword slapping against his thigh.

"Dydd da ich!" he called out, his voice light as if he were saying something vastly amusing.

Roanna looked quickly from Cynric to the man. The stranger must be mad.

The stranger approached Cynric's horse, coming to a stop only a few feet away from Cynric's knees. "What, Cynric," the man said, his voice deep and with a hint of laughter. "No Welsh yet, and no manners, either?" He put his hands on his narrow hips.

"What do you want?" Cynric demanded.

"A pity, such rudeness," the stranger continued. "Thought you might be a little more polite to an old friend." Then he reached up and slowly drew off his helmet.

A brutal red scar ran from his forehead through the empty eye socket almost to his ear. His straight nose and strong jaw were untouched by the ragged welt that puckered the right side of his face.

Cynric's mouth fell open. The heavy silence went on until the man threw back his head and laughed.

Roanna stared in unconcealed wonderment. What kind of man could survive a wound like that and *enjoy* the shock on people's faces when they saw it? As she watched the man, his lips curved slowly into a smile, but not before she caught a glimpse of a naked hatred at odds with the smiling countenance.

"We thought you dead," Cynric said at last, his voice strained.

"Well, Cynric, as you can see, I am not." The stranger's voice was steady, with an undercurrent of scorn, and Roanna realized that somehow Cynric had lost.

"Still, I didn't come to exchange pleasantries with you, boy. Came to see the bride of Beaufort, me."

Roanna's breath caught in her throat as the man chuckled and walked past Cynric. Her betrothed made no move to stop him, but only glared impotently as if he were afraid.

She looked desperately toward her uncle from beneath her lowered lashes, but he was pale and shaking and incapable of helping her. Even Fitzroy moved away a little as the man approached her. She stared down at the white knuckles of her tightly clasped hands, not knowing what else to do.

The stranger's feet stopped beside her horse. "This must be the lady." His deep voice seemed at once interested and intimate. Taking a deep breath, she summoned her courage, made her face a careful blank and looked at him, determined that he would not see her fear.

Slowly he smiled, the action dimpling the sun-darkened skin of his cheeks. Tendrils of brown hair curled on his forehead above the small wrinkles at the corner of his good eye as he gazed at her as if he could see into her very soul.

For a long moment all her concentration focused on the man before her, every sense trying to find his measure. What she saw was a man who had known great pain and suffering. But it had made him strong.

He turned to Cynric. "She's too good for you, boy, no doubt of it."

Roanna tried to subdue the pride that flew through her as he spoke, now all too aware of the stares of Fitzroy and the other soldiers. Pulling her cloak tighter, she hid the blush traveling up to her face.

The man turned and walked to his horse, his long legs covering the distance quickly. He moved with the innate grace of a well-trained warrior, yet she saw the subtle signs of tension and knew he was prepared to fight.

Roanna tried not to watch as he mounted his horse and placed his helmet on the saddle, yet she had to.

The stranger turned his horse, then glanced back. Without thought, she met his steady gaze.

Suddenly he punched the side of his horse with his heels and rode swiftly toward her. Before she could cry out, before Cynric or the others had any notion of what was happening, he grabbed her horse's bridle.

"Time for a lesson in Welsh customs, Cynric!" the man shouted as he spurred his horse and turned along a narrow path through the trees, pulling her horse behind him.

Desperately Roanna clutched the reins, struggling to avoid the low branches, a scream caught in her throat.

Her stomach churned like the mud beneath the horse's hooves. Wet leaves slapped her in the face. Branches caught her cloak, tearing and pulling it from her. Her horse's jolting strides made every breath difficult.

The man continued riding as fast as the underbrush would allow, paying no heed to the mud or rain or trees.

At last they came to a clearing, but still the man rode on, taking her farther and farther away from her party. They rode up a steep path and came to a meadow, where he spurred his horse into a gallop. Roanna felt her grasp slipping and clung tighter.

No. She had to get away. She had been wrong about him. He might even...

Taking a deep breath, she yanked her legs from the saddle and jumped.

She hit the ground with a thud, the air knocked from her lungs. She tried to breathe, but her body would not respond. Everything seemed to be turning around her, and she could hear nothing except a dull roaring sound. A searing pain gripped her chest as she tried to crawl under a bush.

Two long leather-wrapped legs stood before her, and two strong bare arms reached down for her. The one-eyed man hoisted Roanna to her feet.

"Let me go!" she gasped, fighting for breath.

He did, and she stumbled.

Quickly Emryss took hold of her arms again. He didn't want this girl with the amazing eyes to be hurt in any way while she was in his care.

She pushed away and stared at him. "Don't touch me," she whispered, her green eyes glittering like a cat's, but she made no move to run. If it were not for the fire in her eyes and the rapid rising and falling of her chest, she might have been a statue.

"A jest, is all," he said at last, awaiting the inevitable sobs of fear. "I won't hurt you."

"I would rather be dead than dishonored," she said. He was not surprised by the words but by the iron in the soft voice. This girl meant what she said.

"I give you my word that I won't harm you," he promised firmly. The suspicion in her eyes lessened slightly, and he felt strangely pleased.

"Then let me go."

"Thanking me I should think you'd be," he said. He tried to keep his voice light, but it wasn't easy with her steadfast gaze on him. "Only a fool would be happy to marry that lout, and you're no fool."

"You don't know what I want or even who I am." The girl straightened suddenly. The movement took him by surprise, as if a stone had come to life. She took a step toward him. "Take me back."

"Why should I? I wouldn't give a dog to Cynric De-Lanyea," he said.

"I am not a dog, nor am I yours to give." Her voice

rose, and her green eyes flashed with sudden fire. "If you have any honor at all, take me back to my betrothed."

The vein in his temple began to throb as he leaned toward her. "I don't take orders, my lady. Better get that in your Norman head."

She lowered her eyes and clasped her hands together. "Please."

He reached out and took her chin in his hand, forcing her to look at him. "Don't play the simpering girl with me, my lady. It doesn't become you."

By God, she looked at his face then!

He had seen the expression that sprang into her eyes before. In a battle. On a man's face.

His anger dissipated like the mist. In its place came regret, and a deep-seated wish that they had met in a different place at a different time.

"You can throw yourself to that lump of dung tomorrow. For now, you're coming with me."

She didn't move.

"It doesn't matter to me if you're so determined to marry Cynric, but I won't argue about it in the rain." With that he picked her up and carried her to his snorting, prancing beast, his strong arms holding her as if she were no more than a piece of fleece.

Once on the huge animal Roanna was too terrified of falling to do anything except hold on tightly. He climbed into the saddle so that she was in front of him, and his arms encircled her body like iron bands. Warm iron bands.

Roanna tried to remain perfectly still, even when the horse moved off slowly down a path she could barely see through the thickness of the trees.

"No jumping now."

She said nothing.

"Might have killed yourself. Better dead than married to Cynric, of course, but there's other ways to get out of it."

Roanna stiffened.

"Ah, maybe I'm wrong and you want to marry that *am-harchus ffieidd-dra?* I would have thought you were too smart to agree, despite his good looks."

His deep, soft voice, so close to her ear, seemed to force her to answer. "My uncle made a contract."

"But the lady in question has to agree."

"I have no choice."

"You agreed, then? Formally?"

"You don't know about such things."

His hands tightened on the reins in front of her. "If it pleases you to think so."

"You could not know the ways of the nobility."

"Couldn't I?"

Roanna decided at once to remain silent. Already she had said too much to this man—a thief at best and a rebel at worst—who had stolen her away from her betrothed and her uncle. She should be terrified of what he would do with her.

What was wrong with her, that she was not? Had the fall addled her wits?

The man spoke no more. Only the sound of the pattering raindrops and the noise of the horse's hooves disturbed the quietness of the forest as they rode on.

After a time they reached a small river. Willow trees bent over the rushing torrent of water. The bank was rocky and looked treacherous. Roanna's hands tightened on the saddle.

He nudged the horse forward. "Safer than it looks, my lady."

They crossed the river slowly, the horse stepping surely. Obviously this was a familiar way for them.

Once across, she spied a narrow path leading up through the trees. The horse turned toward it and they rode into a wood of willow, hazel, oak and pine. She tried to memorize

the way, in case she could somehow get free, but the path
was so narrow and the trees so close together that she realized it would be like trying to find a path through water.

The scent of wet leaves and pine needles was strong.
Chilling drops fell from the trees onto her. It took a considerable effort not to lean back against the man's warm,
hard chest, but that she would not do.

At the top of the hill the land flattened out into a plateau.
A stone-covered hill rose a short way in the distance, and
in the foreground Roanna saw some small, rough buildings.
A village perhaps.

As they got closer, she saw that it wasn't a village at all.
It was simply four huts, probably used by shepherds.

A dog barked a warning, and a few men, poorly dressed
in woolens and leather, came out. Two were no more than
lads, armed with short Welsh bows; another was an old
man, straight-backed and white-bearded. The others, seemingly empty-handed, looked like men more accustomed to
shearing than fighting as they raised their voices in greeting.

A stocky young warrior with thick black hair stepped
forward and took hold of the reins, looking up at her with
barely disguised loathing.

"God, *brawdmaeth,* what you brought her here for?"
Gwilym said in rapid Welsh, glancing up at Emryss.

"Because I wanted to," his foster brother replied. He
swung down from his horse, ignoring the girl for the moment. "Got a fire anywhere?"

"Over there," Gwilym replied, pointing to one of the
far huts.

"Right, Gwil." Emryss reached up to help the girl down.
He tried to ignore the soft, delightful pressure of her hands
on his arms.

"Come," he ordered in Norman French, taking hold of
her slender hand. It felt as fragile as a tiny bird in his palm,

until she pulled it away. Clenching his teeth, he took her hand and stalked toward the hut, half dragging her along.

God's blood, what was he to make of her, this woman who belonged to the man he despised?

No. What was he to make of himself? Just because of the way she'd looked at him, he'd taken her.

Perhaps he had imagined the shrewd thoughtfulness when she had stared at him before. Perhaps it was only that it had been too long since a woman had looked at him like that.

Lost in his thoughts, he didn't notice that the girl had to run to keep up with his long strides, her soaking gown slapping against her legs.

He pushed open the door to a small hut and yanked her inside.

A fire burning smokily in a shallow pit in the earthen floor made Roanna's eyes sting. She tugged her hand from her kidnapper's and stumbled toward a pile of straw. He made no move to help her this time, but waited until she had regained her balance. Then he slowly crossed his arms over his broad chest and spoke.

"Take off your gown."

Chapter Two

The thin old woman drew back from the narrow window. "Tch, Bronwyn! Fit enough to drown in and those two not back yet!" she said, her voice like a mill wheel in need of grease.

"They might be spending the night up in the hills, Mamaeth," the smiling brown-haired girl replied.

"Or Emryss has got in a fight or other such foolishness," Mamaeth muttered, peering out into the driving rain as if she could see beyond the half-completed fortress wall.

"Gwilym will make sure he doesn't."

Mamaeth shot the girl a knowing glance. "Since when has Gwil been able to stop Emryss? Especially when those Normans been concerned?"

Bronwyn sighed and looked up from her sewing. "Considering Emryss learned to hate all Normans except his da at *your* knee, I don't know why you're blaming Gwilym. He does his best, but it's *not* his place to order around the lord of the manor, as you well know."

Mamaeth looked as if she were contemplating a curse, but fear of the wrath of God held her tongue. She took a few steps toward the small brazier that provided some feeble light and warmth in the large chamber for the female servants of Craig Fawr. "Well, that's as may be," she said, lifting a corner of the linen the young girl was working on, "but he'd do better to leave off thinking of fighting and fortifications and start thinking about getting a wife."

Bronwyn chuckled softly. "I seem to recall you suggested that the first night he was home."

"Aye, and well I did. Your stitches are getting too wide, my girl."

Bronwyn checked her work, saw that Mamaeth's old sharp eyes had been correct, and delicately began pulling out her last few stitches. "Perhaps Emryss hasn't found a girl he likes."

"Him?" Mamaeth cackled. "He's been chasing the girls since the time he was in breeches...and got more than one, too, though not one to brag, him." She stayed silent for a moment, but only for a moment. "Time to get the meal moving, or there'll be no supper tonight for those two, if they come home."

Bronwyn nodded. She, too, was worried about the two men, for she knew, whereas Mamaeth did not, that they had indeed ventured onto Beaufort land.

Mamaeth stalked from the room, her steps fast and light for one of her years. Looking after the interest of Emryss's widowed mother, and now Emryss, kept the old woman perpetually active. Bronwyn watched her leave, then sighed as she bent to her sewing.

Gwilym had not told her where they were bound because he knew of her feelings for him. No, it was only because she was close to Mamaeth, who guarded Craig Fawr like a faithful steward.

Perhaps some day Gwilym would see how much she loved him. Until then, she would carry his messages and pour his wine and keep her love in her heart.

"Fool! Oaf! Simpleton!"

The baron's bejeweled fist crashed down on the arm of

the huge oak chair, the action mirrored by a grotesquely huge shadow on the tapestries. As if trying to hear, the embroidered figures moved and whispered against the cold stone wall of the chamber.

Cynric brushed at the lank hair hanging on his forehead and opened his mouth to speak, but before he could, his father started shouting again. "How the hell could you let that one-eyed, crippled bastard take her from right under your nose? Or were you dwelling on your own looks so much you missed it?"

Cynric stared at the fleshy fist as it smote the dark wood again, suppressing an urge to shout back. When he had conquered such weakness, he let his gaze move upward, to the florid face and quivering jowls.

His father did not look well. Not at all. Perhaps he was ill. Now here was something to consider as his father continued his angry ravings.

"You let him and his shepherds beat you! We need that girl—or don't you want to hold on to your land?"

At the mention of land, Cynric's attention came back to the matter of the girl. Land was power, and he dearly wanted power. "You weren't there, my lord," he said sullenly. "It was impossible to tell how many men he had—and you know how those bumpkins can fight when they want to."

"I know how you're supposed to fight. You're not supposed to sit there like some woman, by God!"

Cynric pushed back his damp hair again. "There was no reason to risk my men."

Noticing how his father's chest heaved with every breath, Cynric realized that his father could die, right here, right now.

"No reason! He's only made you look like an ass! God's blood, I begin to think he's right."

"Why should I give a damn if he took that skinny, ugly hag out of my hands? I'd rather marry my horse."

The baron rose, looking at him ominously. Cynric felt afraid for an instant, but only for an instant. "I don't care if she looks like a corpse! You will get her back from him. You will marry her."

"Not if Emryss takes his pleasure of her."

"You know as well as I do that Emryss has never taken a woman against her will in his life." The baron crossed the floor and stood facing his son, his eyes narrowed into the fleshy folds of his cheeks. "Idiot! What would it matter anyway? What will be left for you if the king takes my land and gives it to another?"

Cynric's hand went to the hilt of his sword, but he smiled with his lips. "You're right, Father. What does it matter? As you yourself have so often said, one woman is like another in the dark, eh?"

The baron looked at his son suspiciously. "Aye, that's right."

Cynric spoke, but more to himself than his father. "If I agree to marry her, no one will dare to raise the question of rape."

His father nodded.

"Then I believe I will take her. Let Emryss have his little joke, but he won't laugh so hard when he realizes he's given me the perfect excuse to march onto his land."

"I begin to think I've underestimated you, my son," the baron said, looking at Cynric with new respect.

"Have you?" Cynric looked back and knew in his heart that it was already too late for his father to make amends. Much too late. Now he was simply a sick old man in the way of Cynric's plans. "I'll start the search at dawn."

Cynric didn't wait to hear his father's response, but walked out of the chamber and into the great hall. He went toward the dais and sat down. In his father's chair.

Suddenly heavy footsteps sounded at the entrance to the stone chamber. Cynric sat up quickly. A large shadow loomed on the wall, but when he saw the figure standing in the doorway that led to the kitchen, he slumped back in the chair.

"Who in God's name are you?" he demanded of the unfamiliar fat man.

"Jacques de la Mere, Lord Westercott's cook," the man said. "Please, my lord, when do you go to save Lady Roanna?"

"In the morning, I suppose," Cynric said, straightening his tunic. He had barely had time to get out of his muddy clothes before his father had sent for him.

"May I go with you?"

Cynric laughed cruelly. "A cook? What would you do, ladle them to death?"

Jacques drew himself up. "I would gladly strangle with my bare hands any man who has harmed her."

Cynric raised her eyebrow. "Would you? Well, I think we can retrieve her without such aid." The young lord stood up, pulled down his tunic and walked down the room toward the steps that went up to the sleeping chambers, brushing past the huge man.

Jacques slowly went back along the corridor to the kitchen. After the attack, he had expected to find the whole castle in an uproar, with soldiers preparing to ride out to save Lady Roanna. Instead, he had been shown the kitchen and told Lord Westercott expected his dinner at once.

This Cynric DeLanyea didn't even seem concerned about Roanna. Jacques' heart sank in his breast. She had seen enough troubles, and now this!

In the kitchen a scullery maid was halfheartedly scraping a large pot in the well-appointed, enormous room. The hearth fires had been banked, although a few glowing coals cast some dim light. The room was quiet, for all the other servants had retired for the night.

Jacques sat down on a bench alongside the wall and put his head in his hands. What was going to happen to Roanna? He was the only person who seemed to care about her fate at the hands of that miscreant.

The scullery maid cleared her throat. Jacques glanced at her. The pretty girl seemed to enjoy his scrutiny, adjusting the low bodice of her dress around her creamy shoulders. She tossed her head, sending her honey-colored hair dancing.

"Not worrying, I wouldn't be. He won't hurt her."

"Eh?" Jacques sat up.

She put down the pot. "Aye. Emryss DeLanyea won't hurt a woman."

"How do you know this? Isn't he an outlaw? Or a rebel?"

She laughed, showing fine white teeth. "Lord save us, no! The one that took her was Emryss DeLanyea. The baron's nephew."

"*Mon Dieu,* what kind of nephew is that?"

"Oh, they've always hated each other. But I was told by them as knows that Emryss DeLanyea never took a woman against her will." She came and sat down beside him on the bench. She continued, lowering her voice. "No need. There was plenty would give up the *amobr* for a night with him, I've heard."

He eyed her suspiciously. "Give up their what?"

The girl laughed kindly. "Money—for their maidenhead. Tch, foreigners!"

She sighed, apparently for opportunities lost, then went on before Jacques could reply. "Right handsome, they tell me he was—but I heard he looks frightful now?"

Jacques nodded. "His face is very scarred, yes."

"Sorry then I am. The lady'll be scared witless, not

knowing he used to treat women like they was all sacred or something.''

Jacques felt some of the worry drop and sat up a little straighter. "His face would not scare Lady Roanna. She is too courageous."

"Well, pardon me, I'm sure." The girl got up as if to go.

"Wait!" Jacques put his hand on her arm. "Sit…"

"Lynette."

"Lynette. Tell me about these people."

The maid hesitated. "Well now, I don't know as I should… There's them pots to be finished, and I'm parched with thirst as it is."

"Never mind the pots." Jacques heaved himself to his feet and went to the cupboard. He produced a bottle of wine and poured two cups full. Setting them on the long wooden table, he drew up the bench and pointed. The girl smiled and sat down, taking a quick sip of the wine. "Oh, that's nice, is that."

Jacques nodded and waited while she took another drink. "Well," she began when she saw that Jacques was not going to refill the cup just yet, "Emryss DeLanyea's mam, Angharad, was a Welsh princess, and a beauty, too. Dark hair, big eyes…and a mind of her own, they say. Well, the king took all the land from the Welsh, 'cepting one piece she could keep to give her husband…who had to be Norman. Not pleased she was, so I heard, until she met Ralf DeLanyea. Like Emryss, him. Tall, bold…a strong man for a strong woman. So they wed."

The girl coughed quietly and glanced at the cup. Jacques poured a little more wine. "Thank you, I'm sure. Well, that would have been that, except that Ulfrid DeLanyea, the baron now, decided he wanted Angharad for himself, marriage or no. Naturally the king was against that."

The girl lowered her voice to a whisper and leaned

closer. "But not stopping the baron, that. Tried to woo her away, married though she was. Anyway, it didn't work. But the baron's a vengeful man, and one day he come upon her and her ladies in the woods. He sent the women away. They got help, but not before the baron had beat her senseless. The families been at each other's throats ever since."

Jacques stared at her in dismay. His Roanna was going to marry into this?

"We all thought Emryss was long dead. He gone off to fight in the Crusade, and others come back, but not so much as a word about him. The baron wanted the land still, but Angharad was some woman—held onto the land like a vixen with a hen in her teeth. She died not long ago, and left that Mamaeth in charge. My God, she's tough. The baron went once to try to tell her the land should come to him, since Emryss was surely dead. She sent him back here right quick. Still, I think the old baron would have got his way at the last, if Emryss hadn't come home."

"How can you be sure this Emryss won't hurt Lady Roanna, if he hates the baron and his son so much? Might he not beat her in revenge? Perhaps he has changed..." Jacques paused as the cold weight of dread settled on him.

"Oh! Not thinking of that, me! Perhaps he has. He was a long time among the heathens. I hear they have strange ways." Her eyes gleamed as if she would like to know exactly what those ways might be.

Jacques stared at her. Cynric DeLanyea might be a conceited coward who ran off at the first scent of danger, but this Emryss DeLanyea was beginning to sound even worse.

Emryss strode across the small clearing to a hut at the other side. He didn't know whether he should curse or laugh at the impulse that had made him take Cynric's bride, but he had not reckoned on finding her such a proud, stubborn woman. He had been expecting some washed-out, simpering Norman girl.

With her big eyes and long hair, she looked like a lost child, until you got a good look. My God, she had iron in her heart, like his mother. How many other women, when a strange man asked them to remove their gowns, would stand and stare with such apparent loathing that he had been ashamed—even though, as he had told her, her wet gown would make her ill if she kept it on.

But unlike his mother, she would not be harmed by a relative with a grudge. He hoped the girl understood that now. Of course, taking the bride would make Cynric annoyed, and that had been the whole foolish goal of his action. As for the girl, he would return her tomorrow, with no harm done.

A flurry of Welsh curses greeted Emryss as he pulled back the cloth covering the doorway of the hut closest to the meadow.

"God's wounds, Emryss, already chilled to the bone I am!"

Emryss looked through the gloom to his foster brother, who crouched before a small fire.

"Leaving her alone, are you?" Gwilym asked, by his expression clearly sure that Emryss had taken complete leave of his senses since coming onto Beaufort land.

"Where are the others?" Emryss asked, avoiding the conversation he knew was coming. Although Gwilym was the younger and a bastard of unknown parentage, he considered it his job to remind Emryss that he should always take the baron and his son seriously.

"Gone home. No time to play your games."

"What about Hu?"

"Oh, he's still here. Can't understand the lad, but he won't leave if you're about. I sent him to take care of the horses."

"Let him watch the hut for a bit, then. Tell him he's the guard. Oh, and he can take her some bread and water. She's only a mite of a thing. He can call if she tries anything."

Gwilym passed him the wine and went to the door. He paused and turned back.

"Emryss," he said quietly, "what are you about, man? Only going to bid good day and let DeLanyea see you was still alive, we all thought. Then you made off with that woman."

Emryss rubbed the scar on his face. "What, Gwil, forgetting the ways of the Welsh? Turning Norman?"

Gwilym's eyebrow rose skeptically and he frowned.

"All right, then, *cyfathrachwr,*" Emryss said with a sigh. "I took a notion to do it. And no, not stopping to think." He shook his head briskly, sending drops of water flying, and ran his fingers through his tangled curls.

Gwilym went out, leaving Emryss to stare at the smoking fire. He took long gulps of the strong wine. Not stopping to think. How many things had he done in his life without thinking first? Too many, Gwilym would say. And yet, the girl had intrigued him. Any other woman would have collapsed in a heap of weeping and wailing, but she faced him like…well, like a man. And a quiet one, too. Maybe that's why he wanted to listen to every word she uttered.

Another gust of wind heralded Gwilym's entrance but Emryss, wrapped in his own thoughts, made no comment. Gwilym reached for the wine and sat down.

"He'll never forgive you this," he said, as if Emryss were a lad.

Emryss threw a stick into the fire and took the wine from him again. "Since when do I care whether Cynric forgives me anything or not?"

Gwilym nodded. "True, true. Is the poor girl terrified out her wits?" He took the wine and drank an enormous gulp of the red liquid.

Emryss shook his head. "Stronger than she looks, her."

Gwilym glanced at him and blinked.

Emryss grinned. He rubbed his scar again and spoke, his words slightly slurred. "A look from her could probably strike a man dead."

Gwilym chuckled, their camaraderie restored. "Just what we're wanting for Cynric, then. Poor fellow—and no meat on her bones, either. No wonder he's proper put out having to marry her. Thought you'd gone mad, when you grabbed her horse like that. Should have seen Cynric's face, boy!"

Emryss began to laugh, remembering Cynric's shocked expression at his sudden appearance on the road. It was easy to imagine his surprise at the old Welsh custom of kidnapping the bride. "You'd think he'd know something of the Welsh by now!" He wiped at his good eye, grinning broadly at Gwilym.

"Taking her back in the morning, are we?"

"Aye."

"Does she know who you are?"

Emryss's grin disappeared. "No, she'll find out soon enough, and that we're going to be related."

Gwilym chortled and stood by, swaying slightly. "Taking the first watch, me. Good night, my lord."

"Good night, Gwil."

Gwilym opened the door and left. Emryss shivered and tossed another stick onto the fire. He lay down, shifting his weight. Too much riding this day, he thought as he rubbed his aching leg. He wondered how *she* was faring, and hoped she wasn't chilled to the bone in the small hut. It would have been too far to go to Craig Fawr, especially when she was drenched with rain.

He hoped she had removed that heavy, ugly gown. Suddenly his breath caught at the sudden vision of masses of black hair around her flushed face, green eyes shining, her slender body beneath the wet clinging gown.

He moaned softly. Why couldn't the Saracen have damaged his imagination as well as his body?

He rolled onto his back and reached up to touch his scar, made sore by the pressure of his helmet. He didn't even know her name. Perhaps that was just as well.

Roanna fed another twig into the waning fire. She had no clear idea of the time, but it was getting colder by the minute. Her body felt as if it had been dipped in ice.

Surely Cynric would find her soon. She looked around at the wooden walls. It could be that Cynric wasn't looking.

Roanna laid her head on her knees and forced herself to face the truth. She didn't care if she never saw Cynric DeLanyea again, or heard his bragging, arrogant voice—except that what could possibly become of her if he didn't come to her rescue? Would this thief, this scoundrel who claimed to be only following a custom keep his word and take her back?

What was she to make of him? When she had refused to disrobe, he had only smiled and said, "Well, knowing how it feels to be at someone's mercy. Just not wanting you to catch your death of a chill. The gown will dry better off than on." And then he had left her alone in the hut.

Maybe her uncle would insist upon a search. Or maybe he would simply be glad to be rid of her, and no dowry to pay, either.

At least Jacques would be upset. He was only the cook, but he was her one friend in all the world. Had been since that first day he had found her crying behind the flour barrel and taught her how to make a roll. He frightened most people with his fiery temper and booming voice, but she would give anything to hear him now.

Suddenly she sat up. Someone or something was outside the door, quietly trying to get in.

She didn't want to think it could be the tall man, but

there were others in the camp who might have scores to settle with the Normans. Moving slowly until she felt the wall of the hut at her back, she waited, scarcely breathing, the hay tickling her nostrils as she tried not to sneeze.

A little boy, not more than eight years old, pushed through the tiny opening. He carried an earthen jug and a loaf of bread and set them down carefully while keeping his huge black eyes on her.

Roanna realized he was as frightened of her as she had been of the noises he made. "Thank you," she said softly.

The lad narrowed his eyes. He was not tall, but well-made, with particularly fine features that made her think of a cherub. "Emryss...says...you's to eat," he said in a voice that matched his angelic face. Roanna realized he spoke the words without understanding them, as a message memorized. She nodded and inched forward. Slowly she broke the bread in two, and offered him a piece.

He drew back as if she had moved to strike him. Then he gave her a parting look full of hate mingled with fear and went out. She would have given much to tell him he had no cause to feel that way in her presence. After all, she was the prisoner, not him.

But then she realized something that made her heart beat faster. The boy had not put back the block of wood on the other side of the door.

Chapter Three

Roanna hurriedly ate the bread and took a gulp of the fresh, cool water, all the while listening to hear if anyone else realized the boy's mistake. Apparently no one did, for after several minutes the camp was still quiet.

Caution counseled her to wait longer, but all she could hear were the sounds of horses stamping and snorting and the occasional call of a night bird.

Roanna moved slowly to the door and put her hand on the latch. With a gentle tug, she pulled it toward her—and it moved.

And then she heard a sound that made despair flood over her anew. Footsteps! Coming toward the hut.

Quickly she moved back, crawled into the straw and closed her eyes. Perhaps they had only come to assure themselves that she was still there.

The door opened. Then closed.

She opened her eyes cautiously.

The scarred man sat near the fire, his long legs stretched out in front of him, his broad shoulders resting against the rough wall. A dagger was thrust into his belt, and a sword lay beside him. Now a black leather patch covered his scar, and the other eye was closed. His chest rose and fell with his slow, even breathing.

She lay motionless, studying him as he rested as comfortably as if in a feather bed. What was he, Welsh or Norman, noble or common? He spoke like a Welshman, although his Norman was excellent and fluent. He might be a Norman, for he was taller than any of the other Welsh people she had seen. Yet he was so poorly dressed, and so familiar with the other men, that he must be Welsh. Then why wasn't he afraid of the more powerful Normans? It seemed Cynric DeLanyea was more frightened of him. She knew bandits had been harassing the Normans ever since they came to their country, but this man didn't seem like an outlaw.

What *was* he like? A bold warrior, well-trained, confident—and those scars could only belong on a man of such will that he would not succumb. She let her gaze travel down his robust body, from his marked yet compelling face, past the strong shoulders, down the wide expanse of chest and powerful arms that had held her as if she were goose down, to the long, lean, powerful legs.

Heat coursed through her veins, slowly moving outward like ripples in a pond. She shifted her legs, aware of a subtle throbbing of blood in a new place. The movement increased the pressure of the fabric across her breasts. She pulled her gaze from him.

Yet the scent of him, of horse and leather and rain-dampened hair, crept to her like smoke from a faraway fire.

She must escape. Her own traitorous body forced her to acknowledge the danger if she stayed any longer. This man tempted her, as surely as if she were Eve and he the serpent holding an apple. She must go, find a horse and get away.

Slowly she sat up, making as little noise as possible. The man remained asleep. She got up gingerly, picked up the cloak and folded it, laying it down in the straw before drawing her still-damp gown on.

Raising one foot carefully, she took a step. He didn't stir. She took another cautious step, and another, keeping her gaze fastened on the man. When she drew near his legs, she hesitated, for she would have to walk around them. She took a breath and lifted her foot.

"Leaving so soon?"

She almost fell over. He quickly got to his feet. She stepped back, watching him warily.

"I may have one eye, but it's a good one," he said. "And I must say I like what I see."

His smile was slow, as intimate as she imagined a lover's might be after a tryst. She stepped back.

Roanna tried to breathe normally as she struggled against the feelings that swamped her. He came closer.

"You gave me your word," she said, moving back.

He crossed his muscular arms over his chest. "So I did."

The smile died on his lips and his expression hardened. "Can't judge the mutton by the wool. Just because I look like something out of a nightmare doesn't mean I'm a fiend in human form."

She lowered her face as the heat of a blush rose to her cheeks. What would he do if he knew what she had been thinking only moments ago?

"Not fooling me with that," he said sharply. "Too late to play the mild maiden. More going on in that head than you want to let on."

Emryss looked at the woman standing before him like a post, head down, hands clasped.

Perhaps he had been wrong about her all along, and she was like every other well-trained noblewoman. Perhaps she thought only of making an advantageous marriage, and was worried that her plans were ruined.

God's wounds, he'd make her look at him again, even

if the sight of his face made her flesh crawl. "Tell me, my lady, do you always play the simpleton? Or only when it suits you?"

Instantly her head flew up and her eyes flashed. "Some men believe all women are fools. Who am I to tell them otherwise?"

Her green eyes shone with passionate fire and her chin jutted out, almost as if offering her lips for his kiss. "I beg your pardon, my lady," he said as he bowed, not taking his gaze from her indignant face. "Now I'm more sure than ever that Cynric's not the man for you."

What kind of man *was* this, Roanna thought. More anger welled up inside her as she looked at his grinning face. Her hands began to shake as she fought to suppress it, but all her usual rectitude had fled.

"Who are you to tell me whom I should marry? What can you know of my life, or any woman's?"

He reached out and touched her cheek, the gentleness of his action shocking her. "I know Cynric will make your life a misery."

Tears sprang to her eyes, but she blinked them back. "What else am I to do? An agreement has been made."

"Did *you* make it?" His voice was soft, and oh, so gentle.

"Honor demands that I keep the pledge of my uncle."

"But what do you want?" He moved closer, so close she could hear him breathe.

She knew she should back away, but she could not. "I...I..."

Before she could move, he took her in his arms. His lips brushed against hers, tasting, caressing as gently as a breeze across a meadow. He pulled her closer. Dizzying sensations traveled to every part of her body as the throbbing beat of her heart responded to his more insistent kiss. A need to touch moved her hands to his chest. Dimly aware of the hardness of his muscles beneath the rough tunic, and of his beating heart, she delighted in the slow movement of his lips over hers.

She would not have believed such pleasure existed. Not for her.

His kiss deepened, and he pressed her closer. His fingers played on the naked skin at the nape of her neck, and then she felt the lacing of her gown give way. The feel of his hand on the flesh of her back brought a low moan to her lips as she leaned into him, her legs trembling and weak, aware only of his lips and hands and her own growing need.

His tongue gently forced her lips apart, seeking the inner warmth of her mouth. The shock and surprise of his action forced awareness of what she was doing, and with whom. She pushed him away. "Please. Stop."

His smile was slow, enticing. "If you wish."

Her face burned with humiliation. She had acted no better than a whore with this stranger! She, Lady Roanna Westercott, so proud and honorable! She turned away, so ashamed she couldn't look at him.

He spoke softly. "A kiss is all. Nothing to cry about."

"I never cry." Her voice was firm. She turned back. "You can't understand." Her voice dropped to a whisper. "My honor is all I have."

Suddenly the lad stood in the doorway. The man turned to him with a brief smile and spoke softly, tousling the boy's curly hair. Anyone could see that the boy worshiped the warrior who towered over him. When the boy scampered off, he turned back to her.

"Is he your son?" she asked without thinking.

A strange expression crossed his face, then he bent to pick up the jug she had left beside the door. "No. I have no sons." Something in his tone pulled at her heart, destroying the heat of her anger. Quickly she tried to tell herself that his lack of sons was none of her concern, that nothing about him was any of her concern.

He straightened slowly and regarded her, his lips a hard line in his face. "I don't need anyone's pity."

Roanna tried to find the vestige of her anger that kept all other feelings at bay, but now it was gone. The silence grew between them, until he finally spoke. "I have no sons, because I have no wife. With little wealth, a small estate and this face, who would have me?"

"As if all women want are money and handsome faces!" she said, for once not stopping to consider her words.

As his lips curved into a smile, the import of what she had said grew clear. She clapped her hand to her lips as the blood rushed to her face. He came toward her, his eye gleaming.

She turned away and began fumbling with the laces at the back of her dress.

"Well, now, there's a pity. No woman in the camp to help." She heard the laughter in his voice, and it humiliated her even more. "Turn around." She heard the note of impatience in his voice and obeyed.

Surprisingly he took up the laces and began threading them through the small holes. She stiffened, trying to retain some semblance of dignity and not think about his fingers as they brushed the thin fabric of her shift and the naked skin at the back of her neck.

"There now," he said as he tied the knot. "It's been a time since I've done that." Roanna turned and eyed him warily.

Emryss suddenly felt as awkward as a lad with his first love. God's wounds, he'd better leave, if she kept looking at him like that. He hadn't meant to kiss her, but she had stared at him with those eyes...

"I want to go to Beaufort."

She would still marry Cynric. He should have known,

should never have gone near her, should have left her on the road. "Very well," he said crisply, "you shall. Now."

He left the hut, pulling the door closed with such force that the wood splintered.

"For God's sake, move or I'll have you whipped within an inch of your lives!" Cynric bellowed as his men hurried to mount their horses. He looked at the sky. For once the miserable weather in this godforsaken country was going to hold. How he hated this country, he thought for the thousandth time. He despised every tree, every rock, every stream and all the ignorant Welsh.

He spurred his horse toward the steps to the great hall of Beaufort, where his father and the girl's uncle waited.

"Don't bother to return if you can't find her," the baron growled. Lord Westercott glanced nervously at the baron and smiled placatingly at Cynric.

"I'm most certain, my lord, that you will find her if anyone can. Of course, I realize there may be... complications to the wedding arrangements, but I'm sure we can come to an agreement."

Cynric smiled slowly. Perhaps he could get the old buzzard to increase the dowry, especially if the girl was no longer a virgin.

"Have no fear, Lord Westercott. I will get her back."

He wheeled his mount and headed to the front of the column of glum-looking soldiers. Cynric almost laughed out loud. Emryss himself, brave, bold Emryss, had given him the perfect excuse to ride onto his land. Perhaps he would thank him, once he had defeated him.

The column rode quickly down to the river and followed the road along its banks. Cynric saw the deep ruts from the cook's cart, which had arrived late the night before.

He pulled hard on the reins, forcing his horse out of a muddy puddle. Damn this place, and damn his father for keeping him here. He'd never been to London, or to the court, and his request to go on the Crusade had been scorned.

"What?" the baron had screamed. "Waste my money and soldiers on some hellish desert? What's to be gained by that, boy?"

No talk of concern for his son's life, of course. Only money.

So he had endured listening to the people's endless praise of the valiant warriors going to save the Holy Land from the cursed infidel and their sly looks in his direction.

Then Emryss had returned, mangled but not broken, to be a thorn in his flesh again.

They came to a fork in the road, one way leading to the more populous south and the other to Emryss. Cynric raised his hand, and the soldiers rode to the north.

A short time later, three people rode along the path leading to Beaufort. Gwilym, riding silently and sullenly behind the girl, saw Emryss glance at her yet again. God's wounds, what had his foster brother done? Did he really think the baron would ignore this?

How could he ever explain to Emryss how much had gone on in his absence? The baron had learned to use money to influence the king and his court. Emryss would never understand the power wealth had, thinking only of valor and honor.

Gwilym had tried to explain the changes in the country in the past several years, but Emryss would not listen. The one time Gwilym had mentioned Richard's name, Emryss had cursed and told him never to speak of kings in his presence, especially that one.

Perhaps he wanted everything to be as it was before he had gone away. Perhaps, Gwilym realized as Emryss glanced at the girl again, he wanted to believe that *he* had not changed, either.

Gwilym could well remember how he would trot at Emryss's heels like a lamb as his foster brother strode through the village, tall, strong, confident, with a smile that warmed even the old dames at their spinning. Many a time Emryss had said he had "business" to attend to, and had sent him away. But one night he had followed Emryss, staying hidden in the shadows, and watched him disappear into a secluded hut. Peeking through a crack in the wall, he had seen a girl with Emryss. She was practically tearing the clothes from him, and they were both laughing. Then the laughter stopped, turned to sighs, and finally to soft moans. Keeping his eye to the crack, he had learned what happened between men and women in the night.

Was it so unusual, Gwilym thought as he watched Emryss's back, that Emryss wanted to relive those days?

Gwilym hardened his resolve. It was, if he wanted that girl. He tried to get Emryss's attention and finally shouted at him.

"Delff!" he called out, for Emryss was sitting there like some dunce.

At the insult, Emryss turned, his brow furrowed. Gwilym rode forward, past the wench who surely was not worth all this trouble, even if taking her would twist Cynric's chausses.

Gwilym spoke quietly as he kept his eyes on the rough road before them. "Not taking her back to Beaufort, are you, brother?"

"Why not?"

"God, man, when you getting any sense? Your life won't be worth a beggar's penny if you go near the place."

"They wouldn't kill me."

"Not sure of that, I wouldn't be if I wore your boots."

Emryss glanced at the girl.

"*Duw Lwyd,* can't you keep your eyes off her and listen?"

"You mean my eye?" Emryss said, his grin breaking.

"Whatever, you nit. I tell you, things is different now. The baron's like a spider who's spun a web of iron in the time you been gone. You just can't ride in there, girl or no."

Emryss looked ahead, his jaw getting the stubborn set Gwilym knew so well. "Even the baron should know it's a common enough custom to abduct a bride," he said.

"Aye, if he chooses to remember. And stop looking at her, man. Hu said she's bewitched you, and I'm beginning to think he's right."

"You're talking nonsense, Gwil," Emryss said, laughing softly. "I suppose Hu thinks she's the White Lady, even though it's nowhere near Allhallows eve?"

"For God's sake, be serious! We have to let her find her own way back. It shouldn't be hard, if she follows the road."

"I won't leave a woman alone in the forest, not even if she's Cynric's. You've said yourself there's a pack of thieves hereabouts."

Behind them Roanna kept her face lowered, hoping to avoid the one-eyed man's penetrating gaze. He kept looking at her, increasing her discomfort. Surely he didn't think she would ride off, for she had no idea where she was. She forced herself to pay attention to their dispute in an effort to forget the effect of his scrutiny.

It was obvious that the dark, stocky man was annoyed with the scarred man. From his admonishing tone, it was difficult to believe that this was a soldier talking to his leader, but that had to be the case.

With the start of yet another rainfall, the leader turned his horse and came toward her. The other man stayed in front.

Her fingers tightened on the pommel.

"Need some help, my lady?" The man reined in and began to put his cloak around her. His knee brushed against hers. Wordlessly she submitted to his assistance, not wanting to get soaked through again and not sure how to tell him to stop. His hands brushed over her lightly.

He finished and pulled his horse back a bit. Roanna clung more desperately to the pommel of the saddle, telling herself it was her fear of falling into the mud that made her heart beat frantically.

The one-eyed man nudged his horse to a walk, but now the way was wider, and he remained by her side. The scent of the damp leaves and earth rose afresh with the drizzle.

"Not liking the rain?" He studied her for a long minute.

"Do you enjoy being wet?" she said at last. Anything to make him stop staring at her.

"When you've been in the desert, you come to love the rain," he said softly.

The desert could only mean the Holy Land. "You were on the Crusade?"

"Aye."

"Perhaps you knew of my father, Edmund Westercott?" she asked hopefully.

He looked at her, the rain glistening on the leather patch. "Aye, knew of him. A man of honor, they said."

"Yes. Yes, he was." Deep inside, the memories of her father stirred. The happy moments with her parents, before her father left on a Crusade, never to return. Her mother's fever. Then her death, leaving Roanna all alone in the world, save for an uncle she had never met.

"A pity, then, he died. We could have used some honorable men in that place."

She looked up to see that he was entirely serious. "Surely all the Crusaders were honorable men. They were going in the service of Christ."

His jaw clenched, and a small vein in his temple began to throb. "Then honor includes thievery, rape, murder, sodomy…"

She gasped in disbelieving horror, and he stopped.

"You must be wrong!" she cried. "How could such men be…"

"My lady, I was there," he said quietly.

She couldn't speak. Surely he was wrong. Surely the Crusaders hadn't been…hadn't done those things. He must be lying.

If he lied, he was not a man of honor. And if he was not a man of honor, she must not have these feelings for him.

But God help her, she did.

He spoke again. "Forgive me, my lady, for shaking your notions. Thought you wanted honesty, so you got it."

"I know you as little as you know me, so it may be that you only want to discredit my fellow Normans."

He laughed, a harsh bark that drew the attention of the other man. "They don't need any words from me. They discredit themselves every day."

"It seems you know little of Normans, no doubt because you aren't one," she said indignantly.

He smiled mockingly. "You know as little about me as I about you. I had hoped to remedy that, but I begin to see you may be as blind as all the rest of your countrymen."

"It may be that I see more clearly than you think."

"Do you, now? Then how can you still be willing to marry Cynric?"

Always he came back to that. Why? What purpose would it serve now? Hadn't he realized she would not be swayed from keeping her word, despite his words, despite his kiss?

He had said he had taken her for a jest. Surely it was time she was returned and the jest finished.

Unless he was toying with her feelings, too.

She would be all too susceptible to a subtle seduction,

she realized as the heat of humiliation crept through her. What a triumph it would be for him, to brag that he had wooed and won Cynric's bride, that he had broken the match so easily, with one kiss.

She clenched her teeth and in one swift motion brushed the damp hair from her face. She lifted her chin.

The leader spoke a few words, and the other man rode down the path.

"My lady," the scarred man said gently, "are you certain you wish to marry him?"

She spoke swiftly, defiantly, the words tumbling out like water from a floodgate. "I have told you. An agreement was made. I must keep it."

"*You* did not agree."

"And if I do not marry as my uncle wishes, what then? I will be less than a pauper at his gate. I will have no place. No home. Not even a chance for happiness."

"*You* must agree for the contract to be legal, my lady," he said, looking at her intently.

"What could you know of the law?" she asked, ignoring the pounding of her heart and the hope that blossomed in her breast. What could he know, indeed? "I must fulfill the agreement my uncle has made. Honor demands it."

He nodded once, but whether it was with understanding or only to acknowledge her response, she couldn't tell.

Suddenly they heard a shout from up ahead. The man grabbed the reins of her horse and spurred his horse into a gallop.

They came out of the trees onto a rocky hill. In the distance she could see a column of men riding down the road in the valley.

"Cynric," the dark man said.

"Aye," the scarred man answered. He turned to her. "Cynric DeLanyea is there, at the front of his men. No doubt he's come looking for you. Well, my lady?"

She looked at the face of the man who had taken her. The rain wet his full lips and the dark skin of his cheeks. At the bottom of the leather patch she could see the ruined flesh. His damp curls glistened around his face. In his gaze she saw all the respect she had ever wanted. And something else, an emotion that made her decision so painful that she knew she would never forget him.

Nevertheless, she climbed off the horse and began to walk down into the valley.

It was the only honorable thing to do.

Chapter Four

"Did he rape you?"

Roanna's gaze swept past the baron, who sat awaiting her response, past her uncle, who looked at her as though everything were somehow her fault, to Cynric, sprawled nonchalantly in a chair at the end of the huge table. The room was cold, but that was not why she shivered.

In the corner sat a priest wringing his ink-stained cassock in his hands. On a small table in front of him a long parchment had been unrolled. The marriage contract, she was sure.

Roanna glanced at her uncle, sitting with his hands steepled beside the baron. So many times she had watched him sit in judgment on his tenants, his face impassive. She might have known she could expect nothing else of him, even for her.

"Answer me!" the baron demanded, his deep voice harsh and impatient. For the first time since she had been brought to this room without even being allowed to change her soiled dress, she looked directly at her interrogator. His tiny eyes gleamed maliciously in the fleshly folds of his cheeks.

"Well?" he said.

"No, my lord, he did not," she replied softly, hoping that she would be allowed to leave soon. She heard the soft chink of the soldiers' weapons beside the door, but forced herself to concentrate on the men in front of her.

The baron grunted and glanced at his son. Roanna, too, turned to look at him. So different from the other man...and yet now, when Cynric sat apparently unconcerned in the chair, there was something vaguely similar in their long, well-built legs and air of concealed strength.

Lord Westercott unsteepled his thin fingers and spoke. "Obviously, Baron DeLanyea, nothing untoward had taken place. I think the marriage may proceed."

The baron glared at Cynric, who spoke after a short pause.

"Very well. It shall be as *you* wish. I will marry her," he said.

Roanna lowered her eyes. So that had not changed. When she had gone to Cynric in the valley, he had said nothing. His lips had twitched into something between a frown and a smile, and he had not spoken to her all the way to Beaufort.

"I suppose Emryss will get away with this insult?" Cynric asked belligerently.

Emryss. His name was Emryss. It sounded like a caress, or a wave brushing against the shore.

"You suppose right," the baron said, then pushed his chair back as if preparing to leave.

Roanna clasped her hands together, took a deep breath and spoke. "Why was I not asked to give my consent to this marriage?"

Her words hung in the air for a moment. Her uncle stared, dumbfounded at her boldness. The baron looked rather startled. Cynric looked at her as if she had announced her intention to murder someone.

Her uncle frowned, and his eyes narrowed with annoyance. "It is not necessary."

Unexpectedly, the little priest stepped forward. As he began tying his rope belt into a knot, he cleared his throat. "Excuse me, my lords, but the lady is correct. She must give her consent for the agreement to be binding."

The baron stood up and the priest scurried back to the corner like a frightened rabbit.

"You lied to me," Roanna said, her voice firm and full of contempt. "You are dishonorable men and less than the stones beneath my feet. I will have nothing more to do with you."

Westercott's chest felt tight. He recognized the voice, the tone, the words. It was as if his younger brother had suddenly spoken, alive again.

For the first time in many years, he was ashamed. Until Cynric pushed back his chair, scraping it against the stone floor, and he realized if there was no marriage, he would get no money. "Now, my lord, don't be hasty," he said, his voice a cross between a command and a plea. "Give me some time to make the girl see reason. And she will, I assure you."

Roanna stared at her uncle, not hiding the scorn she felt for him.

"The north tower room would perhaps be a better place for you to reason with her," the baron said coldly.

Lord Westercott nodded, his face grim, and took his niece's arm, pulling her toward the narrow stone steps. He tasted the bile rising in his throat as he roughly jerked Roanna up the stairs. He hadn't come all this way to have the bargain destroyed by some fool woman. As if a woman's consent mattered.

And to hell with idiot priests, speaking up at the most inopportune times. He'd contrived to get rid of Roanna for

a profit, and now the whole bargain threatened to crumble
in his lap like stale bread.

He reached the small room at the top of the steps and
threw her inside. "Now, you fool, you *will* marry Cynric
DeLanyea. And you'll stay in here and think about the ad-
vantages of this marriage."

He went out and pulled the door shut.

Roanna looked around the barren room. It was empty
save for a pile of filthy straw and a bucket. One small
window provided feeble light. She heard a key turn in the
lock and her uncle's footsteps going down the stairs.

The sky had darkened, and the sounds from the hall had
quieted.

The evening meal must be over, Roanna thought, laying
her head wearily on her drawn-up knees. No one had
brought any food up to her, but she had not expected her
uncle to feed her. It was doubtless his plan to starve her
into submission.

She sat up as she heard footsteps coming toward the
door. Then she stood and prepared to face her uncle's wrath
for a second time.

But it was Cynric who pushed open the door.

"Ah, my lady, lonely?" he said, an unpleasant smile
curling his lips.

Roanna said nothing as he came closer. With an effort
she kept her face serene, although she knew precisely how
a trapped animal felt.

Cynric slowly walked around her. Then he drew out his
dagger and began cleaning his immaculate fingernails.

She waited for him to speak, her hands clasped before
her, feeling the tension build inside her. He wanted something, perhaps only to toy with her, but his studied non-
chalance was no more than a feint. "So, he didn't touch
you."

She looked at the floor, remembering the kiss. How soft his lips were, how gentle.

"He did not dishonor me," she answered quietly.

"So you said." Cynric walked slowly toward her. "You are no beauty, but I find it hard to believe that Emryss didn't take his pleasure of you. He's been many years among the heathen. Perhaps he's forgotten what honorable men are like."

She kept her gaze on the uneven stone floor. "No, he has not," she said firmly.

Cynric walked behind her. His body was uncomfortably close, his breathing too loud in her ears.

"Is that so?" His hand traveled slowly down her arm. She tried to suppress a cringe at the unwelcome familiarity. "Tell me, then, about my honorable cousin."

"What?" She spun around and stared at him.

He smiled slowly, and it was not a pleasant sight. "Ah, that surprises you? Didn't he tell you he is Lord Emryss DeLanyea, the cousin of your betrothed?"

Her mind reeled for a moment. "No, no, he said nothing…"

"Well, my dear, that one-eyed misbegotten barbarian is my dead uncle's offspring. Of course you couldn't possibly guess from his dress, or even his speech. He's a disgrace to the DeLanyea name, and always has been."

His gaze moved over her leisurely. "No doubt he took you to annoy us. He's like that, grotesque simpleton. If he didn't rape you, it would be because he would know *that* wouldn't bother me. This must be some new game of his."

Cynric stepped closer. "Surprise becomes you, my dear. It makes you look alive, and not some cold marble statue."

His lips came crushing down on hers, brutal and plundering. Roanna struggled in his grasp, fighting the terrible fierceness of his kiss. She couldn't breathe, couldn't think.

At last his grip loosened. She broke away and rubbed the back of her hand across her bruised lips.

"Don't!" she said, panting. "Don't do that again."

She saw the flash of anger in the depths of his ice-blue eyes and stepped back. He shrugged his shoulders. For an instant it was so like Emryss's gesture that it seemed a cruel reminder of him, and that other kiss.

"No more for now, if you wish it. I can wait until we are wed."

He began to walk toward the door, then turned. His eyes took on a feral gleam. "Oh, and don't worry if I discover on the wedding night that you have lied." He moved his tongue slowly over his lips in a gesture that turned Roanna's stomach. "I prefer a woman experienced."

"Do you think I lied?" she cried. Her anger blazed up like a smoldering flame touched to dry thatch.

"Yes, I do. But it doesn't matter, does it?" he said, his tone mocking. "Let Emryss have your maidenhead. I get the dowry, pittance though it may be, and your uncle's influence."

"No," she said, her voice now barely under control. "You do not. I will never marry you. Never!"

In a quick move, he grabbed her arms tightly and thrust his face barely inches from hers. "Do you think *I* want to marry *you,* you bony wench? I could have my pick of a hundred women, all more attractive and with richer dowries than yours. But my father wants *this* alliance, so, since I must have this land when he dies, I will wed you. And I will bed you, whether you like it or not." He tightened the grip on her arm, and his thin lips pressed together. "If you hate me, bedding you might not be such a dull exercise after all."

Roanna wrenched herself from his grasp. "I would rather die. I would not allow myself to be sullied by someone like you!" She clenched her fists into tight balls of control.

His lips curved into a fearsome smile. "Only ruined old warriors, like Emryss?"

"At least he has honor. You have none!"

"And you have no beauty. I'm willing to overlook that." Suddenly he lunged for her, pulling her into his arms again. His heated lips moved across her cheek. She struggled for a moment, then stopped. She became as still as a rock. She would do nothing that might please or goad him. Perhaps that would change his mind.

"Ah, Roanna, do you give up so easily? Or do you begin to see the error of your ways?"

He kissed her brutally, then stepped back. His low, dreadful, mocking laugh filled the room. "Perhaps I should invite my cousin to our wedding feast!" he said as he turned and went toward the door.

The next day Emryss stood in the old stone stable of Craig Fawr, his fortress. Slowly he moved the brush over the black mane of his horse as he listened absently to the sounds of the laborers in the courtyard. Night was falling, and it would soon be too dark to work. Everyone would begin gathering in the newly completed great hall for the last meal of the day.

He smiled, content that the work started by his father would be finished soon. Only two sections of the main wall remained to be rebuilt. With luck they would be completed before the winter set in.

Thank God his mother had managed to fend off the baron's avaricious attempts to get the land until he had returned.

His thoughts darkened. Only his mother's strong will had kept her alive to achieve his father's dream of a rebuilt castle on this site that had been fortified for centuries. Not even the Romans had conquered it. Only the ruthless Normans, seeking land at any price, had managed to beat the

Welsh warriors. They had torn down the old fortress. For long years the stones had laid on the ground, for the Welsh would not take them away for their own use. They belonged here, on the Great Rock.

In time their respect and patience had been rewarded. Emryss's father, although a Norman knight, had loved a Welsh princess and recognized the value of the site. He also recognized the value of Welsh loyalty, and in turn earned their love.

His early death might have meant the end to his plans, for his eldest son had died before him. Only his wife, with her will of iron, had kept his dream alive and passed it on to their son. Even when it seemed that Emryss was dead, she would not allow the work to stop. Many had warned her that she was doing the baron's work for him, that he would be the one to hold Craig Fawr when all was finished. She had never given up hope that Emryss would return.

Two months before he had ridden through the gate, marveling at the reconstruction, she had died.

Soon, he thought as he brushed the horse's mane. Soon they would be ready to make the baron pay for the anguish he had caused. The horse whined in protest, and Emryss lightened his strokes.

"Not meaning to take it out on you, Wolf," he muttered. "Best think of something more pleasant, eh, before you kick me."

Something pleasant. The girl. He had watched her for long minutes while she slept in the hut, longing to feel the black mass of her rippling hair, to caress the cheek it sought to hide. Her dark lashes lay spread so delicately on the white, smooth skin of her face. But he had enjoyed watching her even more when she was awake. Her amazing eyes, so green and full of passion! He had seen many beautiful women from many lands, but she fascinated him in a way no other woman ever had.

"Think you back in the heathen desert, boy?" interrupted the scolding tones of Mamaeth, his old nurse. How he loved the sound, he thought as he turned to her with a smile. She glared back, her small dark eyes snapping with annoyance as if he were still a little boy.

"Summer it may be, but needing more on your arms at night now."

"Ah, Mamaeth, right as always!" He tossed the brush onto a nearby stool and went to her, lifting her up and planting a kiss firmly on her leathery cheek.

"Tch, boy! Put me down and no more of that," she cried, although she couldn't keep the pleasure from her voice.

"No more of that?" He stepped back, feigning surprise. "And who was it always demanding kisses from me when I was a lad?" His lips twitched as he tried not to laugh.

"Go on with you!" She slapped his arm lightly. "Did something wrong, we did, when we was raising you. No respect for your elders, boy. And no listening, either. Too chill it is for you to be about almost naked."

Emryss had to laugh. "Mamaeth," he said, "how did I ever manage without you?"

Her eyes lost their sparkle, and he regretted reminding her of the days when no one had known whether he was alive or dead on some far-off battlefield.

"I think," he said lightly, "that as your lord, it's time I found you a husband to fuss over."

"What?" The spark returned immediately as she looked at him. "What would I want one of those for? Got enough to look after, me, with you. Tch! A husband? Like another baby, and me too old for that." Mamaeth looked at him slyly. "It's you needing to be wed."

Emryss struggled to keep his voice lighthearted. "Well, I shall have to give the matter some thought."

Mamaeth straightened her narrow shoulders, then looked

him over slowly. "A girl who's not impressed with you and your title, that's what you need all right. And one that'll give you sons." She grinned and bustled off toward the kitchen.

Emryss watched her leave, then slowly bent to pick up the brush. He sighed heavily. Gwilym would be his heir, or Gwilym's sons. He had told no one at home of the full extent of his wounds, although all saw the scar and the limp when he was tired. How could he tell them of the great gash that had taken a part of his manhood, and the infection that had followed? Abram, who had saved him from Saladin's men on the field and healed his wounds, had told him he might yet father children. But he had bedded a willing tavern wench on the journey home, a venture that had ended with humiliating failure. He would not risk such shame again.

"For brushing the beast, that thing is," Gwilym said with a chuckle, making him start.

He shook his head as if to rid it of unwanted thoughts and turned to Gwilym with an indulgent grin. "Mamaeth says I show no respect for my elders. Seems to be a common failing around Craig Fawr. My men show no respect for their lord."

Gwilym sat down on the stool. "And why should we? Just because your da was Norman?"

"God's wounds!" Emryss lifted the brush as if he would strike his friend for his audacity, but it was impossible to keep his face serious. "Now you're insulting me! Because my mother was a Welsh princess, you nit. And I *am* the lord of Craig Fawr."

Gwilym stood and made a deep bow. "A thousand pardons, my honorable lord. Forgive your humble servant, I beg you."

Emryss clouted him lightly with the brush. "I forgive you."

"Thought you would," Gwilym said, but he quickly ducked out of reach of the brush. "After all, I'm the best fighter you've got." He grinned broadly for a moment, then his face became serious. "Emryss, there's been another attack on travelers near the river."

"No one killed?"

"No, but their goods was taken, even to the clothes on their backs."

"The thieves—Welsh, Saxon or Norman?"

"Don't know."

"And the ones robbed?"

"Normans, but poor enough."

Emryss quickly threw a blanket over Wolf. "Best go on a patrol tomorrow. We'll take twenty men."

Gwilym nodded, then hesitated. "Not expecting any trouble from Beaufort, then?"

"No." Emryss began walking toward the great hall.

Gwilym hurried to catch up. "You truly think they'll let this pass?"

"Why not? She wasn't hurt."

"But the insult…"

"They're cowards."

Gwilym placed his hand on Emryss's arm and halted him in the center of the large courtyard filled with stone blocks, lumber, scaffolding and tools. "Emryss, don't be underestimating the baron, or Cynric."

Emryss placed his hand over Gwilym's. "I know that, Gwil. All the world can see that I underestimated an enemy once. You can be sure I won't make that mistake again."

Roanna scrambled to her feet. She stared at the two small eyes shining in a broad crack in the mortar. With a shudder of revulsion, she moved away, hampered by the stiffness in her legs.

All through the previous night she had sat awake, terrified that Cynric would return, or the rats. Then the daylight had come, and each hour had passed in slow monotony. She looked up at the small window. Now it was night again, and the rats had appeared.

If only she had a light, maybe they would go away.

Without warning the door crashed open. Her uncle, his face flushed, staggered into the room. She could smell the wine on his breath, although she stood at the farthest end of the little room.

"Well, niece, have you reconsh...reconsi...thought again?" he asked drunkenly. He swayed and clutched at the doorposts.

Roanna watched him warily, but spoke with determination. "I will never marry Cynric DeLanyea."

"Are you mad?" He stumbled farther into the room. "You stupid girl! If you don't marry him, I'll send you off to some frozen convent in the north, I promise you. No other man will make an offer for you."

She regarded him steadily, not moving or speaking. He lunged for her, grabbing her arms roughly. She pushed him back, and he reeled until he smashed into the open door. "By God, I'll beat you until those eyes fall out of your head!" he shouted, charging at her.

Roanna stepped out of his way, and his head smacked the stone wall. Stunned, he sat down limply.

"You will do as I say!" he muttered, rubbing his head. "Damn women! Why'd your parents give you to me anyway?" He looked up at her with bleary red eyes. "They didn't make any arrangements for you. They left it all to me. So I make a match. A good match. And what thanks do I get, eh?"

He continued to mumble, holding his head in his hands. "By Jesus and Joseph, I'd beat you, but that'd mark your face." He struggled to his feet as she moved closer to the door.

His next words came in a wheedling whine. "Roanna, my dear, would it not be honorable to marry to please the man who has raised you? To repay him for all the food and clothing provided all these years?"

She was almost at the door. "You mean to prostitute myself?"

He began to blush, the red moving past his chin to cover his face. Suddenly he flew at her, knocking her to the ground.

"Oh, no, my dear!" he said triumphantly, the smell of his breath sickening her. "You'll stay here until you agree."

He pulled her to her feet and pushed her into the room before shutting the door. He laughed as he twisted the key in the lock. "Thought you could trick me, eh, girl? We'll see who wins this battle."

His feet slapped the stones as he went away.

Roanna held her side, fighting the pain and her own despair. She would never agree to marry Cynric. Never. Her uncle could starve her to death.

She went to the straw and sat down, moistening her sore lips with her tongue, but it, too, was dry. How she wanted one of Jacques' sweet rolls and a drink of clear spring water.

She lay down. Jacques would know everything by now. The kitchen servants always knew all the gossip in a castle. He would be worried about her, too. She could almost hear him speaking to her now.

She sat up and hurried to the thick door. It *was* Jacques, calling her name on the other side.

"I'm here, Jacques," she said softly, hoping he could hear her.

"Did he hurt you, little kitten?"

"No."

"That is good. I have brought you some food."

The door had little space under it, but Jacques managed to slip a cloth containing a slice of bread to her. Roanna ate it gratefully, looking at the door that separated her from her friend. She stared at the leather hinges.

"Jacques!"

"Yes?"

"Have you got a knife?"

"You are not planning to fight your way out, are you?"

"The leather holding the door is old and worn. If I had a knife, I could cut it…"

"And it would fall on you and crush you. Or suppose you managed to sneak out of this room, how would you get out of the castle? It is too well guarded. Even if you did that, then what? You have no money."

Roanna knew the truth of Jacques' words and felt defeat settle like a fog over her.

"Unless, of course, I help you," he whispered.

"What?" Roanna held her breath to hear every word.

"I am tired of cooking for a man who will not even buy pepper. I think it is time I left him."

"Where would you go?"

"Where you wish. A cook as good as me will always find a willing patron."

Hope rushed into her heart, but the risk was too great. "Jacques, I can't let you do this for me."

"I do it for me, too," he answered indignantly, and she smiled a little. "I will come back quickly with the knife. They all think I sleep now, and know better than to disturb me. The bread baking will start in only a few hours. We must be far away by then."

"But it might be dangerous for two lone travelers on the road."

"Do you think you would be safer by yourself? Besides, you insult my valor." His voice softened into the tender tone he only used when speaking to her. "Let me do this, little kitten."

She listened as Jacques' footsteps retreated, and looked again at the hinge. She began to pace anxiously, wondering how long it would take him to make the preparations.

She pushed back her hair and felt her cracked lips with her finger. Trembling with abhorrence, she remembered all too clearly the lustful gleam in Cynric's eyes. Dear God, what would he do to her if they were wed?

Perhaps he would decide not to wait. Perhaps he could come here again...

Roanna held her breath as she heard the sound of stealthy footsteps coming toward the door.

"Jacques?" she called out softly.

Chapter Five

"Jacques?" Roanna called again urgently. Fear was growing with every breath.

"Yes, it is I," he answered, and she sighed with relief.

He pushed a long, thin knife through the crack under the door.

"I go to prepare other things. I will hurry. Do not despair!" he whispered, and she heard his steps retreat again.

The remnant of fear gave Roanna a renewed sense of urgency. Cynric had not come...yet. Quickly she grabbed the knife and began sawing at the old leather hinge. It seemed to take hours before she could see even a small cut, but once she had penetrated the outside edge, the work progressed swiftly.

Absorbed by her task, she didn't hear Jacques' return until he called to her.

"I think it's ready, Jacques," she whispered as she shoved dirty straw toward the door to cushion its fall. She took up the sharp butchering knife again. "Another minute, and it will be cut through."

She sawed the topmost leather hinge until it was almost completely cut in two.

"Try it now," she said, standing back as Jacques put his

considerable weight against the door and pushed. Slowly the hinge twisted, and the top of the door turned in toward her. The leather ripped and the door sagged. Its weight snapped the bolt and it fell completely, landing with a dull thud.

Jacques stood on the other side, his broad face smiling. Then he became serious. "Come, kitten, quickly."

Roanna needed no urging. She climbed over the fallen door and joined him. The two hurried silently down the steps.

"I have a cart waiting," he whispered as he led her down a corridor and into the biggest kitchen she had ever seen. The banked fire in the hearth cast long shadows as they moved across the deserted room.

A donkey and cart such as farmers used on market day waited in the courtyard. Jacques motioned Roanna to get into the bottom of the wagon, then he covered her with a musty blanket. She felt the cart tip as Jacques eased his corpulent body onto the seat. With a jerk they began to move.

After only a few moments, Roanna was jostled again as they halted.

"Who are you?" an unknown voice demanded.

"I am Jacques de la Mere, Lord Westercott's cook, and if you want to eat tomorrow you will let me through the gate."

"What do you mean?" the voice responded querulously.

"The flour in the kitchen is full of maggots. Unless you want them in your bread, you will let me through. I myself will choose the flour at the mill. And since it is almost dawn, you had better not delay me, or his lordship will be most displeased. I would have to tell him about the soldier who would not let me pass."

Roanna thought she would suffocate under the blanket, but suffered willingly as she heard the portcullis open. The cart jolted forward again, and the gate crashed down. Deciding to risk a breath of fresh air, she held the blanket up just a little and peered out as they passed through the outer ward. It seemed deserted until she looked up at the walls. Many men stood on the battlements, their weapons gleaming dully in the moonlight.

They came to another gate, and Jacques told the same story. Again he convinced the guard to let them pass. The guards wouldn't be expecting anything unusual. Jacques had told her, as she had sawed at the hinge, that her uncle and the baron had informed no one of her whereabouts. A pretty maid had told him of Roanna being dragged up the stairs and that there was only one room at the top.

Roanna peeked out again as they passed through the town outside Baron DeLanyea's immense fortress. No one stirred, and only an occasional bark from a watchful dog heralded their progress. They turned down a road.

"We must go north first, little kitten," Jacques said quietly, "the mill lies to that way, and it is also wise that we go the way they will least expect should they discover us missing too soon. The little maid said the north road forks and then we can go south, to more civilized places."

Roanna lifted the blanket a little more and gazed at the night sky. The stars twinkled benignly. A moon three-quarters full illuminated the countryside, lighting the slow-moving river beside the road. They passed by the mill, and Jacques began to sing softly. He tossed a bag to her. Inside she found his delicious rolls and devoured one as the cart rumbled down the rutted road.

He had to find food. In the unbearable heat, wearing all his armor, he crawled over the battlefield. Flies swarmed on the bloated bodies of men and animals. A vulture fed off the bloody corpse of a horse covered in maggots. He tried to wet his parched lips with a dry tongue. Food. He must find food. Then the drums began, their pounding growing louder and louder as he crawled, the pain in his thigh excruciating.

He would starve if he didn't find something to eat. The insistent beat of the drums filled his ears. He stood, trying to see. Then he heard the almost silent hiss of a sword being pulled from its scabbard and turned around.

"Allah ackbar," the Moslem soldier whispered, then lifted his sword to strike.

Emryss sat up with a strangled cry, his body drenched in sweat. He rubbed his face with both hands, then lay back. A dream. Another dream. The pounding of his heart subsided slowly as he breathed deeply. Another nightmare of the Holy Land. Dear God, he had hoped he would be free of them once he arrived home.

The first rays of dawn shone through the narrow window of his chamber. He got out of the bed, wrapping a sheet around his naked body. Through the window he could see the pink-tinted sky growing lighter as the sun rose. Fields of nearly ripe grain shifted like the golden sand of the desert. He sighed as he watched for the occasional glimmer of the river winding through the rocky valley. He thought he could see white specks on the farthest hill, a few sheep wandering in their search for food.

He turned and walked to the basin, pouring water from the nearby ewer. Quickly he splashed his face, holding his right hand over the scar for a moment to let the cool water soothe it. Then he went to the chest beside the bed and, removing the sheet, he picked up the chausses he had laid on it the night before. He began to draw them on, pausing to examine his body yet again for any sign of returning infection.

The door burst open.

"Damn!" Emryss said as he quickly drew on the leggings.

"Blasphemy, you learned on your Crusade?" Mamaeth said as she cocked her head to one side. Over her arm she carried fresh linen.

"Sorry," Emryss said, picking up a shirt. "Liking you to knock, is all."

Mamaeth tossed the linen on the large bed and placed her hands on her thin hips. "What?"

"Not a boy anymore, Mamaeth. I'd like you to knock," he said, sitting on the bed and reaching for his boots.

Mamaeth frowned with consternation. Then a wicked grin lighted her face. "Not got a woman about, have you?"

Emryss pulled on his boots, his voice muffled as he bent over. "No, I don't."

"Why not?"

He lifted his head and looked at her.

"Just a simple question," she replied as she began tugging on the sheets. "No harm in it."

Emryss got up and grabbed his leather jerkin.

Mamaeth began to remake the bed with the clean sheets. "Might do you some good," she mumbled.

Emryss tugged the jerkin down. "What did you say?"

Mamaeth straightened and glared at him. "I said, might do you some good."

"No," he said harshly, snatching up his sword belt. He fumbled with the buckle. God's blood, when would he learn to curb his tongue, and his temper?

Finally he succeeded with the buckle. "Has Gwilym eaten yet?" he said, hoping Mamaeth would overlook his peevish reply.

"Had enough for ten, he has. What an appetite! At the stable now, I think, getting ready to leave." Mamaeth picked up a pillow and punched it, giving him a sidelong glance. "You off again, too, then?"

"Aye. Too close, the last attack was."

"Liking to get my hands on them, me." Mamaeth

pounded the other pillow, and Emryss thought the thieves would find her a worse foe than many a man.

"Wish me luck, then," he said as he went toward the door.

"Good luck to you. But keep away from Beaufort land— and Beaufort women."

He left the room without answering. Everyone in Craig Fawr had probably heard of his latest escapade. No doubt they would put it down to old enmity, as it had started. They would forget it soon enough, unless more troubles ensued.

When he reached the hall he nodded at the men gathered for the morning meal and grabbed a piece of bread. He took a bite, then washed it down with a fast gulp of ale. He continued to eat his bread as he went out the door and across the courtyard.

Already masons were climbing the scaffolding to begin work on the walls. He checked the fast-depleting pile of stones. Somehow he needed to find more money to make Craig Fawr strong. His parents had spent far too much out-fitting him for the useless effort of the Crusade. He wished Archbishop Baldwin had stayed safely in Canterbury, or that he had not heard the priest speak that day. How young and foolish he had been, full of the glorious need for ridding Jerusalem of heathens!

At the entrance to the stable Gwilym had Wolf saddled and waiting. The other men making up the patrol sat on their mounts patiently. Gwilym gave Emryss a welcoming smile, then swung onto his own stallion. Emryss finished the bread, climbing into the saddle slowly.

"Not slept well, have you?" Gwilym asked with concern.

"Slept better in my time," Emryss replied ruefully. "Suppose I can't get used to a soft bed."

Gwilym grinned. "Needing a woman in the bed, I think."

A picture of a pale face surrounded by rippling black hair lying beside him unfolded in his mind, but he pushed it away. "Why is it everyone seems to think a little tumble with a willing female is going to make everything well with me? Next thing I know, you'll be telling me my scars will disappear after a good bout of lovemaking." He turned Wolf toward the gate. "Enough of this talk. Where exactly did the thieves attack?"

"A few miles down the road beside the river, where it goes through the deepest part of the forest, my lord."

"Near the ford?"

"Aye."

"Where are the other men?"

"Waiting in the outer ward, my lord."

"Good. Let's get hunting, then."

"Aye, my lord."

Emryss sighed and looked at his foster brother, who sat staring stonily ahead. "Gwil," he began, tempted to explain why all the talk of women troubled him.

Instead he spurred his horse and rode out of the inner gate.

The creak of the cart wheels sounded loud in the mist-enshrouded river valley. Above a brave sun shone, burning over the remainder of the early-morning fog. Roanna looked at the willows bent over the small river like women drawing water and smiled as two squirrels chased each other through the nearby oaks. A few birds sang from the underbrush of gorse and bracken, but everything seemed hushed, as if waiting for the heat of the sun that would drive away the last of the fog.

In the distance, a wall of low rocky hills rose, trying to

touch the white, puffy clouds that scudded across the blue sky.

Roanna drank in the rugged loveliness, so unexpected in a place where all she had encountered had been dreary, damp days of endless rain.

Emryss DeLanyea was like his country, she thought, and like him, the country was proving more attractive than she would have dreamed possible only a short time ago.

She forced herself to face the truth as she sat swaying in the rough vehicle. She didn't want to run away.

Oh, she had to leave Beaufort after breaking the match. To stay would have been intolerable, as well as dangerous. No, she didn't want to go because she had at last met a man who completely and utterly fascinated her.

She thought about his face and the hidden scar. It must have been a clean wound, from a sharp weapon, or he would have died. She remembered her father telling her that the most dangerous men to fight against were the scarred ones, for they had the will to survive. Surely he must be so, or he would never have returned alive from the Holy Land.

What would he think when he heard of her going? Would he even care, except to be pleased that Cynric's plans were momentarily thwarted?

"You must not fret, kitten. Your uncle will not go to that room until after the noon meal, of that I am certain," Jacques said, his voice booming in the stillness. "He stayed up very late sampling the baron's wine." Jacques chuckled.

Roanna smiled at her friend. "It was free, after all," she replied. "I wonder what they'll do when they discover…"

"That we have outsmarted them?" He beamed at her. "They will make chase, of course." His smile turned sly. "They will think we go south, but we do not."

"Can you trust that girl not to say anything?" Roanna asked, wishing she could feel as confident as Jacques.

He shrugged his shoulders. "It will take them time to prepare to come after us. We have some hours' start and I do not think..." His words trailed off and his face began to turn red.

"And my betrothed may not look very hard," she finished for him.

"Well, he's an arrogant braggart, so you're well rid of him. Still, I think it would be wise if we do not stop for some time."

Roanna nodded and turned to reach into the cart for the small cask of water.

Suddenly Jacques cried out. The cart lurched to a halt. Roanna grabbed the side to keep from tumbling out, then turned to him.

"Jacques!" she gasped, reaching for the reins as they slipped from his grasp. An arrow protruded from his shoulder, surrounded by a growing red stain on his tunic.

The cook looked at the arrow and turned a sickly white.

"Don't stop!" he said, his breathing ragged, "we must go..."

Before he could finish, a gang of well-armed men crashed out of the underbrush and surrounded the cart. Their long, tangled hair hung down to their shoulders, framing filthy, scornful faces.

Roanna slapped the reins hard on the donkey's back. Jacques reeled as another arrow struck his leg. The surrounding faces twisted into grotesque grins.

One, who carried both sword and dagger, grabbed the donkey's halter. He smiled, showing his rotten teeth.

Jacques moaned, but Roanna dared not take her eyes from the man holding the halter. She fought the panic growing in her, realizing that she had no weapon.

The man with the rotten teeth walked toward the cart. She stared at him. He must have a weakness. Find the weakness, she told herself, echoing the words her father had said so many times to the men he trained. Find the weakness.

The man's hand darted out, grabbing her arm and pulling her off the cart. He threw her onto the ground.

She knelt in the dirt, watching him through the curtain of her disheveled hair. He paid no attention to her, but began rummaging through the bundles in the back of the cart. She kept watching him, not moving but ready to spring if he moved any closer to Jacques.

Another man, thin and stinking, picked up a strand of her hair. He laughed coarsely and whispered something in a guttural voice to the other men.

At the cart the leader snorted with disgust, but whether at the meagre goods in the wagon or at the other man's word, Roanna could not tell. He grabbed Jacques roughly. Roanna tried to stand, but the thin man clamped his hand to her shoulder, making her stay where she was. Finally the leader found Jacques' small purse. He shook it, then put it in his belt.

Roanna dared to hope that now he would let them go.

The thin man spoke briefly as he hauled Roanna to her feet. His hands were surprisingly strong, and his long nails bit into her skin. She kept her gaze firmly on the leader, as if she could make him let them go by an effort of her will.

The thin man's words became more insistent, and the leader turned and came toward her. His foul breath made her stomach turn. He surveyed her slowly, grinning. Her whole body trembled as she swallowed hard.

Dear God, help me find the weakness! she thought, all too certain of his intentions now.

The leader spoke, and the thin man pinned her arms behind her back. She closed her eyes, too frightened to try to think. The point of a knife touched her throat. She heard a low groan of agony, not sure if it was Jacques' or her own. The tip of the blade pierced her skin.

She gasped as the dagger tugged at the top of her bodice. The knife ripped the cloth. The man holding her drew her arms farther back, exposing more of her naked skin to the men around her.

Suddenly a blood-curdling cry tore the air. Roanna's eyes flew open. The thin man dropped her hands and dove for the bushes. Two riders thundered down the road as the other thieves disappeared. She had a glimpse of a familiar face before the huge horses smashed through the bushes in pursuit.

Roanna clutched her torn gown together and clambered into the wagon where Jacques lay sprawled on the seat. For an instant she thought he was dead, but his eyelids fluttered open and he tried to smile. "It would seem, little kitten," he whispered, "that my valor leaves much to be desired."

She smiled back. If he could speak, surely he would live.

The muffled shouts of the chase sent a fresh wave of fear through her. She listened, not knowing that she was trying to distinguish one voice from the many. Surely he would rout the thieves, she thought, then realized they could not wait to see who would win.

They had to find a village, somewhere other people would be. Then she would try to help Jacques.

She picked up the reins and slapped them against the donkey's back. The animal moved, but as the cart jolted forward, Jacques groaned loudly.

"Are you hurt?" a voice called out. Emryss rode out of the underbrush, ducking beneath the low branch of a huge oak. In his hand he held his sword, which he slid into the sheath. He adjusted the leather patch over his eye as he came closer.

Again, Roanna had the impression of great strength held in check, and this time of barely concealed rage. When he halted his horse, it pranced impatiently. He, too, shifted in his saddle as his gaze swept over her.

"I'm not injured," she answered, immediately aware of her torn garment and the wild beating of her heart, "but Jacques is badly wounded."

Emryss looked at the man on the seat. "Not very serious, I shouldn't think. Seen a lot worse. Had a lot worse." His roguish grin filled her with relief.

He reached down with a strong, lean hand and took hold of the donkey's harness. "My apologies, my lady, that this should happen on my land. I'll take you where your friend can be cared for."

Roanna looked at Jacques, pale in her lap. It was not right that she should feel so unaccountably happy when Jacques was in pain.

"Thank you, my lord," she said softly, raising her face. He looked at her strangely.

"You know who I am then, my lady?"

"Yes. Cynric told me."

Emryss smiled ruefully. "Ah, I'm sure he sang my praises well."

She gazed at him, her heart light. He looked at her for a moment, then abruptly tugged on the reins. The cart began to move.

Roanna's eyes swam with hot tears. She cradled Jacques' head in her lap and held her bodice together. The sounds of the chase in the forest became more distant as Emryss led the cart along the road. He seemed unconcerned with the pursuit and capture of the thieves.

They came to a fork, turned and began to climb a steep hill. The jolting of the cart made Jacques cry out in pain, but Roanna spoke softly to him, assuring him that he would soon be helped. She found the cask of water and tried to get him to drink, but he shook his head weakly.

Roanna hoped a village was close by. Jacques' pain was growing with every toss in the cart.

At last they reached a plateau. In the distance loomed the massive earthworks of an ancient fortress. At the top, in the center, stood a castle. Around its base rose a cluster of buildings that made a small town, and on the edge of the river there was a small mill.

"Is this yours?" she asked, astounded by the size of the fortress. She looked from the building to the man so poorly dressed and back to the castle.

Emryss answered without turning. "My family's, yes."

After a short time they rode through the village outside the fortress. A man called out, and Emryss replied, his words clipped. The man ran off toward the castle.

"He'll fetch Mamaeth. She'll know what to do for your friend," Emryss said, seemingly oblivious to the stares of the gathering villagers.

Roanna tried to ignore them, too, but her face burned with the heat of a blush as she clutched her bodice tightly.

They reached the first gate, then another, then, finally, they came into a courtyard bustling with activity. Scaffolding of poles lashed together and ramps of planks seemed to be at every wall. Hoists and pulleys dangled from them like spiders from their webs. Huge blocks of stones and smaller piles of cut rocks lay on the ground. A gaggle of women stood around a well, their jugs balanced on their hips. A group of children ran under the scaffolding and paid no attention to the scolding of the laborers above.

It's more like a holiday than work, Roanna thought as they rode into the yard.

The cacophony of hammering, banging, gossiping, scolding and shouting ceased abruptly as the workers and servants caught sight of Emryss. Roanna sat up straight, trying to ignore their staring eyes.

Emryss slid down from his horse as a thin old woman

darted out of a low stone building at the base of the largest tower. She arrived at the cart with surprising speed. Ignoring Roanna, she climbed onto the seat and looked at the two arrows. The woman felt Jacques' shoulder, making him groan louder. After she examined the bloodstain, she looked at the wound in his leg, muttering to herself. Roanna watched, not quite sure what to make of her.

Jacques opened his eyes and stared, too. "Can't I die in peace?" he muttered as the woman prodded his leg.

"*I ffwrdd!* Die? You're not going to die, you *ffwl.* Just like a man that is. One scratch and you're planning your wake. Get down, girl, and give me some room here."

Roanna nodded, then looked at Jacques as he moaned again. Mamaeth turned to her. She looked Roanna over slowly. Then she nodded and Roanna discovered that she had been holding her breath.

"No need to look so worried, girl. Nothing but flesh wounds, these, though they've bled some. Rest and food and some of my medicine will have him up soon."

Jacques groaned again, and cursed softly. Mamaeth slapped his wrist. "None of that, now, or you can heal yourself. Emryss," Mamaeth barked. Roanna could scarcely believe the woman would use such a tone to the lord of the manor, but Emryss didn't seem to think it was anything unusual. "Put him in the barracks," the woman ordered. "He should be carried gently. Off for the medicine, me, then I'll get the arrows out. Where's Gwil?"

"Still after the ones that did this."

She nodded and jumped nimbly from the cart. "And take *her* to Bronwyn. Needing some decent clothes, she is."

Roanna blushed at the woman's words and stared at the rough stones of the courtyard. Emryss called to two nearby carpenters, who had been watching with gaping mouths, and passed on Mamaeth's orders.

Roanna watched as her friend was lifted gently from the

wagon and carried away to a nearby building, trying not to think of her gown and the man standing close enough to touch.

She felt the gentle pressure of a hand on her arm. "Now, suppose you tell me what you're doing on my land?"

Roanna clutched her torn gown together. The full import of her state burst into her mind. She was virtually alone, with no relative to protect her, no money to pay for lodging, in an unfamiliar countryside, without even a decent gown. She heard a few snickers and glanced at the workmen nearby.

Emryss turned to them slowly, and the men quickly returned to their jobs.

"Come. There's a more private place to talk inside the hall."

He held out his arm. Embarrassed at being the center of attention, she lightly touched his arm and allowed him to lead her toward the long, low building attached to the most ancient-looking tower. She kept her eyes downcast, all too acutely aware of his bare skin beneath the tips of her fingers.

When they entered the building, she quickly surveyed the room. It appeared to be a recent addition to the old fortress, for a huge hearth yawned in the center of the wall opposite the door. At the far end, closest to the tower, a brightly painted screen created a private space in the vast hall.

But no matter how she tried to concentrate on the unusual construction of the room, Roanna felt the soft hairs of his arm against her fingers, the hard muscle beneath the skin and her own blood pulsing through her body with unaccustomed warmth.

Emryss stopped in front of the screen, then motioned her to go around it. She did, and found a small trestle table and two chairs on the opposite side. She sat in the closest chair, and he sat across from her.

"Now, then, my lady. What happened?" His voice was soft, gentle in a way she had not heard in a long while. For the first time since she had touched his arm, she raised her eyes to look at him.

He stared back for a moment, but his gaze wavered and he looked away. Surprisingly, his face turned pink beneath the brown, tanned skin.

"I beg your pardon," she said. "I...my uncle has told me many times that I shouldn't stare at people."

"No matter," he said quickly, and his mouth jerked into a grin. "Used to getting stared at by now."

She wanted to duck beneath the table to hide her embarrassment. Instead she fastened her gaze on the grain of the wooden table.

"Thank you for rescuing me from those men. And Jacques, too."

"Glad we went that way. But I want to know why you're not in Beaufort. Getting married."

"I refused."

"Why?"

She looked down at her hands.

He spoke quietly. "Sorry to ask, my lady, but I have to know. Old enemies we are, those DeLanyeas and me, and this might be cause to fight. If it is, I have to know."

Roanna stood up abruptly. "I don't wish to be the cause of any more trouble. We'll leave—at once."

"Sit down." She had the sudden impression that he could subdue her with a movement of his eyebrow, but he spoke quietly, almost apologetically. "I'm not saying you have to leave. It's just better that I know the why of this."

She sat down slowly and wondered how much she should tell him.

I must not forget how little I know of him, she reminded

herself as she watched the man's face. Every instinct argued that she could trust him; experience warned her to trust no one.

Flushing slightly, she said, "I did not agree to marry Cynric DeLanyea."

"That's all?" Emryss stared at the slender girl sitting before him.

She turned pinker. "He also…insulted me."

"Cynric insults everybody. Born that way. But what about your kinsman? Didn't he stand up for you?"

"No." She looked away.

Sitting in his hall, holding together her ragged gown, she seemed as weak as a sapling on a rocky hill. But when she looked at him, her eyes challenging, her delicate chin thrust out slightly, it was clear that she had strength no one would guess.

"I'm surprised Cynric let you go, although he certainly didn't spare you much of an escort."

"He doesn't know I'm gone."

"What?"

"I…escaped. My uncle had locked me up, trying to force me to marry. Jacques helped me get away."

Emryss tapped his foot against the stones, unsure how to proceed. This *was* a mess. He didn't want to take her back to Beaufort, although Cynric could well claim that she was being held against her will again. His gaze strayed to the torn bodice of her gown. Her breasts rose and fell beneath the thin white garment, every movement enticing.

He scrutinized his callused hands, trying to think as if she wasn't there, but he felt her steady gaze. No wonder her uncle told her not to stare. He felt almost naked.

"Jacques and I will leave tomorrow, if you will allow us to stay for the night," she said. "I am very grateful for your help."

Emryss glanced at her pale face. "There's no need for

you to go so quick. You're welcome to stay for as long as you like.''

God help him, what was he doing?

''No, my lord. I think it is better that Jacques and I go our own way, where our presence can cause no one any harm.''

He should have been relieved. She was right that she could only bring trouble.

She stood up, and he rose, too. ''There was another reason I would not stay in the house of Cynric DeLanyea.'' She regarded him steadily across the table. ''He accused me of lying when I said you had not...harmed...me.''

He smashed his fist on the table, wishing it were Cynric's face. *''Melltigedig da i ddim!''* he growled. ''He knows me better than to say such a thing, that accursed...'' He hesitated. ''Forgive my temper, my lady,'' he said slowly, trying to control his feelings. ''I should know that accursed blackguard by now.''

He came around the table until he stood close beside her, but before he could speak, a young woman hurried around the screen, her hazel eyes widening with surprise when she saw Roanna's torn gown. ''Beg pardon, my lord,'' she said rather breathlessly as she glanced at them. ''Sent to help the lady, I was.''

''Right,'' he said, turning to Roanna. ''This is Bronwyn. She'll find you another gown. First, though, she'll show you to my bedchamber.''

Chapter Six

Roanna stared at the enormous bed. It took up one whole side of the small room. She had protested using Emryss DeLanyea's bedchamber until he had explained that it was the only room that would give her any privacy.

"Big enough for six, it is," Bronwyn said shyly.

Roanna tore her gaze from the massive piece of furniture and looked at the well-built, dark-haired maidservant.

"Mamaeth says you're to bathe and I'm to fetch you something to wear. We don't got much to offer in the way of gowns, I'm afraid."

"Anything will do," Roanna said quietly. Even a sack would be better than her ruined dress.

There was a knock at the door. Bronwyn answered and other female servants entered the room, bearing a huge wooden tub, linen, buckets of hot, steaming water, buckets of cold water and finally a little girl carrying a small jar. Roanna stood beside the bed and watched as they prepared the bath quickly and efficiently.

When the water seemed to be a suitable temperature, the little girl stepped forward and carefully tipped the jar. A delightful fruity smell pervaded the room when the contents hit the water. The women then trooped out of the room, each eyeing Roanna with frank curiosity.

Bronwyn closed her eyes and drew in the scent. "Wonderful is that. His lordship carried it all the way home." She glanced at Roanna. "Do you want any help, my lady?"

"No, thank you," Roanna said. She was not used to having any servants to assist her, and she suddenly felt utterly weary. She wanted to be alone.

"Very well, my lady. I'll bring a dress." Bronwyn went out, closing the door softly behind her.

Roanna slowly climbed out of the soiled garment. She drew off the remnants of her shift and shivered. The hot tub steamed invitingly, and she gingerly stepped in.

The warm water, smelling of far-off sunny lands, caressed and soothed her aching muscles. It had been a long time since she had enjoyed the luxury of heated water and scented herbs.

She looked around the room. It was sparsely furnished, if one didn't look at the bed, containing only a small table with a basin and ewer, one chair, two unlighted braziers and the small chest.

Bronwyn had been absolutely right about that bed. Six would fit easily, let alone one tall, well-muscled man. He had said he had no wife, but that didn't mean he slept alone, she realized. Surely she couldn't be the only woman who considered him an attractive man. Everything about him was so vital and alive, his face so strong and handsome despite the imperfection. Perhaps the full-figured Bronwyn had found favor with her lord.

Roanna moved around in the tub until her back was to the bed and she faced the closed door. She splashed her face with water. What did it matter whom he took to his bed? It was none of her concern, none at all.

Roanna leaned her head back and closed her eyes, trying

to make her mind blank. Usually she could shut out the worries of the day if she tried hard enough.

The door banged open. Roanna sat up quickly and opened her eyes. Mamaeth darted into the room, carrying a garment over her arm.

"He'll do, your friend, if he lies still like I told him to and drinks the potion I gave him, but being a man he'll probably ignore everything and kill himself."

Roanna's eyes widened with concern.

"Don't trouble yourself, girl. I've told him plain enough what will happen if he acts like a dolt, but since when did a man listen to a woman's wisdom?" Mamaeth suddenly sniffed. "Ah, that's good, that is. Using the herbs like I said. No doubt you're feeling better?"

"Yes, I think so," Roanna replied. She had the impression she was trying to talk to a windstorm and would be listened to about as much.

"Good, good. Now, out of there before you catch your death from the cold."

"The water's warm," Roanna demurred, not willing to be naked in front of a total stranger.

"No modesty now, my girl. Seen it all, I have, man or woman, so you'd better step out. Here's a cloth big enough to keep your secrets safe, if that's what's worrying you."

Roanna took the proffered linen, which indeed was bigger than many a blanket, and stood up, wrapping it around her body.

Mamaeth scrutinized her, then laid the garment on the bed. "It's Bronwyn's and not going to fit, I'm certain. I've got no eyes for a needle now, or I'd fix it."

"I can sew," Roanna said.

"You can?"

"I've spent most of my time sewing. It was the only thing my uncle let me do."

Mamaeth nodded briskly. "Good. I'll fetch the things

you'll need." She stepped closer and looked into Roanna's face. "You're tired, my girl, so why not have a rest? We won't be having the evening meal for some time yet."

Roanna nodded her agreement. In truth, the bath had made every limb as heavy as iron.

Mamaeth scuttled out the door. Roanna looked at the garment. She didn't want to be seen in any more things that hung from her slender figure. It was bad enough that her shape resembled that of a boy more than a woman.

She lay down on the bed. The mattress was soft, and she sunk down into it gratefully. In a few minutes, she fell into a deep, dreamless sleep.

A short time after that, Mamaeth opened the door cautiously. She peered into the room. The girl lay on the bed, her long black hair spread out around her and the cloth wrapped tightly around her body.

Mamaeth crept inside and put needles and thread on the small table. She looked at the sleeping girl.

"Thin, but some good food take care of that. Hips perfect for children. No simpering nonsense about her, either. And the way she looks at him..."

Her eyes grew misty. "The way *he* looks at her, you old fool. Yes, she's for him."

She walked slowly to the door. The girl stirred, moving her legs so that the cover rose closer to her waist. With a sly grin, Mamaeth silently went toward the bed and adjusted the sheet so that almost all of Roanna's long, slender legs were exposed. Then, even more carefully, she pulled the cloth down until the tops of Roanna's creamy breasts, pushed together by the tight wrapping, showed above the sheet.

"Now, to find Emryss," she muttered as she tiptoed out.

Emryss and Rhys, the steward, stood together outside the storehouse. Emryss leaned on his right leg, while his left foot moved back and forth in the damp dirt.

"Not liking this, me," Rhys said, his usually smiling face clouded with concern. His fingers plucked nervously at his long, black beard. "The baron's been waiting a long time for a lesser excuse than this, my lord."

When Emryss didn't respond, he spoke more deliberately. "She should go, I'm thinking, although sorry for her I am. Very bad, all this business. And with harvest time coming, too."

"Mamaeth said her friend will die if he moves now," Emryss said.

"What about taking her to the convent? The sisters would take her in," Rhys said, his round face brightening. "Then she's out of our hands, see, and safe, too."

Emryss's foot still moved in slow circles in the mud.

A door banged and Mamaeth's voice could be heard across the courtyard as she hurried toward them. "Oh, you men! Talking to no purpose, as usual. And what about?"

"Rhys is worried about keeping Lady Roanna and her friend here. He's afraid the baron might attack."

"*I ffwrdd!*" She darted a glance at Rhys, who blushed bright red. "That spider's too old now to move off his web. Of course they'll have to stay, at least for a few days. The girl's near exhausted to death, and that fat fool will bleed like a stuck pig if he's jolted in a cart again."

Emryss shrugged his shoulders. "Well, that's it, then. They stay."

"We've not got the stores to withstand a siege," Rhys said defensively. He gestured to the unfinished storehouse. "Not nearly enough."

Emryss glanced at Mamaeth, his hand beating against his leg as he considered. Then he sighed. "You're right, Rhys. When the man's well enough to travel, they'll have to go. Meanwhile, tell everyone this is to be kept quiet."

Rhys's pleasant smile dawned across his face, and he nodded, relieved.

"Well, that's settled," Mamaeth said quickly. "I best try and get that big oaf to have another draft of my medicine. Oh, Emryss, the girl wants to see you. Probably wanting to know what's going to be done." She bustled off toward the barracks.

"Gwil and the rest of the men should be back soon, and with the outlaws, I trust," Emryss said. "Let me know as soon as they ride in the gate."

"Aye, my lord," Rhys replied, watching his lord limp toward the hall.

As Emryss climbed the stairs to his bedchamber, he wondered if Roanna had decided to tell him more about her abrupt departure from Beaufort.

He knocked softly. The door creaked open from the pressure of his fist, and he went in.

Roanna lay asleep on his bed, barely covered by a white linen sheet. The pure whiteness seemed to make her hair blacker, her skin more pink.

Dear God, he wanted to touch her. To run his hands up her long slim legs. To kiss the tempting top of each rounded breast. To stroke her rippling black hair. To press his lips to her eyelids, her cheeks, her rosy lips...

With a low moan, he backed out of the doorway, pulling the door shut behind him.

Without any clear intention except to get away from Roanna's disturbing near-nakedness, he walked out of the hall and toward the barracks. As he drew closer, he could hear Mamaeth's insistent voice and a man's response. Not surprisingly, Mamaeth was arguing with someone. Mamaeth's voice grew louder and more insistent as he reached the door, which was suddenly wrenched open.

"Go ahead and get blood poisoning!" Mamaeth muttered as she brushed past Emryss. "Men!"

Emryss would have smiled if he had not been preoccupied. With sudden determination he entered the barracks and went toward Jacques, who sat propped up in bed.

"How are you, my friend?" he asked solicitously.

"Well enough, unless that witch makes me drink more of her infernal brews! *Mon Dieu*, they are an insult to my palate!" Jacques cocked his head and looked at Emryss. "The Lady Roanna. How does she fare?"

"She's well. Only tired, Mamaeth says." Emryss sat on a low stool beside the bed. "Tell me—Jacques, is it?" The man nodded. "How did you come to be in this predicament?"

"She has not told you?"

"She told me she refused to marry Cynric DeLanyea. Her uncle locked her up and you helped her escape."

"That is what happened, my lord."

Emryss leaned forward. "As simple as that?"

"If that's all Lady Roanna wishes to say, that's all I will say, too."

Emryss reminded himself they had little reason to trust him, but the man's refusal irked him nonetheless. "What did she expect to do next? Does she have family to take her in?"

Jacques shook his head. "Only the uncle, of that I am certain."

"And he wouldn't help her?"

Jacques sniffed eloquently. "He cares nothing for Lady Roanna. Nothing at all." He leaned forward and whispered. "He treated her worse than a servant, when he didn't ignore the poor girl."

"Is there another man she hopes…" Emryss's heart began to pound strangely as he waited for the man to answer.

Jacques' sly smile disturbed him almost as much as his inability to breathe properly. "No, my lord. Although any man should be pleased if she paid him the compliment."

Emryss tried to return the conversation to its proper course. "Where were you going?"

"To the south. Lady Roanna has had enough of being a noble nothing, my lord. She is proud, as any noblewoman should be, but also practical. She can sew very well, and she intended to make a living with her needle."

"I see." Emryss looked at the big man and saw shadows under his eyes. He had asked enough questions for now.

He stood up to go, but Jacques reached out and clutched his sleeve. "She will not ask you for help, my lord, so I will. Let us rest here awhile. This has been more trying for her than she knows."

"Of course you may stay."

Jacques sighed and dropped his hand. "Now we must convince her of that."

"Tell her. Won't she listen to you?"

Jacques shook his head. "You do not know her, my lord. She has great wisdom for a woman, but, also like a woman, great stubbornness. I cannot simply say to her, 'Do this.'"

He saw the other man's skeptical expression. "She has a mind of her own, Lady Roanna."

Jacques settled down into the pillows again, his eyelids closing. "Even when she was a child, she was thus." His eyelids flew open. "When her uncle didn't send for her when her parents died, she *walked* to his estate, because she decided it was what she must do. Think of that, my lord, only nine years old, and alone..." Again his eyelids slowly lowered. "When she has decided a thing, it stays decided."

"Except who she'll marry," Emryss muttered softly as he stood up.

Jacques' eyes opened again, and when he spoke, his voice was determined. "No, my lord. You still don't understand. She would have married that piece of... An agreement had been made, by the man who stood in the place of her father, undeserving though he may be. She would have abided by that, but not when she learned they had lied to her. I wonder how she came to have such knowledge, eh, my lord?''

Emryss looked at Jacques. ''Thank you for telling me about her.''

''I tell you, my lord, because I think we can trust you.''

Emryss nodded once, then turned and walked into the courtyard. A voice called his name from the battlements and he looked up.

''The patrol—they're back!'' one of the masons shouted.

Emryss hurried toward the gate hoping Gwilym and the others had captured the outlaws who had the audacity to come onto his land. He would deal with such men as was his right as the lord of the manor.

His first concern must always be Craig Fawr and its tenants.

When the girl and her friend were well enough, they would have to leave.

After all, he had nothing to offer a woman. Nothing at all.

Raynald Westercott moaned softly. Deep in the warmth of the bed, he turned away from the sunlight streaming in the unshuttered window. He smacked his dry lips together, the taste in his mouth foul. The wine had been delicious, but he was paying for the pleasure now.

The slight thump of a log slipping in the fire made him open one eye. In the hearth a small blaze burned brightly.

A terrible waste of wood, he thought sourly, then burrowed down into the equally wasteful coverings and feather bed.

A pretty maid, buxom and blond, opened the door tentatively.

"Well?" Westercott growled. She smiled, but he paid no attention to her wiles.

"Good morning, my lord," she said. "Do you need anything?"

"Go away," he snapped. "Wait!" he called before the door completely closed. When the maid peered around, he said querulously, "Send me some of my cook's special broth. He'll know what I mean."

The girl bobbed again and disappeared. Westercott laid down on the pillows. His head continued to pound fiercely.

Where the hell had that wench got to, he wondered several minutes later when she hadn't returned. Servants! Miserable, untrustworthy lot, always trying to steal from you...

He heard a knock at the door.

"About time!" Westercott called out, and sat up, pulling the fur coverings around his chin.

Cynric DeLanyea strode into the room. "Good day, my lord," he said.

His insolent tone was insufferable, but Westercott's head hurt too much to complain.

"Or rather, perhaps not so good," Cynric continued. "It seems my dainty little bride has seen fit to abscond with your cook."

"What!" Westercott sat up quickly. A pain coursed through his brain. "What did you say?"

"Lady Roanna is gone. And your cook, too. I must say it's not very flattering to have one's betrothed run away with a fat, middle-aged servant, but there it is."

"I'll ring her scrawny little neck," Westercott muttered as he climbed from the warm bed.

Cynric leaned nonchalantly against the back of a chair. "Do you think she's worth the effort?"

Westercott stopped putting on his fur robe and stared at the young man.

"Perhaps, Lord Westercott, we should just call off this whole arrangement. Obviously, the girl isn't interested."

Westercott drew himself up. "Your father and I have signed a contract. There's no more to be said."

Cynric walked over to Westercott's open chest of clothing. He ran his hand over the edge of a velvet tunic that lay on top. "Well, I could swallow my pride, I suppose, if the dowry were larger. But as it is..."

Westercott narrowed his eyes. "Very well. I'll pay... more."

"How much?"

"Twenty head of cattle."

"I want gold."

"Fifty pieces."

"Two hundred," Cynric said.

"What? Are you mad? I don't have that much." Westercott walked over and slammed the lid of his chest shut.

"One hundred and seventy-five."

"One hundred."

Cynric smiled slowly. "Very well, my lord. One hundred gold pieces and twenty head of cattle."

"Wait one moment, you arrogant puppy! No cattle!"

"Then our deal is off. Good luck finding someone else to marry that skinny wench." Cynric turned and walked to the door. "I understand it can also be quite an expense to keep a woman in a convent, especially if she lives to a ripe old age."

"Wait," Westercott said. Cynric turned back. "You drive a hard bargain, DeLanyea. But as you say, the girl may have ruined her reputation. Therefore, I will give you what you ask."

Cynric nodded and turned again to leave. Westercott detained him with a hand on his sleeve. Cynric looked at the older man's hand, then into his face. Westercott withdrew his fingers.

"Naturally I'm pleased that you are willing to overlook my niece's peculiar behavior," Westercott said slowly. "I'm sure nothing of a shameful nature has taken place with the cook. He dotes on her like a daughter, I've been told."

Cynric's smile offered no comfort. "Naturally I believe you, my lord. Perhaps her mind was addled from lack of food. Yes, that's it, I'm certain. Perhaps she even now realizes her mistake. And when I find her, she'll be more than grateful that I'm willing to have her, don't you think? Every man should have a wife so beholden to him."

Westercott looked at the handsome young man. "That's why you'll marry my niece?"

Cynric brushed his sleeve where Westercott had laid his hand. "My reasons are no concern of yours."

Chapter Seven

Cynric looked around the darkening clearing. His horse danced nervously, as if it, like the men in the troop behind, expected a pack of howling Welshmen to leap from the trees. He yanked on the reins, and the horse became still.

To his left, Cynric saw the oak, split long ago by lightning, leaning perilously close to the rocky ground. To his right, outcrops of stone thrust upward like fingers trying to grasp the thin branches above.

This was the right place.

"Wait here," Cynric said to Fitzroy, who nodded and moved back to join the rest of the men.

Cynric smiled as he dismounted. Urien Fitzroy was a valuable soldier—as long as he always obeyed unquestioningly.

Cynric leaped the shallow stream and disappeared into the bush on the other side, bending low to avoid the branches. He found the barely discernible path and began climbing up the wooded hill, stepping carefully over the hidden stream that emerged from beneath two rocks. About halfway up he spotted the two stones and large thorn bush. Biting back a curse at the thorns that caught his tunic, Cynric pushed through the undergrowth and into the small cave beyond.

The slight silver flash of daggers caught his eye. "Put them away," he barked to the men huddled in the cold dampness. The crouching, disheveled men smirked, but they sheathed their weapons.

"Good even', m'lord," their leader said with forced joviality. As always, the stench of his foul, rotting teeth repelled Cynric, but he sat on the earthen floor.

"What can we be doing for ye?" the man continued.

The man's accent bespoke his humble origins, adding to Cynric's distaste, but he needed these outlaws, landless, titleless men who could be counted on to do any job for the right price. "I want you to find a girl."

The man's mouth twisted into a leer. "Another one, eh, m'lord?"

"A *special* one."

"Oh, gettin' particular now, are ye?"

Cynric's dagger was at the man's throat in an instant. "Listen, you gallow's bait, I want you to find a girl, young, black-haired, thin, who's traveling with a fat man. I want you to get her and bring her to me—without so much as a scratch. Do you understand?"

"Easy, m'lord, easy."

Cynric put his dagger away and the man moved back slightly. "Black-haired, you said, and with a fat man?"

Cynric saw the greedy gleam in the man's eye. "Yes. What do you know?"

"Well, maybe I knows somethin', m'lord, and maybe I don't."

Cynric reached into the bag at his belt and threw some coins back into the cave. The men scrambled for the money, but the leader stayed still.

"Now, tell me what you know."

"Well, m'lord, we did see two like that. Had them in our hands, so to speak."

Cynric's eyes narrowed, but he said nothing.

"Leastways going to have a little fun we was, till we was interrupted." The man reached for the wine. "All this talking be thirsty work, m'lord. Care t'join me?"

Cynric watched impatiently as the man took an enormous swig. "No, I don't. Get on with it! Who interrupted you?"

"Them ones from Craig Fawr, it was." The man heard the sharp intake of breath. He'd have to ask for more money for this job, if it was that important. Usually the young lord DeLanyea gave his orders with as much feeling as one of the rocks in the wall of the cave.

"That's right, proper troop they was. Must have been fifty, sixty men. They had a new one with 'em—good fighter, blind in one eye, but he took off soon enough."

"And the girl?"

"Don't know, m'lord. Didn't wait to find out, if you know what I mean. Came back here. Almost didn't make it, but we give 'em the slip."

Cynric reached into his pouch again and pulled out a gold piece. The man's eyes lit up.

Cynric tossed it to him. "They'll be a lot more if you get me that girl."

"What about our other job, eh, m'lord?"

"Do whatever you like on Emryss's land, just so long as you stay off mine. But find me that girl."

"We'll do our best, m'lord—seein' as you're most generous. And what should we do with the fat man, if we finds 'em?"

"Kill him."

Gwilym stood beside Emryss in the great hall. Around them servants bustled, harassed by the ever-present Mamaeth, as they set out the bread and cups and bowls.

Emryss rubbed a hand along his aching jaw. He had to fight the urge to clench his teeth again, angry that the outlaws who had attacked the Lady Roanna and her friend had managed to escape. His men had searched until the light began to fail, then turned for home.

Gwilym reached for a piece of bread, only to have his hand slapped by Mamaeth as she passed by with fresh candles. "So, she took it into her head to run off, eh?"

Emryss's fingers tapped the oak table worn smooth by many meals. "Why not? They tried to force her to marry Cynric. She's a lot better off here."

"For now maybe."

"Aye, for now." Emryss's fingers stopped tapping and clenched into fists. He kept his voice low, for now his people began filing into the hall, talking and laughing, ready for the evening meal. "Cynric said she must be lying, when she claimed I had not raped her."

"Liking to get my hands on his throat!" Gwilym growled angrily.

"You'd have to climb over me first," Emryss said softly.

And then Roanna appeared in the doorway.

The new gown molded itself to the slender body he had seen so nearly naked. Her hair, now brushed, seemed to flow around her like a dark mist. He glanced at her face, his gaze drawn to her soft green eyes.

He reminded himself that she would soon be gone.

Roanna blinked in the bright light from many candles—fine candles, not the cheap ones favored by her uncle—that filled the hall. A hush fell over the waiting crowd as she entered.

She paused, uncertain where she should sit. She had no place here in this hall. She was an unwelcome intruder, not friend or invited guest or...anything. In her old gesture of self-defense, she lowered her gaze to the floor and waited.

The whole room seemed to sigh at once, and she raised

her eyes. Emryss, tall, strong, his face grave, walked toward her.

Her lungs ceased to breathe as he held out his arm. Demurely, her fingers quivering, she placed her hand on the offered arm and let him lead her. She was to sit in the place reserved for honored guests, beside him and to the right hand. He escorted her there as a matter of course, too, as if his action were completely natural and to be expected.

Her surreptitious glance saw no surprise on anyone's face. Not the round, smiling face of the man nodding to her from the closest place at the next table. Not Bronwyn's as she moved to the side of the hall. Not Mamaeth's, sitting at the far end of the high table, her beady eyes darting about constantly.

The hall was crowded with so many people, and not one expressed any shock at the lord's action, although they all stared at her frankly. Perhaps their respect for Emryss made his every decision acceptable, but she knew—none better—that she had no right to be so honored.

As Emryss sat, everyone else took their seats silently. Roanna looked at all the people, wondering how the few paltry fields they had passed as they rode into Craig Fawr could support such a multitude. It might be that this estate's wealth lay in the flocks of sheep that grazed on the hills. Or perhaps there were other sources of wealth.

She craned her neck, searching for the priest who would bless the meal. The places were laid, the wine poured, the aroma from the kitchen most enticing, but yet no man of God rose to say a blessing. All around, the people began to break their bread, the sound of their several voices swelling through the room.

''Excuse me, my lord,'' she ventured softly, aghast that they would dare to begin, ''but isn't the grace going to be said?'' She looked at him fully for the first time since she had entered the hall, and for the first time realized she sat

on his blind side. He would have to turn his body to look
at her.

Emryss kept staring at his chalice, which Bronwyn filled
with wine. "I will have no priests in my hall. I had a belly-
ful of them in the Holy Land."

Roanna tried to control her shock. She, too, looked at
her chalice. Even her uncle kept an old priest on his estate,
and the baron had spent considerable sums, or so Cynric
had bragged, to build a large monastery on Beaufort land.
The church was too important to offend in such a manner,
and surely the tenants' spiritual well-being called for a res-
ident priest.

But his tone had been one of absolute finality.

The aroma of freshly baked bread filled her nostrils. It
had been a long time since she had eaten, she realized, and
the food spread before her seemed more appropriate for a
banquet than an ordinary meal. Hoping God would understand, she crossed herself and silently blessed the food before her.

As the meal progressed, she tried to concentrate on the
people in the hall. She listened carefully, using all her skill
to understand the nuances even if she couldn't understand
the language. She wanted to know who smiled with their
lips but not their eyes, whose joviality was forced, who
bore grudges, who was an enemy and who a friend.

It was not easy with Emryss sitting beside her. She was
all too conscious of his lean, strong fingers so close to hers,
of his lips against the rim of his chalice, of the rising and
falling of his chest as he breathed. Even the slight scent of
leather that arose from his clothes could not be subdued by
the delicious smell of the food.

And what food! Roanna could scarcely believe the va-
riety and quality. The bread brought to the high table was
white and delicious, rivaling Jacques'. Even at the farthest

tables, the bread seemed to be above the usual standard for those at such a place in the hall.

As she took another bite of the bread, she glanced at Emryss. Maybe she had spent too long at a miser's table and had forgotten the usual generosity of most noblemen. Platter after platter passed by, and the people all seemed so genuinely happy and guileless that she finally gave up her subtle scrutiny and gave herself in to the pleasure of a wonderful meal.

The high table partook of a dizzying array of meats, mutton, pork, chicken and beef, each in its own sauce. There was a delightful dish of beaten eggs mixed with the crumbs of bread and shaped like dumplings that had been simmered in chicken broth. Many kinds of fruit sat on the table, and the bread was always plentiful. Wine and beer flowed abundantly, as well, but Roanna was most careful not to over-indulge, no matter how tempted. She was having enough trouble avoiding staring at her handsome benefactor; a little more of this delicious wine, and she might be tempted to loosen her rigid self-control.

As the servants hurried around, Roanna noticed that Bronwyn always moved most slowly as she passed by the high table, the jug of wine cradled against her ample bosom. For a brief instant Roanna frowned with consternation, until she told herself it shouldn't matter to her that Bronwyn had a prettier face and finer figure. Nevertheless, when Bronwyn apparently felt it necessary to replenish the wine goblets yet again, Roanna kept her covert gaze on the girl.

Bronwyn ignored Roanna's chalice and barely glanced at Emryss's. It was at Gwilym's cup that she lingered, letting the wine trickle into his chalice. Roanna felt like a simpleton as she realized she was most inordinately relieved that Bronwyn obviously cared more for the younger man. A few minutes later, however, Roanna found herself moved to pity the maidservant. Despite Bronwyn's tardiness, Gwilym never so much as acknowledged her presence. He kept talking to Emryss, as if the girl, whose eyes fairly brimmed with love, were invisible.

"May I have some more wine, please," Roanna finally said, when she could no longer stand to see Bronwyn ignored.

Emryss tried not to look at Roanna, although he had been wondering for some time when she would speak. And then it was only to ask for more wine. In fact, she seemed so interested in the food that he was a little dismayed. She ate as if she were starving, but maybe that wasn't too far from the truth, from what he had been told.

It wasn't, he told himself, that she should be interested in him necessarily. Yet there had been a time when the maidservants squabbled over who would pour his wine, and he, young fool, had assumed it would always be so. Now, however, a loaf of bread was proving more intriguing than he was. The idea was most unsettling, although he should be used to such changes by now.

Trying not to watch Roanna's slender fingers as she reached for an apple, he toyed with the base of his goblet and half listened to Gwilym recount a long tale of some sheep thought stolen and then found to be "borrowed."

"Emryss!"

He turned toward Gwilym, whose face wore a bemused look. "Stop playing with your cup, man. Either take a drink or not, but you're going to drive me mad if you don't quit your fiddling!"

Emryss mustered a grin and picked up his goblet. He very nearly succeeded in looking nonchalant, but his fingers brushed against the sleeve of Roanna's dress. He jerked as if she had slapped him, spilling some wine on the table.

Fortunately, Gwilym had been occupied with his own

goblet, so Emryss was spared his foster brother's wry comments.

"The outlaws must know the land," Emryss said. He had more important matters to think about than this woman at his elbow.

"Aye, to judge the way they disappeared. Like snow in the sun, it was, and we had the best trackers with us, too. Unnatural, almost."

"Could they have had help from our people?" Emryss hated to consider this possibility, but it existed nonetheless.

"Not likely—not them. Rob anybody, they do, Welsh or no. Our folk wouldn't hold with that, I'm certain. But—" he paused and his look was meaningful "—the De-Lanyeas..."

"You think they would stoop to such measures?"

"I think they'd be using any means they could, no matter how low. Don't think of honor and them at the same time."

Emryss let his breath out slowly. "My God, I knew Cynric was a lout, but at least he used to have some principles."

"That was long ago, *brawdmaeth.*"

Emryss sat back in his chair and cursed in eloquent Welsh.

"I beg your pardon, my lord?"

Emryss sat up straight and looked at Roanna. Her brows were furrowed with charming bewilderment.

"It was...nothing important, my lady." He glanced at the empty platter before her. "You seem to be enjoying the food."

The pink of a blush tinged her cheeks. "It is wonderful." She looked down at her lap, robbing him of the sight of her eyes. "Jacques would surely give ten years off his life to work with such food as you supply."

It took a mighty effort not to touch her cheek.

"Even without a grace?" he said.

"It would have been appropriate to thank God for such

bounty," she replied. At least he got her to look at him
again, even if it was a glance intended to make him feel
ashamed. He fought the urge to tell her he had no need to
apologize for the lack of holy hypocrisy in his hall.

Suddenly Rhys, his round cherubic face grinning, cried
out a slew of Welsh. At once everyone in the hall began
to call "Emryss! Emryss!" They slapped the tables with
their palms, and their feet stamped on the stone floor until
the noise was deafening.

Roanna looked around, wondering what had brought on
such a demonstration. Emryss raised his hand for silence
and spoke a few words. Another shout answered him, and
he bowed his head in acquiescence.

He rose from his chair, downed a gulp of wine and went
to the corner beside the hearth. Only then did Roanna see
the small harp placed there. Voices continued to shout out
a cacophony of Welsh as he picked it up.

Roanna could hardly believe her eyes as the lord of the
manor grabbed a small stool and, setting it down in the
middle of the hall, gently stroked the harp as if it were a
lover reluctant to speak. Then he began to sing, his bass
voice low and soft.

After the first few notes, Roanna was overwhelmed. The
music and the voice, quiet yet powerful, were filled with a
sweet yearning that reached deep inside her to a place long
guarded. Although she couldn't understand the Welsh, his
song tugged, pulled, demanded that she understand the feeling. And she did. Dear God in Heaven, it was as if he had
seen the loneliness inside her very soul.

The last, lingering notes echoed off the stone walls. No
one spoke for a moment, then the clamor of clapping and
shouts began again. Emryss nodded and called for
Mamaeth.

He began to play a lively tune. The harp danced in his
hands as if it had a life of its own, and Mamaeth, as spritely

as a child, began singing in a creaking, wavering, thin voice. To judge by her winks and gestures, the song was clearly bawdy, but all the people in the hall laughed and began to join in the words.

Roanna looked around at their smiling, singing faces. They all belonged here. Only she, the outsider, the dispossessed Norman, had no place in this hall.

She choked back a sob as she realized the man Gwilym was speaking to her.

"Fine song, eh, my lady? Our Emryss makes a fine *bastynwr*—minstrel, that is!" His words were slightly slurred, and he leaned toward her as he spoke.

"It was lovely," she said, looking down, suddenly ashamed that a song could almost make her cry.

"It's his, you know, my lady. Made it up himself." Gwilym laughed loudly. "Now if he could fight as well as he makes music!"

"If you will excuse me, I think I need some fresh air," Roanna said feebly as she rose to her feet. Quickly she made her way down the outside of the hall and slipped into the quiet stillness of the summer night. The moon shone in a cloudless sky, and the stars, her old friends, beckoned her closer.

A ramp led to the battlements nearby, and Roanna, holding her skirts, climbed up. When she reached the top, she looked at the village below. She took deep, cleansing breaths and soon felt calmer. The muffled singing from the hall rose to her, but it might have been phantoms singing and she the only living person here. Beyond, the land spread out like a dark, unmoving sea.

"You're not ill, I hope?"

She hadn't heard Emryss approach, and his unexpected nearness brought a flush of warmth to her body as she turned to him. The moonlight shone on his features, the patch over his eye like only another shadow.

"I wanted some cool air."

He nodded and turned to look out over his land. "Beautiful, isn't it?"

"Yes."

"God, how I missed it!"

"Were you away for a long time?" Somehow, it didn't seem wrong to ask him things now that they were alone, away from everyone.

"Eleven years." He turned to look at her, and she saw no self-pity on his face. "They left me, you see. At Acre, one of Richard's 'glorious victories.'" His expression showed quite clearly what he thought of such a glory, but then he grinned. "Thought I was dead, I suppose. Fortunately Abram found me trying to crawl off the field and healed my wounds. But by the time I could walk, Richard had sailed."

"Was there no one to help you?"

"It was dangerous even for Abram, after what Richard did to the Moslem garrison he defeated."

"What was that?" she asked softly, trying to picture Emryss near death. It seemed impossible that he should ever be weak and helpless.

"Richard ordered them all lined up outside the city, bound with rope. And then he had them slaughtered. Like animals." Emryss closed his eye, his brow wrinkled as if in pain. As if he could hear the screams of the dying men even here. "After that, a Crusader's life wasn't worth a copper to Saladin." He shook his head. "Richard was a good man in a battle, but what a dolt he could be!" He turned to her with a small grin, but now she could see beyond his smiles, to the pain that he carried deep within. "Anyway, I had to make my own way back to Wales, with no money, no horse, not even my armor."

"What did you do?"

She thought he blushed for a moment, but perhaps it was only a trick of the moonlight.

"I sang my way home." He spoke quickly. "I had no weapons, so I couldn't hire myself out as a fighter. Besides," he continued ruefully, "I wasn't sure how my leg would hold out in a battle. But I lived—and that's enough about me. Jacques said you made quite a journey yourself, once."

Roanna moved away slightly. His presence made it almost impossible for her to think clearly.

"Did you really do that?" he pressed, his voice a little doubtful. "Walk to your uncle's by yourself?"

She turned to face him. "Yes."

"That was a brave thing to do." His voice, gentle and soft, was like a caress. She moved back.

"It was the *only* thing to do."

He took a step closer. "Weren't you frightened?"

She turned her back to him, hoping he would leave but at the same time afraid that he would. "I was terrified." She looked at the sky. "I told myself that every star in the sky was an angel, watching over me."

His hands touched her shoulders. "I think, Roanna, you had a harder journey than I, for at least I was going home." His lips were beside her ear, his breath warm on her cheek.

Facing him, she said, "I hope to find myself a home, when we leave here."

He smiled, his warmth reaching out like a mantle to cover her. "Jacques won't be able to travel for a while yet. In the meantime…"

He was going to touch her again. And she knew if she allowed it, she would beg him not to let her go. "Jacques and I must leave here as soon as possible. It is too dangerous."

"Why don't you let me worry about this trouble?"

"Because, my lord, I *am* the trouble. I'm not a child to be patted on the head and sent to bed."

Her chin quivered, but he was certain it was not because she fought back tears. She was angry; he could see that clearly enough.

"I'm sorry," he said. "I know you're not stupid."

"No, I'm not. Nor are you, my lord, but you seem to think of Cynric and his father as some ignorant imbeciles incapable of beating you in a fair fight. That may be—if it came to such a battle.

"I owe you much, my lord, so please listen to me now. Do you know that your enemies have been cultivating powerful friends at court? Friends that have no use for those who served Richard? John has the power now, and he doesn't hesitate to use it to his advantage."

"So? What is that to me? I'm finished with Norman kings."

"The baron won't fight you with arms and men. He will fight you with law and influence. *That* was why the baron wanted Cynric to marry me, because my uncle has powerful friends who owe him many favors. Cynric also told me how cleverly they have lured the most learned monks to the monastery they have built, monks well versed in all forms of law. They can take your land without raising a finger if they have the law and power in their hands."

Emryss rubbed his lips thoughtfully, his head lowered. "Then how do I fight them?" he asked softly, as if to himself.

"By learning the law yourself, or finding someone who knows it."

He lifted his head and her breath caught at the intensity of his gaze. "Do you know the law, Roanna?" he asked as he took her hands in his.

"No," she whispered. "I cannot even read."

He pulled her closer, until he stood as close as a breath.

"I would that you did, for then I would ask you to stay and help me."

His whispered words hung between them as his firm, soft lips met hers gently. Warmth spread outward from some place deep within her. Pressing against him, she wanted to be close, needed to feel the hardness of his chest against her own, craved his deepening kiss. His body moved against hers, insistent and yet oh, so patient. Demanding nothing. Asking everything. Instinctively, her hands reached up to touch his face.

Perhaps, at last, she had found the end to loneliness.

But at what cost, to him and the people who depended on his strength? And what of her honor, if she let him make love to her now?

With a sound that was almost a whimper, she pulled her hands away. "I...I cannot!"

"Bear to touch my face?"

Her heart twisted at the pain in his voice and the anguish on his face.

"No, no, Emryss. I love you! But God help me, I cannot. I must not!"

Then she turned and fled down the ramp.

Chapter Eight

The rain swooped down out of the dark sky, striking like pebbles against the wall. Roanna climbed out of the huge bed and went to the window.

She had watched the clouds blot out the stars as the night progressed. Sleep had come only after many hours, and then it was a fitful unrestful sleep, filled with dreams.

She couldn't stop thinking about Emryss and the feelings that churned inside her like a rolling river. She loved him, but how could she have been so weak, to let him touch her?

And what did he think of her? Did he care for her in the same way? And if so, what then? The thoughts twirled and twisted in her brain, with no answers to give her peace. Clad only in her shift, with her feet bare against the cold stones of the floor, she shivered.

She needed to go to Mass. Surely the comfort of the service would help, and perhaps then she would know better what to do.

A rap on the door heralded the entrance of Bronwyn, who carried in a steaming ewer. She set it on the small table and bid Roanna a quiet good morning.

Roanna gave her a sidelong glance as she pulled on her one and only gown. "Where is Mass said?"

"Pardon, my lady?"

"Where do I go to hear Mass?"

Bronwyn's face went red when Roanna turned to look at her. "My lady," she began, then hesitated. Roanna waited patiently for her to continue. "My lady, we don't have Mass here, except on Sunday."

Roanna considered this for a moment. "You break the fast without hearing Mass?"

"Yes, my lady," Bronwyn said quietly, still blushing furiously.

Roanna digested this new piece of information. For some reason Emryss DeLanyea obviously had very little use for the church in his life, but that was still no reason for him to deny his villeins.

He might be able to excuse his need for religious guidance and peace, but she could not. Not today.

She said no more about it to Bronwyn but nevertheless she left the bedchamber determined to hear Mass.

As she neared the great hall, she heard the clang of sword on sword and quickened her pace.

A group of men, cups of ale in their hands, stood exhorting and cheering two men fighting in their midst. The sounds of clashing sword and grunting opponents grew louder as she ventured closer. Standing on tiptoe, she struggled to see who the fighting men were.

Emryss and Gwilym, both stripped to the waist, circled each other warily, bent low as if weary. No patch covered the awful welt on Emryss's shining face, and she suppressed a gasp at the myriad small scars covering his chest. On his torso there was a long, red welt that began at his left nipple and disappeared into the top of his chausses.

The men's heavy broadswords hung almost to the ground, but she knew the seeming looseness of their grasp was deceptive. Their fingers could tighten and swing the huge weapons in the blink of an eye.

Shouts of encouragement grew and mingled with the sound of the rain pounding on the roof, but they couldn't drown out the labored breathing of the swordsmen. Powerful thigh muscles strained against leather chausses as they circled in a low crouch. Beads of perspiration gathered on their foreheads and ran down the sides of their faces. Then, as if by some sense unknown to her, they lifted their swords at the same time. The blows glanced off, and the men moved slowly around, not taking their eyes off each other.

Roanna cautiously moved forward as she watched Emryss. He favored his right leg, and his head was constantly turned a little to the right. To compensate for the missing eye, undoubtedly. His shoulders were broad and powerful-looking, and she could almost count his ribs as he moved past her. She knew full well how firm and strong his muscular arms were.

Then he saw her.

He stood up abruptly, ignoring Gwilym's startled protest, and came toward her.

She wished they had never been together on the battlements, for now she hardly knew what to say to him.

"Yes?" He waited as she stared at him. And then she saw his face soften. It lasted but an instant, but it made her bold enough to ignore the rest of the men gathered around.

She straightened her shoulders. "Where do I go for Mass?"

Her question caused a slight rise of his eyebrows. Out of the corner of her eye, Roanna saw the other men glancing at each other. Moving leisurely, keeping his gaze fastened on her face, Emryss handed his sword to Gwilym.

"To a church, I suppose." The men snickered, and it suddenly struck Roanna that perhaps his manner was due to the number of onlookers. It could very well be that he had no wish to appear tenderhearted to a Norman, least of all one whose presence inflamed an already volatile situation.

"Where is that?"

He slowly drew on his shirt. "There is a chapel in the town, along the road near the woods. A lay brother says the Mass there on weekdays."

"Thank you." She walked past him, determined to seem as cool and unconcerned as he did. Nevertheless, she felt happier than she had ever been in her life.

He did care for her. In his own way, perhaps, and only for a short time, but he cared for her.

"You'll drown in that wet!" His words brought a hoot of laughter from the men, which ceased when she grabbed the first cloak on a peg near the entrance and threw open the door. The rain and wind buffeted her, but she continued out into the muddy courtyard.

"God's wounds, what a stubborn wench!" Gwilym said as the door banged behind her. "Is she mad?"

Emryss took a cup of offered ale and walked toward the high table. The other men, realizing the practice was over for the time being, sat at the benches along the side of the wall. If they discussed their lord and his guest, they did so guardedly, and Emryss could not hear them.

Emryss threw himself into his chair. Gwilym sat down beside him. "And is she planning to be a nun as well, seeing she's so willing to get drenched?" he asked, hoping perhaps to replace Emryss's glowering expression with his more usual grin.

"How should I know?" was the answer he got for his trouble.

"Mamaeth'll be nursing the both of them soon. Maybe she'll turn back."

Emryss said nothing, only ripped his loaf of bread into smaller and smaller pieces. He was exhausted, from a sleepless night as much as from the practice. He had hoped to work himself until he couldn't think because all his thoughts revolved around a slender, dark-haired woman who loved him.

And whom he loved in return. Only she could never know it.

Gwilym, apparently deciding it wiser to leave Emryss to his mood, ate his loaf silently.

Suddenly the door blew open. Emryss sat up quickly as a small bedraggled figure staggered in.

"My lord!" Little Hu's exhausted voice could barely be heard above the wind, but Emryss was quickly at the boy's side.

"What? What is it, Hu?" He pulled the shivering boy into his arms.

"The sheep. Ianto's flock. Killed." Hu managed to say as he drew in great, ragged breaths.

Mamaeth appeared in the doorway, concern lining her face as she saw the boy.

"Mamaeth, take him and get him food and dry clothes. Gwilym, get a patrol together." Emryss pushed back Hu's sodden hair and smiled at the lad, taking a moment to calm the boy's fear and sorrow. "There's a good boy you are, Hu."

Mamaeth shrouded the boy with a cloak and hustled him off toward the kitchen. Emryss grabbed his leather jerkin and reached for his cloak.

Gone. *She* had taken it. With an oath he grabbed his sword and belt and went into the courtyard.

Gwilym and the others were already on their horses. One of the grooms was hurriedly adjusting Emryss's saddle. He mounted quickly and raised his hand. The column rode out of the gate at a gallop.

It was a hard ride in the driving rain to the pasture where Ianto grazed his flock. All along the way, the men searched for any signs of thieves, or a pack of wolves, or anything amiss, as well as keeping an eye on the treacherous, rock-strewn path.

At last they reached the pasture. A short way in the distance they could make out the figure of Ianto, standing like a beacon at the far edge of the meadow. Emryss took the lead, and they rode toward him.

As they drew near, they saw the decapitated carcasses of several young sheep on the ground. It might have been the work of a fox. They sometimes did such things, although no one really knew why. The only other animal capable of such wanton killing was man.

Rage built up inside Emryss, matching the winds howling around him. Such waste. Hungry, needy men would have taken the sheep, and that he could understand. But to simply leave mutilated corpses...

Ianto, accompanied as always by his dog Mott, came forward. "Hu ran fast, did he?"

"Aye. When?" Emryss asked quietly.

"Hard to say, my lord. Dry the ground is under 'em, so before the rain. Searched since I sent Hu to you, but finding nothing."

"Fox?"

"Maybe."

"Any missing?"

"Could be. I got at least ten other ewes range round here. Could be they've moved off a far ways, if they smelt a fox."

"Aye." Emryss looked about. The sheep might have wandered, for they were not herded. Each sheep learned its grazing place in the hills from its mother, generation after generation, and seldom strayed unless forced to.

A red-brown burst of fur streaked past. In an instant Mott was after it, barking.

"*Cadno!*" The men cried out as they gave chase to the

fox, dismounting and running when the way became too rocky. Ianto, familiar with the rocky hill, kept sight of the fox as it dashed over the rocks followed by the black and white dog. But their prey was too fast, and clever. It ran through a small stream on the edge of the meadow and disappeared on the other side. Mott splashed through the water, but he lost the scent on the far side. Sniffing, he turned this way and that, then lifted his eyes to his master with a look of mute apology.

The men followed across the shallow water, but they could find no trace of the animal, either. Emryss took more time to climb down the rocks.

"That it, do you think?" Emryss asked the shepherd.

"No way of knowing now, my lord. Might have been. Might not."

Emryss nodded. "I'll send some men to keep watch for a few days, just to be certain."

"Aye, my lord."

"I'll bring Hu back myself."

"Thanks, my lord. That'll please him no end."

Emryss smiled. Hu had been the first one to spy him when he rode home, and he seemed to feel that made Emryss his personal property. Emryss couldn't deny that the boy's adoration pleased his vanity.

"And best to have the gathering as soon as the grain's in, I think," Ianto added, referring to the culling process. The yearling lambs were kept in the valley during the winter, for they were not hardy enough to withstand open grazing on the hills.

"Right," Emryss agreed. He clapped his hand on his old friend's shoulder.

The two men stood on the bank and looked at each other, drawn together by the loss. Emryss knew that although he had lost valuable possessions, Ianto felt as if he had lost his children.

Ianto whistled for Mott, and Emryss watched him walk away with the deliberate tread and bent knees of a man born and bred in the hills. The men of the patrol straggled back, with no dead fox. Emryss had them pick up the carcasses of the sheep to be shorn and butchered.

As he walked toward his waiting horse, Gwilym caught up to him.

"Best to have Old Daffyd take a look, eh, Emryss?"

"Aye."

The old shepherd might be better able to tell them what to hunt for, animals or men.

The patrol mounted and turned down the path to Craig Fawr. The rain slowed down and eventually ceased as they reached the valley.

Emryss reached up to wipe the droplets from his face, his fingers touching the deep scar. He stifled the urge to curse. God, he didn't need to remember her touch on that same ruined place. He had lost enough sleep already.

A shiver ran through him. Too bad he'd been so long from Wales, he told himself, if he couldn't get used to a summer rain.

He glanced around, hoping none of his men had seen. They would think less of him for such a weakness. Rather than risk their finding out, he spurred his horse into a trot. The sooner he was back at Craig Fawr and into dry clothes, the better.

Roanna had been cold since she reached the leaking wooden chapel, but at last the Mass had come to an end. Rising to her feet, her knees aching, she went to the door of the small chapel.

The rain had stopped. She looked at the path that led up to the fortress with some distress, for there seemed to be no way to avoid muddying her shoes again.

Several well-wrapped villagers made their way past her

cautiously, saying nothing. She couldn't blame them. She must be an odd sight, with her wet, unbound hair and damp gown.

She pulled the borrowed cloak around her head, pausing for a moment at the scent of leather and metal. One of the soldiers was going to be upset if he had to face more rain without his cloak. It had been most impetuous to take it.

Still, she was glad she had come to the Mass. For a little while she had been able to clear her mind of him, his touch, his kiss.

She walked quickly, lost in her thoughts, but the way was slippery and treacherous, especially with chilled, soaking feet. Roanna pulled the cloak, which was not quite as muddy as her dress, around her and walked regally toward the gate.

She hurried under the portcullis and made her way cautiously across the slippery cobblestoned courtyard to the barracks.

"Kitten! A delight for my eyes. How happy I am to see you!" Jacques' voice boomed through the empty building. Roanna took off the cloak and shook it, sending little droplets flying.

She hung it on a peg near the door and walked to Jacques' bedside. "How are you, Jacques?" she asked softly.

"Better, in spite of that hideous woman and her poisons." He leaned forward, the bed creaking ominously. "I myself think it was the food. Such bounty! Such a meal!" He clasped his plump hands together, leaning back and sighing. "Just think what a genius such as I could do in that kitchen!"

Roanna pulled up a stool and sat beside him. "I'm happy that you're feeling better."

Jacques suddenly lowered his head and looked at her carefully. "And you, little kitten, how are *you?*"

"Very well," Roanna replied, after only a short hesitation. "Lord DeLanyea is most generous."

"A generous man, a noble man, a man of great honor, wouldn't you agree, little one?"

Roanna stood up and moved toward the narrow windows. She looked out at the yard. "Yes, I think so."

"And a most intriguing one, too, is he not?"

"Yes."

"A pity we must go from here." He sighed loudly.

"We can bring nothing but trouble to these people."

"Lord DeLanyea is not concerned, I think."

Roanna whirled around. "Then he should be."

Jacques' eyes widened with surprise at her flushed face, but he quickly resumed his jovial expression. "Well, we shall not worry about that today. It is enough that we were rescued from those brigands." He looked at her gown. "I think you have visited me long enough, my lady. You will catch a chill in that wet dress." Mamaeth appeared in the doorway, a steaming chalice in her hand. "*Mon Dieu,* not more of your infernal brews!"

"More of my *medicine,* you big lout. But you're right." She stopped in front of Roanna. "Needing to be out of that, you are, or I'll be nursing the both of you."

"A fate worse than death, I assure you," Jacques muttered.

"I don't have another dress," Roanna began to protest, but Mamaeth interrupted her.

"The one you came in's been cleaned and mended. Bronwyn's taken it to the bedchamber. Not much of a dress, I grant you, but better than nothing."

Roanna nodded. "Thank you." She leaned over and kissed Jacques on the forehead. "Take care. I'll be back later."

"If I survive this woman's medicine," Jacques said sourly.

Roanna smiled briefly and went out, taking the cloak with her.

Mamaeth turned to her patient. "A fine girl, I'm thinking. Respectable, and knowing when to listen and when to speak."

"There is no finer *lady* on this earth, I assure you."

"I like her. My boy likes her, too."

Jacques frowned. "Should I be impressed with what some bumpkin thinks?"

Mamaeth looked down at Jacques with a withering expression. "Lord DeLanyea, I'm talking of, you ninny."

Jacques nodded thoughtfully. "Naturally everyone who meets Lady Roanna is impressed by her." He gave Mamaeth a narrow-eyed, sidelong glance. "What exactly do you mean, he likes her?"

"*O'r annwyl!* Could you be that dense, man? He likes her the way a man's supposed to like a woman. What a dolt you are!"

Now it was Jacques' turn to be withering. "If you speak of a grown man as a boy, I think *I* am not the dolt. However, I thought that was what you were trying to say."

"What does she think of *him?*"

"How should I know? A lady would not speak of such things." It was no business of this creature what Roanna thought of her "boy," but if he had answered, he would have said that Emryss DeLanyea affected her in a way no man ever had before.

Mamaeth glared at him, then thrust the steaming chalice under his nose. A most unwelcome, familiar odor drifted into his nostrils.

"Are you trying to kill me with your disgusting preparations?" he growled.

Before she could respond, the door crashed open.

"Ah, Mamaeth," Emryss said as he shook his soaked

hair like a dog. "Needing my other shirt. Did you bring it?"

Mamaeth spun around. "No, in your bedchamber it is."

"Fetch it, will you?"

Mamaeth looked indignant. "Got to see to the noon meal. Not your slave, me, and no forgetting it." She stalked angrily toward the door. "Men!" She turned back to Emryss, her arms akimbo. "Ungrateful wretches, the lot of you. Fetch it yourself!" She slammed the barracks door as she went out.

Emryss let out a groan and looked at Jacques. "God's wounds, I only asked for a shirt." He turned and went out.

Jacques absentmindedly took a sip of the brew in the chalice, then made a face and set the cup on the floor beside the bed. He hoped someone would trip and spill it.

He rubbed his jaw thoughtfully. Roanna and Emryss DeLanyea. They would make a fine couple. Of course, she would be a good wife for any man, but she needed someone like *him,* a generous, good-natured person who could make her come out from behind the walls she had built around her heart, to reveal herself.

He sat up suddenly. She had gone to change and so had *he*—and all his clothes in the room she now used! His broad mouth turned up into a roguish grin.

Chapter Nine

By the time Emryss reached the steps leading up to his bedchamber, his anger at Mamaeth's outburst had diminished. He even began to chuckle as he remembered the shocked look on Jacques' face. Probably he couldn't believe Emryss would permit his underlings to talk that way to the lord of the manor.

Well, he wouldn't, if it had been anyone but Mamaeth. She had no respect for any man simply because he *was* a man, let alone one she'd raised from infancy. And of course, he knew that she loved him more than her own life.

He opened the door to the bedchamber, then halted in confusion.

Roanna, dressed only in her shift, was bent over the small basin, a mound of wet, muddy fabric in her hands. She straightened quickly, clutching the sodden mass to her breasts.

Emryss was out of the room in an instant, pulling the door shut behind him. He held his breath, half expecting to hear her screaming for Mamaeth or Bronwyn. When nothing happened, he marched to the top of the stairs. ''Mamaeth!'' He shouted so loudly that Roanna, pulling on her gown with trembling fingers, flinched.

At the thought of how she must have looked standing there in her shift, she felt the heat of a blush travel up her neck. Going to the door, she peered around it. Emryss stood stock-still at the top of the stairs, his foot tapping rapidly on the floor, his arms crossed and his shoulders tense. Roanna closed the door and went to the window.

She looked at the courtyard, glistening from the rain, and tried not to think of the embarrassment of being seen in her undergarment. Below, the masons were supervising the arrival of huge blocks of limestone in the inner yard, and their musical voices reached her ears like a chorus of song.

After the initial flood of heated shame, she remembered the startled expression on Emryss's face when he came in, his chest bare, holding a limp, wet shirt in his fist. The corners of her mouth began to twitch, and soon she was giggling despite her efforts to remain calm. No doubt she had looked just as foolishly surprised.

She stopped laughing at the sound of angry voices, followed by a series of rapid knocks on the heavy door.

"Enter," she said, wondering what was happening.

Mamaeth came hurtling in as if pursued by a mad dog. "Pardon, my girl. Got to fetch a shirt."

She went to the chest, threw open the lid, leaned down until her head quite disappeared, then pulled out one of Emryss's shirts, all the while muttering fiercely in Welsh. She shot a glance at Roanna.

"Emryss says to tell you he's sorry for intruding before, but he needed this, and no one saw fit to tell him you might be here."

"I assumed that was what had happened," Roanna replied gravely.

"And *I'm* sorry he's too ill-mannered to knock!" Mamaeth fired off as she went out.

Poor Emryss, Roanna thought as she smiled at the closed

door. Mamaeth would certainly talk him to death about this!

She went over to the small table, where the dirty dress lay in a heap. She would have to go to the kitchen and get more water if she was to wash it properly. She hoped Bronwyn would be otherwise occupied, for she hated to think how the girl would feel if she saw the state of her garment.

Cynric DeLanyea reached across the sleeping woman and poured himself another cup of wine, emptying the jug. Sipping the drink slowly, he leaned back in his disheveled bed and smiled to himself. Things were going just the way he had hoped after that ridiculous Roanna had managed to slip out of her uncle's fingers.

Last night his father had ranted and raved again, calling Lord Westercott a knave and an imbecile for letting her go and threatening to cancel the marriage contract.

When the baron finally calmed down, Cynric had pointed out that it was very possible that their enemies had taken her. After all, no noblewoman would run off with a penniless drudge of a cook! It would surely be more of Emryss's doings. So they had decided to send a messenger to Craig Fawr.

Cynric glanced out the window. It was long past dawn. By now that fool Father Robelard would be near his destination. The dimwit would hardly be able to speak when facing Emryss, especially if the stories were true. It was rumored that Emryss, after his mother's death, had forbade any priests to set foot in the inner ward of his castle. It would suit Cynric's plans exactly to have Emryss send their emissary packing.

The figure beside Cynric stirred under the mound of sheets.

"Lynette!" He shook her with his foot. "I want more wine."

When her only response was to snuggle deeper into the sheets, Cynric raised his foot and shoved her onto the floor. "I said, I want more wine!"

Lynette scrambled to her feet, holding a sheet to her naked body. "Yes, my lord." She looked frightened, and that pleased him greatly.

"If you hurry, I may let you join me again."

He grabbed the sheet and tugged, laughing harshly at her squeak of modesty. Hurriedly she pulled on her gown and left.

Cynric chuckled. Ah, think what enjoyment he'd get from making that skinny Roanna suffer!

She would be a wonderful excuse for an attack on that half-built fortress, and Emryss would surely see that. They could even avoid a direct attack, for the law would be on their side in this. So he would have Craig Fawr easily and completely. Of course, there was still the matter of that homely wench.

If she were not at Craig Fawr, well, who could blame him for suspecting his old enemy in this matter? And once he had Craig Fawr, it would be hard to get him out.

If the wench *was* there, he might still marry her. Then he would have the influence of her uncle, and the dowry. He lay back and stared at the ceiling.

Marriage to her might even have some unexpected excitement, for he would dearly enjoy making her pay for the insult to his pride her running off had caused. Later, it wouldn't be difficult to make her early demise believable. And while some "mysterious" malady weakened her, he had other sources of pleasure. Then he would find a wealthier and more beautiful second wife.

He finished the wine in his chalice and contemplated the empty silver cup. "Lynette!" he bellowed.

There was a brief knock at the door.

"Come!" Cynric called petulantly. Instead of a contrite Lynette, however, Urien Fitzroy hurried in.

"My lord, you must come quickly. Your father—he's had a fit!"

Cynric stared at him. "What do you mean, fit?"

"He was yelling at the steward, and suddenly he went limp all down one side of his body. Then he fell. No one's been able to rouse him."

Cynric climbed out of the bed and pulled on his chausses and tunic. As he bent down to put on his boots, he smiled.

Father Robelard stared up at the massive earthworks of Craig Fawr.

Oh, dear God in Heaven, why me? he asked in silent prayer as he prodded his donkey forward. Why did Baron DeLanyea have to send *him* to find out if the girl was in Craig Fawr, and if she was, to insist on threat of disownment, that she return to her uncle and her betrothed? He was no diplomat. And Lynette had said only the other day that Emryss DeLanyea *hated* priests.

He had tried to protest, but the baron had only fixed his harsh eye on him and said, "We want somebody neutral. And that's you!"

And then there was the poor girl's uncle! Sitting there like a carrion crow, saying, "Tell her to come back, or I'll have nothing more to do with her—ever!" Fine sentiment for the poor girl's only relation.

He rode through the village. The people all stopped and stared at him coldly.

He shifted uncomfortably. One heard things about these barbaric people, but one didn't like to believe them.

He arrived at the first gate, and one of the guards nudged the other, grinning and whispering something in Welsh.

"I bring a message from the Baron DeLanyea," Father

Robelard said, trying to sound confident. The guards only chuckled.

"I said, I bring a message from the Baron DeLanyea," he repeated.

This time the guards nodded and let him pass. After other humiliating delays, he finally reached the last gate. From inside the courtyard he could hear the banging and hammering of laborers. It was no secret that Emryss DeLanyea was strengthening his stronghold, and to judge by the sounds of it, he was in a hurry.

As Father Robelard rode into the inner ward, the tools fell silent while everyone turned to look at him. One man, standing inside the stable door half-naked, pulled on a shirt and stared openly. Father Robelard stared back for a moment, until he realized the man was half-blind. Poor fellow, he probably had to stare to see anything at all.

He climbed off the donkey and cleared his throat as the man from the stable—a groom probably—walked toward him. "What do you want?" the man asked most rudely.

"I bring a message from Baron DeLanyea," Father Robelard repeated.

"What is it?"

The priest drew himself up. "It's a message for Lord Emryss DeLanyea," he said indignantly.

The man sniffed and turned toward a long, low building attached to a huge tower. "This way."

Father Robelard trotted along behind the tall, arrogant fellow.

Suddenly the little priest ceased in mid-step. Blind in one eye! That was what Lynette had said about the returned Emryss DeLanyea. Oh, surely this person with his plain shirt untucked could not be a nobleman! Perhaps there were two blinded men in such a large place as Craig Fawr.

As if reading his thoughts, the man turned, his annoyed expression the very mirror of Cynric DeLanyea's, minus the eye and plus the scar, of course. The priest groaned softly and followed as Emryss DeLanyea entered the building.

Several servants bustled about the hall. Trestle tables, taken apart during the day, lined the walls.

The man, or, more properly, Lord DeLanyea, continued on toward a screened partition at one end of the room. He paused and waited impatiently as Father Robelard reached him.

"Wine," Lord DeLanyea barked at no one in particular. "And everyone out!"

He motioned the priest to a seat on the other side of the screen, then slumped into a chair on the opposite side of a battered oak table.

"I...I beg your pardon," Father Robelard began as he gingerly sat down. "That is, I assume I have the honor of addressing Lord DeLanyea?"

"You do. Now, what does my uncle want?"

Father Robelard cleared his throat nervously.

"Well, out with it. What?"

"Baron DeLanyea requests that you return Lady Roanna Westercott immediately."

"Does he? He thinks she's here?"

The small man began to twist the belt of his cassock. At Beaufort they had all seemed so absolutely certain she was at Craig Fawr that he hadn't even stopped to consider the possibility that she wasn't. "Well, yes, my lord, he does. Her uncle and her betrothed were also of that opinion. Isn't she?"

Suddenly a skinny old woman appeared around the screen, bearing a jug of wine and two goblets on a silver tray. She set them on the table with a clatter.

"Fetch Lady Roanna," Lord DeLanyea barked.

Relieved, the priest sighed softly, although he could feel

the perspiration forming on his back under the man's un-
yielding gaze.

The woman seemed to make some kind of sound as if
indignant, but nevertheless she left without a word.

"My lord, I am, of course, happy that Lady Roanna is
under your care. It was most impetuous of her to abscond
in such a way…"

"She escaped," Lord DeLanyea interrupted bluntly.

"Well, my lord." Father Robelard shifted uneasily.
"Whatever words one chooses to call the unorthodox manner of her departure, we are all relieved that she didn't
come to any serious harm."

DeLanyea laughed harshly. "Are you?"

At this moment Father Robelard had no difficulty be-
lieving that this man was a relation of the baron.

"Well, naturally her uncle is pleased that she was not
harmed. That is…" Father Robelard felt the fear-sweat
trickling down his sides. "She *is* unharmed, I trust?"

A slight movement near the side of the screen drew his
attention. Lady Roanna, looking exactly as she had the last
time he had seen her, stood there.

Father Robelard got up quickly. "Ah, my lady. You are
well, are you not?"

Lord DeLanyea rose to his feet slowly.

"Yes, Father, I am quite all right."

DeLanyea motioned her to his chair. After a slight hesitation, she sat down.

"This priest has something to say, and since it concerns
you, I thought you should hear it," he said.

Lady Roanna nodded once, then fastened her steady gaze
on the short man.

Father Robelard cleared his throat. "Ah, my lady, this is
most difficult." He looked up at DeLanyea. "I think, perhaps, that since I have now seen for myself that Lady

Roanna is uninjured, you and I could best discuss the baron's message in private.''

DeLanyea nodded his agreement.

Roanna placed her hands in her lap and looked from one man to the other. So, it was to be no different here. She was being dismissed, as if her fate mattered nothing to her. She pressed her lips together and made no move to leave.

After a long moment, Father Robelard raised his hands in a pleading gesture. ''My lady, the baron's words may upset you.''

''I have a right to listen, since they concern me.''

''But my lady…''

''She stays.''

Roanna didn't look at Emryss. She fastened her gaze on her hands, so that she could concentrate fully on what Father Robelard had to say.

''My lord, the baron requests that Lady Roanna be returned to Beaufort forthwith, there to comply with the terms of the marriage contract.''

''No,'' Lord DeLanyea said.

Roanna's hands tightened in her lap.

''Then, my lord, I must tell you that her uncle, Lord Westercott, has threatened to disown her. He will have nothing further to do with his niece.''

''He had little enough to do with her before.''

''But my lord, she will be *penniless.*''

''She won't marry that dog.''

''Perhaps she could persuade her uncle to nullify the contract, on payment of a small penalty or some such expediency.''

''He's locked her up once for refusing. Do you think he'll listen to her now?''

Roanna stood up abruptly. ''Gentlemen, I am not a bone to be wrangled over. Father Robelard,'' she continued, regarding him steadily, ''I will not marry Cynric DeLanyea.

I am leaving here as soon as my companion is able to travel. I ask for nothing from my uncle, and I expect nothing. That is an end to this matter. Good day.'' With her head held high, she began to walk past the two men.

"One moment, my lady," Father Robelard said, but he turned toward Lord DeLanyea. "Your cousin told me that if the lady refused to return, I was to tell you he will be most displeased to lose the apple of his eye."

Roanna paused to look at Emryss, and what she saw chilled her to the marrow of her bones. His face showed such incredible hatred that she could scarcely believe she was looking at the same man.

"Wait down by the door, priest. I want to talk to Lady Roanna alone."

Father Robelard scuttled around the screen, and Roanna heard his feet clatter down the length of the hall.

She stared at Emryss. He rubbed his hand up and down the table, gazing at the wood.

"What did he mean?" she asked.

Emryss looked at her with a strange expression. "What, don't you believe you could be the apple of his eye?"

"This is not the time for riddles. I know I am not pleasing to look at. What does he really mean?"

"God's wounds, you keep a cool head," he muttered. He turned his back to her and went to the window. "Once, when I was a child, I climbed into the orchard of Beaufort to steal some apples. Just a childish prank, really. But Cynric saw me and started a fight. I beat him—bloodied his nose, and no worse. Nothing much would come of it, I thought.

"And nothing did, not for about a year. I had a dog, Cil. Ianto gave him to me and helped me to train him. Spent hours in the hills together, we did. Cil even slept in my bed. Then one day I found him, dead. And beside him a poisoned apple."

"I don't understand..."

"Cynric had killed him because I had bested him. And what he's saying is, unless you go back to him today, he may not move against me directly, but he will try to kill *you*."

"Then Jacques and I must leave here at once. Today."

Emryss took a long step toward her and grabbed her arm as she turned to go. "Roanna, you don't understand. You don't know that *diawl* like I do. He won't forget about you, or the fool you've made of him. He may not come after you tomorrow or next month or even next year, but one day, he'll send someone for you. And if you're *lucky,* you'll die quickly."

Roanna tried to ignore the pressure of his hand on her arm and the intent expression on his face.

"I am leaving here at once," she said firmly.

He frowned. "You can't go alone."

"Jacques will be with me."

"He can't protect you from Cynric."

Roanna pulled away from his grasp. "Well, then, my lord, since you seem to have all the answers, what do you suggest I do?"

"Marry me."

Roanna stared at him incredulously. If she had been struck by lightning, she would feel like this. She took hold of the back of her chair, grabbing onto the cool wood as a drowning man to a floating spar.

He was offering her the vision she had fought to keep at bay. She could ask for nothing more than to be his wife, wanted nothing more, indeed, had dreamt of this in the still, small hours of the night when all such thoughts seemed hopeless and sinful.

"I realize a proposal from a disfigured, poverty-stricken nobleman whose own family is trying to destroy him is less than gratifying, but I can keep you safe."

"Why should *you* wish to marry *me*?" she asked softly.

He grinned crookedly. "Well, if nothing else, it will annoy Cynric for the rest of his life."

She stepped toward him. "Please, my lord, can't you be frank about this? I assure you, it is a very serious matter to me."

"As you wish, my lady," he said, his face flushing slightly, "I will be frank." He planted his muscular legs and crossed his arms. "All the other noblewomen I've encountered never impressed me as anything other than an unsavory combination of weak simpering and voracious greed. You don't whine, smile stupidly or weep false tears. Even now, you stand here discussing these matters as calmly as if we were speaking of a new fashion.

"I tell you plainly that I have little to offer besides my protection, since everything else I have I intend to use to strengthen Craig Fawr. If you are willing to accept that, I will gain a quiet, unselfish wife who can maintain a cool head, and one who has a similar interest in keeping this land. Satisfied?"

Roanna stared at the floor. She had wanted his honest reasons for such a proposal, and he had given them.

He had said nothing about caring for her, or even liking her. And the kisses they shared…to him, they must be unimportant.

If that was so, then she must consider them—and the feelings they created—unimportant, too.

Logically, reasonably, then, what else could a woman do but choose the most acceptable, least intolerable husband?

"I will marry you," she said flatly.

He made no move toward her. "Roanna, circumstances will make me a less than proper husband, but you will have your independence as much as possible. I will not question what you do, and you will not question me. Is that agreed?"

"Yes."

"Good. The ceremony can be tomorrow. I'll tell Mamaeth, and I'm sure Father Robelard can be compelled to bless our union."

He disappeared around the screen as Roanna sank down onto the chair.

Chapter Ten

"*O'r annwyl!* Mad you are, Emryss!" Mamaeth's sharp voice echoed through the empty hall. He waited for her to protest that he couldn't possibly marry a Norman, especially one who only a few days before had been betrothed to Cynric DeLanyea.

"Tomorrow! It can't be done!" Mamaeth looked at Emryss defiantly, her whole body trembling with suppressed indignation. "That's not near enough time to make the food even, and needing new clothes, the girl will. Just like a man, that is, no thinking about how much time it takes to do things right. And you a lord, with everyone there to see and talk if something's forgotten!"

"Two days then, and no more."

He waited for an explosion of Welsh curses, but they didn't come.

"Very well, my son. Being a man, and impatient like all the rest, and leaving everything to the women. Still, two days and we might manage it, if that fat fool of a cook will get out of bed and help with the cooking." Suddenly a broad grin creased her wrinkled face. "Glad I am you're to wed, my son. Needing babes about, and could do a lot worse than her." The grin grew even wider and she leaned closer. "It'll put Cynric in a proper twist, eh?" She straightened quickly. "But by all the saints! No time for me to stand here flapping my gums!" With that, Mamaeth rushed down the hall.

"Send Rhys!" he called as the door slammed shut. He sat down, letting his breath out slowly. He knew how the captain of his ship to the Holy Land must have felt the day he made all hands prepare for a storm, only to have the wind veer suddenly and become no more than a strong breeze.

He glanced at the stairs, remembering how Roanna had gone up to the bedchamber while he "persuaded" Father Robelard to remain in Craig Fawr to bless their union. It hadn't taken much, for clearly the fellow was terrified to take the news of the impending marriage to Beaufort.

She always moved with such supple grace, like a willow branch. Yes, she was very like the willow, able to bend far, and hard to break.

God, he needed some wine.

He stood up and began to pace. What was he doing, marrying her? He couldn't be a true hùsband. Not to her. Not to any woman.

Gwilym would have plenty to say when he heard what Emryss had done. He would say it was his impetuous nature clouding his judgment.

Indeed, Emryss wasn't fully convinced it was a wise decision himself, but he knew that while the actual proposal may have sprung to his lips without conscious effort, the idea had been lurking in his mind ever since he had looked into her face that first time.

Rhys came bustling in, his round face wreathed in smiles.

"Ah, my lord, good news I have. The last load of stone's in the courtyard, and lovely it is. One block was a little damaged, so I talked the fellow into lowering his price. A hard man to bargain, he was, but I did it.'' Rhys's face fell. ''Troubles, my lord?''

''No,'' Emryss said, putting on a smile. ''There's to be a wedding.''

''Oh? Who?''

''Me.''

''Congratulations, my lord,'' Rhys said when he'd recovered. ''Who's the lucky lady, may I ask?''

''Lady Roanna Westercott.''

Rhys blanched, then cleared his throat. ''And when is the joyous occasion to take place?''

''In two days. And in those two days, I want you to make sure I have two hundred pieces of silver and twenty pieces of gold.''

''Two hundred pieces…'' Rhys's voice trailed off. ''But my lord!''

''Is it a problem, Rhys?''

''Well, my lord. I've just spent…let me think. With the money I saved, fifty pieces of silver on the stone. And until the grain comes in, I don't think…''

''Sell this.''

Emryss lifted the leather pouch from around his neck and placed the contents on the table.

Rhys stared at the jewel-encrusted crucifix as it gleamed on the dark wood. ''I can't, my lord. It was your dear mother's.''

''Sell it.''

Rhys gently picked up the cross. ''As you wish, my lord.''

''Thank you, Rhys.''

The steward walked slowly down the hall. Emryss picked up the empty pouch and fingered it. He sighed deeply, then thrust it into his belt.

After Mass the next morning, Roanna hurried through the courtyard. All the workmen stopped to nudge each other and smile, but she did her best to ignore them.

What could she expect, after all, when Emryss had announced their wedding as he had?

Last evening, he had stood up after the food had been cleared and begun to speak in a loud voice. Everyone listened very carefully to the Welsh speech, then suddenly, as all the people cheered, he'd pulled her up and kissed her quickly on the lips. Before she could recover from the shock of such a public display, men and women swarmed toward them, slapping Emryss heartily on the back. The women, more shy, offered what she supposed were congratulations.

But not everyone was delighted. Gwilym especially had scowled blackly, and never came near them.

Roanna would have expected more people to react as Gwilym had. She knew that this marriage would anger Cynric and his father, and surely everyone else should be concerned. Yet even Mamaeth had smiled delightedly.

Did they think themselves invulnerable? As she stood next to her future husband, she could understand why they would feel thus. He seemed to bask in an aura of invincibility. She, too, had felt she would always be safe if she were near him.

Nevertheless, she wondered what was really prompting this marriage. It would seem he was approaching the forthcoming nuptials almost as if it was an alliance rather than a wedding. He said no word of love or even affection.

But she would be safe. And perhaps, in time, he would come to love her. That was, she knew, the best any woman could hope for.

She didn't linger over her bread and ale in the hall, deciding to return to her solitary bedchamber.

But when she got there, it was as if the room had become a merchant's stall. Bolts of fabric, spools of thread, needles

and scissors lay on every available surface, including the
bed, which was stripped down to the feather tick. Even
Emryss's wooden chest lay open and empty.

Before she closed the door, a mob of women swarmed
in. Without so much as a beg your pardon, they began
turning her around, clearly taking measurements. Roanna
looked at all the faces, but although they were familiar from
the hall, she didn't know anyone's name.

Then she spotted Bronwyn coming in with a bolt of
white linen. She called out to her, and with a huge smile,
Bronwyn came toward her.

"My lady, off with your gown, please," she said.

"But, Bronwyn…"

Mamaeth burst through the crowd. "No more chatter,
you silly geese. Get to work!" she said. She looked Roanna
up and down.

"Bronwyn!" she said, although she still looked at
Roanna, "why haven't you got Lady Roanna undressed
yet? Can't try on her new clothes over her old."

Roanna knew there would be little point in arguing with
the feisty woman. She reluctantly drew her dress over her
head. There was a smattering of giggles and some whispered Welsh from the maids. Mamaeth, her hands on her
hips, slowly turned and stared at them all until they fell
silent.

"Forgive them, my lady," she said, her voice withering.
"No manners." She went on in Welsh and Roanna was
sorry she was the cause of such a reprimand.

"Now, no more talk about her," Mamaeth finished in
Welsh. "You can see her hips are good for children, and
her breasts might be small now, but wait till she gets some
good food in her. She'll fill out right enough. Should be
enough for you that *he* likes her. So quiet now, and get to
work." She hesitated for a moment. "Still…" She winked.

"Make the gowns to show her to good advantage. The
honor of the lord of Craig Fawr is important."

Roanna caught sight of Bronwyn wistfully eyeing some
soft blue wool. An idea came to her, and she pushed her
way through the protesting women.

"Bronwyn, I'd like you to have that piece," she said,
pointing to the fabric.

"Oh, my lady, I couldn't! It's yours. What would his
lordship say, if giving it to me you were?"

"I ruined one of your dresses. It's only fitting that I
should replace it. And perhaps you would have time to
finish a dress for my wedding. I would be very pleased if
you'd accept this small token of my thanks."

Bronwyn looked doubtfully at her for a moment and
glanced at Mamaeth.

"A very fine weave, that is, taking a poor woman many
hours at her loom," Mamaeth said.

"*I* want you to take it, Bronwyn," Roanna said, keeping
her tone innocent. "You'll look lovely in a dress that shade.
Everyone will be sure to notice your beauty."

That was the perfect thing to say. Bronwyn nodded shyly
and picked up the fabric, rubbing its smooth nap with her
fingers.

Roanna waited for Mamaeth's comment.

"Get back to work now, all of you," was all she said,
however. The women stood aside to let Roanna return to
the center of the room. Slowly, they began to smile.

Then began a flurry of sewing, trying on, ripping out,
trying on again, putting on part of a sleeve, a skirt, a head-
dress. Roanna barely got to sit down when someone wanted
her to try something else.

When she finally did get the chance to point out the
missing bed linen, she wished she hadn't.

"New sheets you'll be having, for luck, and the furs beat
well, too," Mamaeth said with the most distressing leer.

"Hard put we are, to hem such large sheets, especially when they'll probably be cast onto the floor anyway."

Bronwyn giggled. Roanna picked up a half-sewn undergarment and threaded a needle. She could at least concentrate on something. She hoped.

Then Bronwyn whispered something, and the women struggled to suppress more laughter.

"Oh, a terrible creature you are!" Mamaeth cried in mock horror. "Surely he'll let her have a few minutes' rest, the first night!"

Roanna looked at the fabric in her hand to hide her alarm. These women all seemed to assume she knew what was going to happen on the wedding night.

Instead, she was woefully ignorant of what would be expected of her.

Her only information of what actually transpired in the nuptial bed she had derived from overheard conversations in the women's apartments at her uncle's castle.

Unfortunately, it was scanty at best. Apparently it was a pleasant experience and best enjoyed naked, although one maid, the boisterous one, had considered clothing no hindrance, but an additional element of excitement.

Of course, Roanna reflected, that girl evidently enjoyed the activity anytime, anywhere, and with almost anyone.

The women chattered on in their musical Welsh, their words flying as fast as their needles. Roanna found, to her dismay, that she had become singularly inept. Perhaps it was because the room had grown very warm.

There was another howl of laughter from the women, and Roanna looked at Mamaeth for an explanation.

"Ashamed of themselves they should be, my lady. Imagine, trying to guess what he'll do first!"

Mamaeth obviously was not ashamed, but clearly enjoying the banter.

"Well, Mamaeth," Roanna said, managing to keep her voice level, "what *do* they think he'll do first?"

The women bent over their needles silently. Mamaeth raised one eyebrow and stared at her for a moment. "A word of warning, Lady Roanna. He was always an impatient, impetuous lad."

"I take it then, Mamaeth, slow is better?"

One by one the women began sputtering with laughter.

Roanna felt the beaming smile blossom on her face when it appeared that they all understood Norman. It was a wonderful thing, to join in the laughter and to be feeling, for the first time, that she might come to belong here.

For the rest of the day, she enjoyed herself immensely. As the time passed, the women spoke more and more freely to her, and in her own tongue. It was only at the evening meal, when she was sitting beside Emryss, that she again felt so completely outside his world.

They sat side by side at the high table, saying nothing. Finally, she asked him how all his people had come to learn her language so well.

"To know their enemies," he replied brusquely.

After that, she kept silent, slipping away to visit Jacques shortly after the last course had been cleared.

Jacques looked much better, and sat up quickly as she drew near.

"Ah, little kitten!" he cried. "To think you are to be married, and to one who deserves you!"

Roanna smiled a little, wishing she could feel completely happy instead of filled with doubts.

"What is it, little one? Why are you not singing and dancing with joy? *This* DeLanyea is quite a man."

Roanna stared at her hands, locked together in her lap, and felt the hot blush on her face. She cleared her throat. "I...I'm not certain this is the right thing to do, Jacques." She shifted, wanting to tell him her feelings and yet constrained. It had never been easy for her to voice her inner-most thoughts.

She took a deep breath and looked at her friend. "Do *you* think it is right to put all these people in jeopardy, to risk Baron DeLanyea's ire? Lord DeLanyea assures me that the baron will be powerless to do anything, but I wish I could be so certain."

Jacques reached over and took her small hand in his huge one. "Lady Roanna, your life has not been a happy one. And now, here is happiness waiting for you." He tightened his grip. "Take it! Embrace it!"

Roanna wanted so much to believe him. She wished that her choice would affect only her and the man she married, not an estate that supported many people.

Jacques let go of her hand and sat back amongst the pillows. "Well, let us be happy!"

Seeing Jacques' pleasure, Roanna decided to keep her worry to herself.

Jacques talked at great length of the delicious delicacies he was going to prepare for the wedding feast until, feeling tired and weary of all the talk of the wedding, Roanna excused herself.

Jacques patted her hand and smiled kindly. "Have no fear, kitten. Trust him."

Roanna nodded.

After she left Jacques, she went to the hall, which was still filled with most of the men. Obviously they were con-tinuing to offer toasts to the groom.

Keeping along the wall, she managed to get to the stairs unnoticed.

But even in the bedchamber she could still hear the loud, boisterous voices of the men. After a while, they began to sing with great gusto.

I won't get to sleep *this* night, she thought, remembering Bronwyn's jest. The bed had been remade with the old sheets for now. After removing her gown, she climbed in and pulled the covers over her head.

Nevertheless she caught herself straining to pick out Emryss's voice from the others, and every time she closed her eyes, she beheld in her mind's eye the vision of him half-naked as he practiced with the broadsword.

The men grew quiet by the time the first streaks of dawn colored the eastern sky. She got out of bed and, pulling a fur cover about her shoulders, went to watch the sun rise.

How many times, since her parents' death, had she waited for the huge yellow globe to rise from its sleep each morning? She felt so lonely and unloved, it comforted her to pretend that it rose only to give her warmth, and that the myriad breathtaking colors were displayed only for her pleasure.

Emryss was like the sun. Bright and bold, once thought gone into eternal night, only to rise again and return to the land he loved.

What would her father have made of him? He would have admired his prowess as a fighter, without doubt. And been impressed by his will to survive. "Watch the ones with scars," she had often heard him caution his men, "for they are the mark of those who refuse to accept defeat."

But other than that? Her father would not have admired his abilities to play the harp and sing, for he would consider such skills beneath a lord and warrior. If she were to be honest with herself, her father would also look askance at Emryss's easy rapport with his men, thinking it would lead to diminished respect.

But did it? Once she would have agreed with her father that any man who joked and laughed like one of the foot soldiers could never be a strong leader. Now she knew that wasn't always the way. Emryss's people loved him, and he cared deeply for them. Was this not part of respect, and the best part?

She looked down at the misty valley, where already the sun was beginning to work its ancient magic. Pieces of green and, here and there, the deep gold of the ripening grain began to show.

This *was* a beautiful land. *His* home, and she began to understand how he could love it só.

Roanna whirled about as a series of rapid knocks banged at the door. Mamaeth entered, followed by Bronwyn carrying the big tub. Some other women trotted behind, laden with various bundles.

"A lovely day we'll be having, for Old Daffyd says no rain today, and he's not been wrong these twenty years."

A perfumed bath came first, then her hair was washed with scented herbs. Mamaeth provided a lovely scented oil that she rubbed into Roanna's skin as Bronwyn brushed her hair to satin smoothness. Roanna put on a new shift of white linen that was so fine it was almost transparent. A simple white tunic of a fabric Roanna had never seen before was put on next. It had taken many fittings to insure that it fit her body snugly and flared fully below her hips.

"Silk," Mamaeth explained when Roanna commented on the lightness of the material. "Brought back from the East. Emryss meant it as a gift for his mother. He said you were to have it."

Roanna ran her fingers down the unique garment as Bronwyn came forward with the burgundy gown she was to wear over top. It was a beautiful dress of soft thin wool. Around the neck and wide cuffs the women had sewn looped patterns of gold riband.

Mamaeth and Bronwyn put the gown over Roanna's head, then arranged the folds of the skirt. The bodice fit over her breasts and hips to perfection, and was cut neither low enough to be too bold nor high enough to seem overly modest.

Bronwyn brought more gold riband and arranged it

through Roanna's long, dark tresses. Finally Mamaeth brought forth a supple leather girdle, decorated with golden rings. She tied it around Roanna's waist and stood back to look at the girl.

"A beauty you are, and no mistake."

Roanna was flattered by her kind words. Bronwyn said nothing, but with a smile held up one of the polished metal ewers that had contained the hot water for her bath.

"It's not much, but you might see for yourself."

Roanna peered at the distorted figure looking solemnly back at her. To be sure her lustrous hair shone, her cheeks had a becoming flush of pink and the gown was a delight for the eyes, but her? She would never be beautiful, although Mamaeth was kind to flatter her.

Mamaeth glanced out the window. "We'll be leaving you, my lady, to get dressed ourselves. Not quite noon yet, but it'll be here soon enough."

The two women went out.

Noon. That was the time they would make their progress to the chapel.

Not daring to sit in the new gown, Roanna walked toward the window. There was no work being done on the walls this day in celebration of the marriage.

She listened carefully, and heard Jacques' roar in the kitchen. He would be having a marvelous time, even if he did have to use a stick to hobble about. She could almost see him terrorizing the kitchen servants.

Then she heard another sound, and looked over to the road leading into the fortress.

Two men rode through the gate, wearing mail beneath their plain black tunics.

"Begging your pardon, my lady."

Roanna turned to find Bronwyn standing in the door wearing her new blue dress. She must have stayed up most of the night to get it finished, but it was worth the effort. "Yes?"

Bronwyn began to wring her hands, and her smile was tentative.

"Is everything...are you... I mean to say, Mamaeth said I was to make sure you're ready for the ceremony."

"Yes. Your dress is lovely." Instead of relaxing, Bronwyn seemed to become even more upset.

"What is it?" Roanna demanded quietly.

"Nothing, my lady," Bronwyn replied hastily. Too hastily.

Roanna swept past the startled girl, down the stairs and outside.

Cynric DeLanyea and Urien Fitzroy sat astride their horses in the center of the ward. When he saw her, Cynric's mouth curved into a smile.

"You look very beautiful, my lady," he said. He dismounted. "It would seem that Wales agrees with you."

Others had heard the commotion, and now the yard began filling up with curious people. Suddenly the door of the barracks crashed open. Emryss strode into the yard.

He was finely dressed in a long tunic of woven black wool with gold trim reaching to the top of supple boots. Under this he wore a shirt of pure white. He stopped several feet from Cynric and crossed his arms, leaning his weight casually on his right leg. "What do you want?" he demanded, his voice ringing in the silence.

Cynric smiled again at Roanna before turning to Emryss. "I thought I should inform you, cousin, that your uncle is ill and quite possibly dying." Roanna knew that Cynric cared little for his father, but his matter-of-fact tone chilled her.

"Thank you, *cousin*," Emryss replied, his mocking emphasis matching Cynric's. "Now get out off my land."

"Tsk, tsk, tsk. Such manners to a relative who only

comes bearing news. You see, my lady," he turned to her, "what kind of barbarians these Welsh-raised men become?"

Roanna said nothing, keeping her face carefully blank.

Cynric walked toward her. "If only your uncle had seen fit to furnish better garments for you, I would never have said those incredibly unfeeling things when we first met. Can you forgive me for seeing the pitiful garments and not the exquisite woman inside them?"

Emryss laughed scornfully. "You waste your breath, Cousin, playing the lovesick lad with my wife."

"Wife?"

Cynric wheeled to face Emryss. For a moment, his shoulders betrayed anger, but when he turned to Roanna, she saw only sorrow on his face. "I am too late, then?"

His earnest expression startled her. "We are not yet wed."

His eyes flashed for an instant. "Roanna." His voice was soft, almost apologetic. "I...I acted badly before. I am sorry, and most humbly beg that you come back to Beaufort." He reached out and took her hand. "All will be forgiven, and the wedding can take place as we planned. And as I now wish with all my heart."

Emryss came toward them and grabbed Roanna's hand from Cynric's, his grip crushing her fingers. She freed her hand from his and stepped back. The two men glared their hatred at each other for a long moment before facing her.

"You are free to do as you wish, Roanna. Go or stay. It is your choice," Emryss said harshly. He stood with his legs apart, his arms crossed, defiant as if it mattered little which man she chose.

Cynric raised his hands pleadingly. "Please, Roanna, give me another chance. I beg you."

Chapter Eleven

Roanna would no more believe Cynric's words than if a viper spoke. Silently she walked toward Emryss, took his hand in hers and smiled into his face.

There was a brief flicker of emotion that thrilled her, a look that told her that no matter how coldly he might be acting, inwardly he *did* care for her. Then she turned toward Cynric. "Get off our land," she said softly.

"I hope, my dear, that you don't come to regret this," Cynric growled as he mounted quickly and galloped out the gate, followed by Fitzroy.

Roanna glanced at Emryss, hoping to see that spark of feeling in his face again. Instead he picked her up, crushing her against his hard chest. "I love you, Roanna," he whispered, and if she had thought a look was reward before, she now knew that she had been wrong.

"By Mary and Joseph and all the host of heaven, not time for you to stand about gawking at each other!" Mamaeth suddenly bellowed. "There's a marriage to be made!"

With that, the people began to move toward the gate. Emryss grabbed Roanna's hand and strode off, out under the portcullis and down through the town toward the tiny wooden chapel. She almost had to run to keep up with his long strides.

Roanna halted, even though he almost jerked her arm from the socket. "I will not be dragged like some donkey to my own wedding," she said, panting.

Emryss turned to her, his eyebrows raised in surprise as if he hadn't realized the briskness of his pace.

"*Twt ei gywilydd!* Shame on him!" Mamaeth whispered loudly to the crowd that followed. "Can't even walk, but got to run to the chapel. Ah, every woman should have such an eager groom!"

Roanna felt a blush burning its way from her chest up to her forehead. She glanced at Emryss and saw that he was trying to maintain a look of calm dignity, with not much success. Nevertheless, when he took her arm in his and proceeded to the chapel, his pace was more leisurely.

Father Robelard stood waiting nervously on the steps of the chapel. When they got there, he nodded slightly. Roanna's heart went out to him, for he surely wanted to be anywhere else. She would have to make sure he didn't suffer for blessing their union.

"Lady Roanna Westercott," Father Robelard began, twisting his belt, "before I proceed any further, I must ask you if you do this of your own free will and in full knowledge that you will be joined to this man for the rest of your life."

"I do."

Father Robelard nodded.

"Lord DeLanyea, do you take this woman to be your lawful wife, to endow her with all your worldly goods and to keep you only unto her until the death?"

"I do swear." Emryss pulled out a small, plain gold band and took Roanna's left hand. Placing the ring at the top of the fourth finger, he waited for the priest.

"In the name of the Father…"

Emryss moved the ring past her first knuckle.

"And of the Son..."

He pushed the ring past her second knuckle. Poor Father Robelard looked about to faint as he spoke the last words. "And of the Holy Ghost, I now pronounce you man and wife."

Emryss turned to her. "We should kiss, my lady," he said quietly, the twinkle in his eye making her tremble with anticipation.

His kiss, this time, was quite chaste, and Roanna had to remind herself that there was a crowd of people watching. A murmur of disapproval reached her ears. With a rueful smile Emryss shrugged in a gesture of apology to the people, then yanked her closer, his hands almost encircling her tiny waist as he brought his lips to hers with more enthusiasm.

"Call that a kiss?" one of Emryss's men called out when they moved apart.

Giddy with happiness, Roanna decided to take up the challenge. Putting her hands on Emryss's shoulders, she kissed him with all the passion she dared show. And today, right now, she dared quite a bit.

His eye widened for an instant, then shut as her tongue reached tentatively inside his warm, moist mouth.

"They'll be a babe by next spring!" Mamaeth's voice and delightful cackle brought Roanna back to reality. The forgotten crowd began to cheer lustily again before filing into the chapel for the nuptial Mass.

As Roanna knelt next to Emryss, she kept her back straight and tried to keep her eyes on the altar. Nevertheless they kept straying to the man beside her. Her husband. He seemed so different in his fine garments. Harder. More lordly. More aloof.

Father Robelard brought forward the host, but before he could give it to him, Emryss shook his head. The priest halted in confusion, then, obviously shaken, proceeded to Roanna.

After the ceremony, the people rushed out of the chapel and up the hill toward the fortress, jostling the bride and groom with hearty congratulations and wishes for future happiness.

Over and over Roanna heard snickering references to her *amobr* and was beginning to wonder what the people were referring to, especially since it seemed to be money of some kind. At any other time, she might not have asked, but walking up the hill, surrounded by happy, friendly people, she grew bold. "Emryss," she began, almost forgetting her question when he turned to her smiling, "what is an *amobr?*"

To her surprise, he blushed. "Well, Roanna, it's a sort of bride price."

"For your maidenhead," the ever frank Mamaeth said bluntly. "And right generous, too."

Roanna flushed to the soles of her feet and tried to look as if she discussed her virginity every day.

When they reached the hall, everything was ready. The rushes had been cleared, and new ones, smelling of fresh herbs, had been spread on the floor. More tables than Roanna would have believed could fit in the large room were set with white linens, and flowers had been strewn around them.

Emryss took her hand to escort her to the high table. As his slender fingers enveloped hers, she felt his warmth and strength. She tried not to tremble at his touch, but she could no more control that than she could the rapid throbbing of her blood or the sudden tightness in her chest.

They arrived at their seats, and Emryss raised his hand for silence.

He began to speak, but in Welsh. Since she couldn't understand the words, Roanna scanned the hall. Jacques, his work finished, stood just below the dais. She was pleased to see that he had been placed there, an honor few cooks ever attained. Father Robelard was squeezed in beside him, and looked in danger of falling off the platform. He had twisted his belt into such knots that Roanna doubted he would ever be able to untie it.

Mamaeth, fidgeting like a knight preparing for a battle, stood next to the entrance to the kitchen corridor. Her beady black eyes watched everything and everyone.

Behind Mamaeth stood Bronwyn. The new gown flattered her voluptuous figure, and her cheeks were a becoming shade of pink as she hovered near the warmth of the kitchen. Roanna felt a slight surge of satisfaction. If Gwilym failed to notice her today, he was hopeless.

The rest of the people, even to little Hu at a far table, all listened carefully to Emryss's speech. Roanna suppressed a sigh. It was, she supposed, to be expected that he would address them in their tongue, even though she had no idea what he was saying.

Her gaze roved over his familiar features. Here, in the hall, he was relaxed and more the man she knew than the stranger beside her in the chapel.

She watched his full lips as he spoke the lyric Welsh. Incredible to think that their pressure on hers could arouse such pleasure. Roanna twisted her fingers in her lap, trying not to imagine what else his lips might accomplish.

At last Emryss lifted his chalice.

"Cymru am byth!" he finished, and drank.

Everyone sat down, and Emryss leaned toward her. "Wales forever. Now you're pledged to the land, too."

Rhys stood up, his goblet raised. "Health, long life and an heir to Lord DeLanyea of Craig Fawr!"

Emryss's response, and the accompanying leer in her direction, made everyone laugh, to Roanna's slight chagrin. She had no wish to have jokes made about what was going to happen later, and she was beginning to worry that Emryss might laugh at her ignorance.

Maids scurried to fill the goblets as the meal began to be served. Everything was wonderful, and she recognized Jacques' special touch in many of the dishes, but she could not eat. She made an effort to pick at some of the daintiest morsels, but it seemed that every time she moved her hand toward a platter, Emryss would, too. Once they accidentally touched, and she began to tremble so violently that she spilled her wine.

No matter how she chided herself for acting like a foolish child, she couldn't bring herself to look at him again.

He apparently found nothing amiss. He laughed and jested with Gwilym, who sat to his left, saying very little. Gwilym alone, of all the people, seemed to realize how dangerous a thing this wedding might be. Roanna hoped he would not begrudge their happiness and vowed to prove to him that she was his ally.

The meal went on all the afternoon, with the cake arriving as the sun set. Roanna could scarcely believe the amount that was consumed, and was even beginning to wonder what this would mean come the deep winter months. Surely they wouldn't waste too much for one feast.

Then Roanna heard Gwilym speak to Bronwyn, and she glanced up. Gwilym was looking at the blushing Bronwyn as if he'd never seen her before.

"Beginning to think you were sick, me," Emryss said softly. Roanna jerked and looked at the table. "Or is the linen that fascinating you can't keep your eyes off it?"

She shook her head. If she spoke now, she was certain her voice would tremble, too.

"A nice new dress on Bronwyn. Mamaeth tells me you did that."

Roanna nodded.

"My God, woman, knew you were quiet, but is it a mute I've married?"

"No, my lord."

"Good." He chuckled softly. "Have to keep an eye on them now, for it's sure to be *caru yn y qwely* from the way they're making eyes at each other."

She looked up at him quizzically.

"Courting on the bed." He laughed. "Don't look so shocked. The Welsh take a more...shall we say, natural view of love. Why shouldn't two people who love each other show it?"

She felt uncomfortably warm. "It isn't...right. And surely it isn't fair to the girl, if she gets with child."

"Oh, none too concerned with that, either. He'll either marry her or not, but she gets the *amobr* regardless, and the child is treated like legitimate issue. And so it is, if you think about it. Don't you think that's fairer for the child, who never asked to be born?"

Roanna squirmed uncomfortably. She couldn't deny that what he said made sense, but she wished they could speak of something other than children. Unfortunately, her mind seemed to have gone completely empty.

"Take Gwilym. He's what the Normans would call a bastard, for he's really the illegitimate son of my father's oldest friend. Sent to us to be fostered. According to Norman law, he couldn't inherit any land from his father, even though he's his eldest child."

"Did he? Inherit anything, I mean."

"Not a copper. But he'll have Craig Fawr."

"Unless you have a son of your own." She spoke without thinking. As he looked at her, his gaze held hers and he smiled very, very slowly.

Then Gwilym called him. He turned away and she began to breathe again.

There had been something unusual in his smile, beyond the way it made her heart race.

She took a bite of the light, delicate wedding bread. It wasn't strange for a man to expect sons when he got married, and yet his smile seemed to be somehow unhappy, like the smile of a man who hopes for the impossible.

Did he think she would refuse him his rights as her husband? The very suggestion of what would happen tonight in the huge bed waiting above made her flush hotly. No, she wouldn't deny him anything. Not anything.

Perhaps he thought she was barren. What if Mamaeth had said something to him that would make him think that?

Suddenly she was filled with dread. Old women were wise in such matters, knowing many things by many ways. For the first time Roanna realized how much she longed for a child, a child who would love her. And more than that. His child.

She thought of Mamaeth's laughter and the sparkle in her eyes as she had prepared Roanna for the wedding.

With a sigh of relief and thrill of hope, she realized that Mamaeth would never have acted thus if she thought her beloved Emryss was marrying a woman who would be incapable of giving him children.

Before she could think any more, Emryss suddenly stood up.

"Y rhibo!" he cried, and instantly people jumped up and began to push the tables in the middle of the hall toward the walls until there was a clear space. Several brawny men engaged in a heated discussion, until six stepped into the empty space. They stood face to face in two rows of three, holding hands like children forming a bridge, and turned expectantly to Emryss. He nodded and pointed to Gwilym.

Gwilym whooped and ran over to Bronwyn, pulling her to the center. Roanna watched in dismay as he picked her up and threw her across the arms of the six men. With a shout Gwilym jumped into the men's arms, too.

Roanna stared as the men tossed the couple up and down as if they weighed no more than a feather tick. Gwilym was so tangled in Bronwyn's new dress that it was difficult to tell whose limbs were whose.

Emryss's voice sounded beside her. "A game is all, Roanna. They won't drop them. Used to carrying blocks of stone that weigh a lot more."

The men threw Gwilym and Bronwyn again, affording everyone a clear view up the girl's skirt. They landed with Gwilym on top of Bronwyn, and everyone except Roanna screamed with laughter.

At last the men set the out-of-breath Bronwyn and Gwilym down carefully. As Gwilym reached for his wine, he shouted to Emryss.

Emryss stood up and looked slowly around the room. Several names were called out, but he raised his hand and pointed…at Jacques.

The six men bellowed angrily, but Jacques rose majestically and paraded around the hall. He stopped in front of several women, eyeing their giggling faces, and even winked at one or two.

Then, with unexpected energy, he ran across the room and grabbed Mamaeth.

"Take your hands off me, you brute!" she cried as he dragged her toward the center of the room. "Going to crush me to death, you're thinking? If that's so, got another thing coming, you do!" Mamaeth shook herself free and glared at Emryss. "Emryss DeLanyea, I won't end my days flattened by some fat foreigner!"

Emryss shook his head sadly. "Well, Mamaeth as you wish. I'm sorry, Jacques. Next time maybe you'll find someone more willing." He stood up. "Now it behooves me to pick someone else."

Roanna waited as he scanned the room again.

"No," he said after a long moment, "I think it will be...my turn!" He leaped onto the table and jumped down on the floor, then strode quickly to the center of the room.

"Now, who will go with me?" he said, smiling broadly. Roanna stared at her hands. Really, this whole thing was the most childish custom she had ever heard of. What kind of woman wants such a spectacle made of herself? It wasn't decent, not at all. Why, everyone could see...everything.

And then, to Roanna's horror, Emryss ran around the table and pulled her out of her chair.

"I won't! I can't!" she cried in vain as he hauled her toward the men.

"Please, Emryss, don't make me!" she pleaded. "It isn't dignified. It isn't proper."

He stopped, and a devilish grin lighted his face. "Maybe not, but it's fun!" He lifted her and seemed about to throw her into the men's waiting arms, but instead he slung her over his shoulder, knocking the breath from her lungs.

"My friends, my wife has other plans for us this evening, so if you will excuse us, we shall retire."

As she started to protest this new indignity, he smacked her on the bottom and carried her toward the stairs.

It was no use to struggle, for he was very strong. Roanna lay limply slung there, trying to capture her breath, aware of the babble of people's voices as they followed them up the stairs, laughing and talking. She raised her head slightly.

"Going to make me fall, if you don't lie still," Emryss said loudly, then gave her posterior another sound whack. He staggered a little as if to reinforce his command.

They rounded a corner and she felt him raise his foot. He kicked open the door, crossed the room swiftly and flung her on to the bed. Roanna had no sooner raised her shoulders to complain about his method of escorting her to the bridal chamber than a mob of women, laughing and chattering like birds, crowded through the door. Roanna looked around quickly for Emryss, but when she saw him, he only shrugged his shoulders and made way for them to pass.

In the next instant Mamaeth grabbed her wrists and with a grin that was absolutely wicked pulled her to her feet. Roanna craned her head around as she was pulled forward into the center of the circle of women, but Emryss was nowhere to be seen.

A cup of mulled wine was held out to her, and she saw Bronwyn, her face flushed, giggling.

It seemed to Roanna as if a thousand hands reached out to undo the lacing from her dress. She gasped and tried to slap them away.

"Have no fear, my lady," Mamaeth said loudly, her voice carrying across the room. "Getting you ready, we are is all…for bed!"

The room exploded into gales of laughter.

Bronwyn, still flushed from the *rhibo,* tried to suppress her mirth as she undid the laces of Roanna's gown.

Thankfully they took great care with the silk tunic, for Roanna could easily believe they were all drunk.

Then she heard steps approaching, lots of them, accompanied by loud masculine voices and snatches of song. The door burst open.

The women moved aside to reveal Emryss swaying in the frame. He no longer wore the long tunic, but only the full white shirt laced at the neck, fine linen chausses and the soft leather boots.

Gwilym pushed him forward and he staggered into the room, his face flushed. His hand clutched a chalice, and wine slopped over the rim. He made a clumsy bow, which set all the women giggling again.

Mamaeth spoke, and in the next moment Roanna, wear-

ing only her shift, felt herself being pulled toward the bed.
A shout went up from the men, and she realized they were
coming into the chamber.

Surely these people didn't intend to *watch?*

She struggled to get away from the bed, but the women
moved to block her view.

"No looking, my lady," Bronwyn chided.

The men began shouting and, it would seem, scolding.

Bronwyn, giggling, whispered, "They've got his shirt!"

Mamaeth pulled back the sheets on the bed, and Bronwyn gave Roanna a gentle push backward. Her legs hit the
side of the bed, and she lost her balance, falling on top of
the huge piece of furniture. She tried to scramble up, but
Mamaeth shoved her down.

Another shout went up from the men, but this time
Roanna heard Emryss shouting, too, and he didn't sound
pleased.

Bronwyn leaned over to her. "Not letting them have his
chausses." Roanna lay back on the bed astounded. What
was about to happen was inevitable, and his right as her
husband—but not with such an audience.

A murmur of approval sounded from the women. Roanna
was about to give up in despair and prepare for the worst
when the crowd silently began to depart. She uttered a brief
prayer of thanks.

And then she saw Emryss, shirtless, standing at the foot
of the bed. They had not succeeded in removing his
chausses, but the fine linen wrapping only made the con-
trast between his skin and the cloth more compelling. His
scarred, naked chest gleamed in the glow of the candles.

Desire, hot and liquid, flowed through her, free of any
constraints of honor and duty. It was as if she could breathe
fully for the first time since she had seen him.

"Well, *brawdmaeth,* we give you good night," Gwilym

said drunkenly from the doorway. "Good night, good night, *good* night."

Mamaeth also went out, saying, "Mind, sons first, daughters later." Then, with a gleeful cackle, she was gone.

Chapter Twelve

The next morning, Roanna lay in the bed. Alone.

Last night Emryss had stood at the foot of the bed for several long minutes. Then, with an abrupt, ''I need some air,'' he had turned and left.

And never returned. Not in the night. Not when she finally fell asleep. Not at dawn, when she awoke after a fitful rest. Not yet.

Why? she kept asking herself. Why? Was there something wrong with her? Or was this another strange Welsh custom no one had bothered to explain?

At the sound of someone entering the room, she lay back down and closed her eyes. She didn't want to talk to Mamaeth or Bronwyn, who were sure to ask any number of embarrassing questions or make lewd remarks.

The person crept into the room, as if searching for something. Suspicious and tense, Roanna couldn't keep up the pretense of sleep.

Emryss, in his shirt and chausses, was pouring water into the ewer. She sat up. ''I trust you've had enough air at last, my lord?'' she said coolly.

''Yes,'' he said without looking at her.

He splashed the cold water over his head, then reached

for fresh linen. He started to rub his damp curls briskly, but stopped and swayed forward. A low curse escaped his lips.

"Are you...all right?" Roanna asked as he leaned against the table. Perhaps he had merely imbibed too much at the celebration.

"Been better." He straightened. "Been worse." He turned toward the bed. "Roanna, I..."

Before he could continue, shouts and singing erupted in the hall below, then several clumsy footsteps sounded on the stairs like the sudden tolling of a loud bell.

"Emryss, *brawdmaeth!*" Gwilym called out. "Good morning. Time to rise, though certain you're exhausted I am!"

His words were followed by guffaws and chuckles that grew louder, until Roanna realized that most of the men of Craig Fawr must be outside their bedchamber. Emryss walked toward the closed door and stood with his hands on his waist, waiting.

Unsure just what was going on, Roanna pulled the covers up to her neck and waited, too.

A new voice spoke, in words that were like a song without a tune.

"Cheating, is that, to bring a bard for the *pwnco!*" Emryss shouted to the men on the other side of the door.

"Not fair to make us do it now, in the morning, either. But make haste, bridegroom. We're listening!" Gwilym teased.

"What is it?" Roanna asked quietly.

"The *pwnco,*" Emryss responded absently, staring at the door.

"I heard the word. What does it mean?"

"It's a contest of sorts. Quiet. I've got to think."

Roanna climbed out of the bed and began to wash. If he wanted quiet, he'd get it.

After a moment, Emryss began to speak, the cadence of

the words matching that of the man beyond the door. When he stopped, he turned to her with a boyish grin. "That'll take them some time, now, to answer."

Roanna stayed silent.

Emryss glanced at her and frowned. "Sorry to be rude, but I had to think. It's a contest of poetry, you see. Supposed to happen at the bride's door *before* the ceremony."

The bard began to speak and Emryss turned to listen, his face a study in concentration. When the voice stopped, he scowled and muttered what she supposed was another Welsh curse. She lifted the lid of the chest, looking for a suitable dress. His clothes lay beside hers, and she stared at them stupidly for a moment before spying Bronwyn's old dress. A white wimple lay folded and ready for her to put on her head. She picked up the dress.

Abruptly Emryss turned, tore the dress from her hands and dragged her toward the door, which he threw open. Gwilym and several other men from the castle stood there gaping at Roanna as she twisted, trying to hide herself behind Emryss.

"Go away and leave us," he said cheerfully. "Can't you see we want to be alone?"

"Right," Gwilym said with a stunned look on his face. "Begging your pardon, my lady. Only making sure he's been a proper husband." The men turned and clamored down the stairs.

Roanna twisted from Emryss's grasp as he slammed the door shut.

"How dare you?" she asked, her voice ominously low. "How dare you show me almost naked to your men? Have you no sense of decency? Of dignity?"

Emryss went to the chest and pulled out his leather tunic and chausses.

"I wanted them gone. That was the quickest way."

Roanna walked up to him and grabbed his arm so that

he turned to face her. "And me? Do you want me gone, too? Is that why you stayed away all last night?"

His mouth hardened. "I married you, didn't I? I wouldn't have done that if I wanted you gone."

Roanna picked up the dress, reaching in for the wimple. It was quite possible she would never understand this man or his people.

She kept her back to him as she pulled on the dress. "Would you please help me?" she asked softly. She heard Emryss come close.

"I'll call Mamaeth," he said.

"It's only to be laced," she said, remembering well the other time he had assisted her.

With a hard tug, he pulled the laces tight. He tied the knot quickly, as if he had no wish to help at all.

When she turned around, he was sitting on the chest, pulling on his leather leggings. Roanna braided her hair swiftly, ignoring him as he was ignoring her, and set the wimple on her head. She took the long white chinband and fastened it around her chin and on the other side of the wimple.

"What's that damn thing for?" Emryss barked as he picked up the leather jerkin.

"I'm a married woman now, so I should cover my hair."

"Makes you look like a dried up old nun."

"I might as well be," she couldn't resist replying.

"What?" His voice was muffled as he pulled off his shirt.

She slipped on her shoes, determined not to look at his half-naked body. His head appeared and he frowned at her. "What did you say?"

"I simply said I might as well be."

He glared at her. "Let's get one thing settled between us. I am the lord here. You are my wife, not my master. God's teeth, if I want to stay out all night, I will!"

Roanna nodded submissively. "Of course, my lord. How foolish of me to expect otherwise," she said, turning away. He would get no arguments from her. She had learned that was the best way to deal with angry men, especially when they were angry at her through no fault of her own.

He crossed the floor and whirled her around. His face was full of rage. "Don't *ever* play the simpering fool with me and don't you ever treat me like a dolt, do you understand?"

Roanna stared at him, aghast at the extent of the anger she saw. He let go of her, his chest heaving. She ran to the window and stared out, seeing nothing. That he should look at her like that! And for what? For stating the truth?

"Roanna, please don't cry."

She turned to him and saw that his anger had fled as quickly as a leaf blown in a strong wind.

"No *man* can make me cry," she said firmly. "And now, if you'll excuse me, my lord, I would like to attend Mass, especially when a priest is here."

"He's gone. He left at first light. I thought it best, considering he took the *amobr*." He looked at her for a long moment. "Don't worry, he had a guard."

That was not what had surprised her.

"I shall attend Mass at the chapel, my lord," she said slowly. "And then I shall speak with Mamaeth about running the household."

He sat on the bed and picked up his jerkin. "Why? Mamaeth does everything."

"Then I shall speak with Jacques about the meals."

"Mamaeth and Rhys decide that."

"But those are *my* duties now."

"I should think you would enjoy being free. And your only duty is to do as I wish."

His gentle words made her knees soften like freshly churned butter.

"Emryss," she pleaded, her reserve cracking. "All I want to do is please you."

A strange look crossed his face. "Good," he said, his voice as cold as his broadsword. "Leave me now."

Roanna obeyed, hurrying out the door and up the narrow stairs leading to the roof. Outside the air was chill and damp, the clouds a dull gray that meant rain would come soon. A pile of cut stone covered in straw lay ready to repair the crumbling parapet, which would no longer afford an archer protection.

She leaned her head on her arms against the cool stone.

Why, oh why, had he asked her to be his wife? So he could humiliate her? So he could kiss her in such a way as to set her heart throbbing with lustful desire, then leave her?

Dear Lord in heaven, she had practically begged him to take her, and he had sent her away!

Nothing had changed. Nothing. Still she would have to watch and wait, dependent on a man, waiting for him to decide.

She stood up slowly and looked out across the land.

No. Not any more. She had decided to become his wife, and she would. If he didn't want to touch her, so be it. Never again would she humiliate herself before him. But in all else, she would be the mistress of Craig Fawr.

Let *him* try to understand *her.*

With her head held high and her back straight, Roanna went down the stairs.

A few nights later, Cynric DeLanyea stared down at the wreck of his sire as Father Robelard hurried from the room. The old man's flesh hung loose and pale, and the body, once overpowering in its very size, now seemed like the hollow hulk of a fallen oak.

So, it has come to this, Cynric thought, subduing a smile.

He, young, strong, in the prime of his life, standing over the man whose massive chest moved only slightly with shallow breaths. Soon his father would be merely lifeless flesh and bone, his secret gone down into the grave.

A pity the priest and Urien, who still leaned against the wall, had to hear the shocking secret his father had revealed as his end drew near. Well, no matter. The priest would be easy to terrify into keeping quiet. And Urien would stay silent as long as he was paid enough.

For once it was good that he had been forced to remain in Wales as his father's lackey, to see who came near the dying man and who learned the truth about Emryss De-Lanyea's parentage.

Cynric looked about the room, admiring the fine tapestries—much finer than the cast-offs in his room above. His particular favorite had always been the one opposite his father's bed that depicted the temptation of Eve. The light from the several candles made the naked figures dance in and out of shadows, almost as if they moved. Soon these, and everything else in the opulent chamber, would be his— the fine silver, the thick rugs on the stone floor, the large mirror, the soft linens, the bed.

Urien Fitzroy shifted slightly as he waited by the door. Cynric glanced at him, then looked at his father.

Suddenly the baron opened his eyes and tried to sit up.

Urien rushed to the baron's side and supported his shoulders as he lay back. "Emryss," the old man whispered. "I want…Emryss…my son."

Urien looked at Cynric questioningly.

"Leave us," Cynric barked, and Urien, after a moment's hesitation, lay the baron on the pillows and walked out.

The baron struggled to sit up again. "Emryss…my son." The once booming voice had grown quiet again, but Cynric decided the time had come.

"Good night, father. And *goodbye*." He picked up a

pillow and held it over the baron's face until his father's chest ceased to move at all.

So simple, Cynric thought. So simple that I should have done this hours ago. But who would have thought the old man would take so long to die?

He placed his father's hands across his chest. Best to make things look as if he cared, a little. He strode across the room and pulled open the door.

Urien straightened expectantly.

"Tell the abbot the baron is dead. I want High Mass at the funeral," Cynric said, hard-pressed to keep the satisfaction from his face.

Urien's eyes narrowed and he looked about to speak, but he turned and walked away.

Cynric shouted for a servant, and when one arrived, gave a brief order that his father's body should be washed and dressed in full armor. Then he slowly sauntered down the corridor and up the stairs to his own room.

Free at last. Free at last. The words echoed and reechoed through his brain, like the beat of a war drum.

Free at last to do as *he* willed.

Free at last from the fear that his father would acknowledge his bastard son Emryss, whom the Welsh would see only as the eldest son of the baron, regardless of the rape that created him.

Free at last to have his revenge on Emryss, and her, too.

Free at last from the pain of never being good enough.

He pushed open his door. A rustle from the bed broke into his thoughts, and a glimpse of bare leg made him smile.

"Ah, Lynette, you are most wonderfully enthusiastic."

The girl poked her head out of the sheets. Her lips curved into a seductive smile. "Aye, my lord."

Cynric sat on the edge of the bed. He ran his hand around

the full curve of her breast. "I am in need of solace, my dear. The baron is dead."

Lynette moved away and pulled the sheet up higher. "Oh, sorry I am, my lord, to hear that."

Cynric grabbed the edge of the sheet and drew her closer. "If you are, I'm sure you're the only one who is."

"Oh, surely not, my lord. I'm certain Father Robelard will be sorry, too."

Cynric stood up slowly. "Father Robelard," he whispered. He looked at Lynette. "You like Father Robelard, don't you, Lynette?"

"Yes, my lord," she replied, her eyebrows knitting together in puzzlement. He began to pace the length of the small room.

"And he, I think, likes you?"

"Father Robelard likes everybody."

"But not as much as he likes you. Isn't that right?"

"Well—" Lynette grinned "—most men like me, my lord."

"As well they should." He stopped and looked down at her. "I want you to do a favor for me, my dear."

"Anything you like," she said, lying down on the pillows.

"No, not that. At least not yet." He sat beside her and toyed with a lock of her thick blond hair. "I want you to show Father Robelard how much you like him."

Her eyes widened. "What do you mean, my lord?"

He bent down to nibble on the lobe of her ear as his fingers continued to play with her hair. "What do you think I mean?" he whispered.

Lynette gasped. "You want me to.... But he's a *priest!* I couldn't."

"I think you can. Actually, I only want to know *if* you could. Rumors have reached me that Father Robelard is, shall we say, straying from the fold? And if that is so, it's my duty as the new lord of Beaufort to make sure this isn't the truth.

"So, dear Lynette, it may all come to nothing. The rumors may only be rumors.

"And of course, my dear, I shall be suitably grateful."

Lynette stared at the handsome face. He was grateful, when she pleased him. And there was Granny to think of, her knuckles swollen and painful in the damp. A new cottage would make things much better for her. And Gwenyth, her younger sister, so infatuated with the wool merchant's son, who wouldn't look at her twice because she had no dowry. After all, many mistresses of noblemen were given houses and land and lots of money. All she had to do was try to seduce a man who was her friend, and a priest.

"If you don't wish to help me, you can leave right now."

Lynette reached up and touched Cynric's face. "I'll do as you ask, my lord."

The door opened and he pivoted on his heel to see who dared enter without knocking. Urien glanced at the girl, then looked at Cynric.

"Some men have come and demand to see you, my lord," he said.

"Demand?" Cynric put his hands on his hips. "Who dares *demand* to see me?"

"One of them says his name is Dolf, my lord." Urien obviously was not impressed by these intruders, and Cynric chuckled softly.

"Well, I shall see them. Wait here," he said to Lynette. He caught her appraisal of Urien. "Alone."

He left, followed by Urien.

The motley group of ragged men stood awkwardly in the chamber. When they saw Cynric and Urien approach, the leader pushed his way to the front, a sly, rotten-toothed smile barely discernible beneath the unkempt whiskers.

"I told you never to come here," Cynric said coldly.

"So you did, your lordship, so you did. Thinking we needed a chat, is all, me and the men here."

Urien closed the door as Cynric faced them, his hands clasped behind his back, making no pretense of hiding his distaste.

"What about?"

"Been doing some thinking, we have."

Cynric raised his eyebrow.

"Thinking we deserve more…reward."

"You do?" A more discerning man would have noticed the slight narrowing of Cynric's eyes.

"Aye, my lord. Seeing as how we takes all the risks, as it were. And having to leave the sheep there…well, not practical for working men, is it?"

The other men nodded and mumbled their agreement. "I see." Cynric walked slowly toward the leader.

The next thing the bearded man knew, he was clasped in an iron grip with a dagger pointing at his throat. His men moved forward.

"One step and I slit his throat. And then I call the guards."

The men hesitated.

"You stupid Saxons are paid more than you deserve." He released the leader, who stumbled into the nearest man. "I am willing to overlook this most inappropriate intrusion, however, since it saves me a trip to you. There is something I wish you to do."

When Cynric described the nature of their task and the amount he was willing to pay, the men glanced uneasily at each other.

"I don't know, your lordship, sir. It seems a mite risky, going so close to the castle," Dolf said cautiously.

"Of course it does, you fool. Why else would I pay you so much to do it?" Cynric said harshly. "Do you wish to refuse?"

Some of the men nodded quickly, but Dolf waited.

"Because if you do," Cynric continued, "I shall have you taken now, and I shall turn you over to my cousin. His wife will certainly recognize you, I will also tell him that you are the men responsible for the death of his sheep."

Dolf took a step forward, but the sound of Urien's sword being pulled from its scabbard halted him. "And I'll say you paid us for everything—even to trying to get the woman."

Cynric sat in one of the large wooden chairs and crossed his outstretched legs at the ankle. The dagger dangled loosely in his fingers. "I don't really think that would be wise."

His cold, vicious tone persuaded Dolf that it was too late to change boats in midstream. "As you like then, my lord," he said. "But that'll be twice the pay."

"Give the lovers a little time, to lull them into thinking that I have accepted their misalliance. Now get out. You stink, all of you. And if you ever dare to come anywhere near Beaufort again, I'll slit your throats as easily as you do the sheep. Do you understand?"

He waited until he heard the muffled ayes of the men.

"Good."

Wordlessly, the men left the room. Dolf, still rubbing his neck, pulled the door shut behind him.

"Soon I won't have to deal with those simpletons," Cynric said as he replaced his dagger. "A swift death will be more than they deserve."

He watched as Urien replaced his sword.

"You don't approve, Urien? Of the men, or the tactic?"

"Either." Urien raised his dark eyes to meet Cynric's pale gaze.

"Well," Cynric said slowly, looking about the room. His room now. "A fire in their mill will provide good cover for firing the weapons store. And then my dear cousin's castle will be ripe for the plucking."

Chapter Thirteen

Roanna shifted impatiently on the chair on the dais. She knew Emryss had returned, for she had seen him from the bedchamber window. For the first time in several days he had come back in time for the evening meal.

Her gaze strayed to the parchment on the table. Today had been bad enough, she thought peevishly, without being reminded of her inability to read even the simplest words.

This afternoon, a messenger had brought the plainly sealed parchment, saying only, "For the Lord and Lady of Craig Fawr." It galled her to have to wait for Emryss before she could find out what it contained. She wished that her uncle had allowed her even the most basic lessons of reading and writing.

With a sound that was a cross between a sniff and a sigh, she watched the tenants enter and take their seats, chattering away in their unintelligible language. Surely more of them understood her better than they let on. How many times had she caught their sidelong glances at Mamaeth for *her* agreement when she had asked them to do something?

The knuckles of Roanna's fingers turned white in her clasped hands. Even Jacques seemed too happy to notice how miserable she was, although he battled with Mamaeth constantly about every item in the kitchen.

She looked around the hall for Bronwyn. The girl was absent from her duties more and more; she should have kept to her own business and let Gwilym ignore her.

Roanna tried not to look up when she heard the men enter but couldn't help glancing at Emryss as he came down the hall.

How tired and drawn he looked! He limped badly, although she could see he was trying to hide the pain. Concern surged through her, and she tried desperately to subdue it.

What else could he expect, when he rode out on patrol every day from dawn to dusk, returning only to eat and then collapse, exhausted, in their bed?

Emryss sat down in his chair heavily. At once the maids—except the missing Bronwyn—jumped to begin serving the meal.

Roanna pushed the rolled parchment toward Emryss. "A messenger arrived, bearing this."

Emryss said nothing as he picked it up, broke the seal and unrolled it. Feigning unconcern, Roanna crossed herself and began to nibble on a piece of bread.

With a disgusted grunt, Emryss tossed the scroll aside.

"Well, my lord?" Roanna asked after a short time, unable to control her curiosity any longer.

"Read it yourself." He pushed the parchment to her.

"I…" she flushed hotly, but continued. "I cannot read."

"Oh," he said absently. Perhaps he had also forgotten the way they kissed that night on the battlements, when he had asked her if she knew the law.

"The baron is dead."

She looked at him quickly.

"My esteemed cousin," he went on sarcastically, "invites us to attend a memorial Mass tomorrow.'' He grabbed his chalice and took a deep drink.

"We shall go, of course," Roanna said.

"Of course *not*," he said coldly.

"But we must go, out of respect."

"Respect?" Emryss said hotly. All the people turned to look toward the high table. "I had no respect for that blackguard living, and I won't give him any now he's dead!"

"He was your uncle," Roanna insisted quietly.

"It is to my shame that I was ever related to that grasping piece of dung."

Roanna raised her eyes to his face. "Are you and Cynric always going to squabble like children?"

He stared at her, his jaw jutting forward and his lips pressed together. "Listen to me, wife," he said slowly. "I will hate that brood of vipers for the rest of my life for what they did to my mother. And no soft words or meaningless gestures will ever change that. Do you understand?"

"Yes, my lord."

"Therefore we will *not* go."

"As you wish, my lord," Roanna said softly. *We* will not, she finished in her thoughts.

"Woman!" Jacques roared, "get those evil-smelling weeds off my table and out of my kitchen!"

"*Your* table? *Your* kitchen?" Mamaeth screeched. "Gall you have, my man, to order me here! Why don't you take your fat belly out?"

Jacques threw back his shoulders. His stomach flattened a little. "I am the best cook in all of Europe, in all of England and certainly in all of this godforsaken wilderness, so you should treat me with proper respect."

Mamaeth walked up and poked him in the stomach. "Listen, you lump of lard, not caring if you were the king himself. This is *my* kitchen and has been since you were slobbering on your mother's shoulder. So you get out!''

''I will not. I will speak to Lady Roanna about your lack of respect, and end this once and for all.''

''Do that, because speaking to Emryss, me, and he's the lord here.''

The two of them, one as skinny as an empty pea pod, the other as fat as a rainwater hogshead, tried to get out the door at the same time. Mamaeth made it first, then stopped abruptly.

Emryss sat on his horse, his face filled with anger, as Roanna, dressed in her burgundy gown, walked toward the stable. Jacques halted beside Mamaeth. ''What is it?''

''Sh! And listen, you big oaf!''

''Where are you going?'' Emryss asked coolly.

''To the monastery,'' Roanna replied, her voice equally unemotional.

''The hell you are.'' Emryss climbed down from Wolf. He planted himself in front of her, his feet wide apart and his hands on his hips.

''I cannot live all my life inside these walls. Cynric has made a gesture of goodwill. I am going to the monastery.''

''On foot?''

''If I must.''

Mamaeth put her hand on Jacques' arm. ''Not going to back down, is she?'' she whispered incredulously.

''No, she will not. I have seen that look before.''

Apparently Emryss recognized her determination, too.

''Gwil!'' he called sharply. ''You and one other. Go with her to the monastery. And have a horse saddled for her.'' He grinned slowly, mockingly. ''We mustn't give dear Cynric any cause to hate us, must we?''

Roanna stood expressionlessly as Emryss swung himself onto Wolf and rode out of the courtyard.

Mamaeth glanced at Jacques. "What's wrong?" she said softly. "What's she done, that he treats her so?"

Jacques frowned. "Lady Roanna is blameless, for a certainty."

Mamaeth gave him a disgusted look. "It can't be Emryss. Why, I used to have girls begging me for love potions, just so he'd look at them, let alone take them to his bed. But *she's* still a virgin."

"How can you know this?" Jacques asked, clearly skeptical. "Lady Roanna would not share such things with you."

"I know it, is all. And it's not right. The lad's smitten, but he rides out every day like he's possessed of a demon, and looks terrible. She must be denying him his rights."

Jacques shook his head. "No, that I do not believe. She cares a great deal for him. He must be tiring himself out too much, whatever you may think."

"Well, something's not right, and I'll be finding out what it is," she said firmly. "Two people looking like they used to at each other getting married, and then acting like this!"

Jacques nodded. "I agree with you. Perhaps together we can help them."

Mamaeth grinned. "For a lump of lard, Jacques, you might have a brain after all."

The vibrating notes of the Mass came to an end, echoing through the massive church. Roanna glanced to where Gwilym lounged near the door, still angry at having to escort her.

Cynric sat at the front of the crowded church, his head bowed as if in prayer. His dark-haired, silent friend was close by, but paid no attention to the service whatsoever, except to kneel at the appropriate times.

The abbot himself had performed the Mass, assisted by Father Robelard. He had smiled at her as he'd given her the host, and she had been warmed by it. Just as she had been chilled by the realization that Cynric had stared at her the whole time she knelt before the altar.

Roanna stood up to leave. She had done her duty as a relative, and wanted to get out of the huge, cold building that was so obviously built more for the glory of the DeLanyeas than the glory of God. Gwilym went out the door, to make the horses ready, she assumed.

As she reached the back of the church, she heard fast steps approaching.

"My lady!" Cynric called out softly.

She turned to him as he pushed his way through the crowd of slow-moving tenants. When he reached her, he pulled her into a quiet, dark alcove. Stairs curved up out of sight, to the belfry, probably.

"Thank you for coming, my lady," he said with a wistful smile. "I am most pleased you did."

"It was my duty," she said stiffly, aware that his hand was still on her arm and that his face was uncomfortably close.

"I had hoped, foolishly I know, that perhaps you realized that I meant it when I apologized before. If I'm wrong, don't tell me. Let me keep my little delusion."

Roanna felt uncomfortably warm. She *had* doubted his sincerity before; now she was not so sure.

She smiled a little and pulled her arm from his grasp. "I do hope, Cynric, that all this anger and hate between our two families will end now."

He took her hand in his. "That is my dearest wish, too, Roanna."

She heard a sound nearby and tried to look past Cynric, but he blocked her view.

Suddenly he lifted her fingers to his lips. "It is my dearest wish," he said forlornly, "because there is little hope I can have the other dream I keep."

She was sure she heard someone just outside the alcove. "What is that?" she asked, leaning away from him.

"You," he whispered.

She pushed her way past him. With relief she saw no one near, and hurried out the door. How stupid she had been! She rubbed her fingers against her skirt where his lips had touched them.

Cynric walked slowly out of the alcove and out the door. He saw Roanna riding away, and began to whistle.

Gwilym said nothing as they rode back, and it was late by the time they returned to Craig Fawr. The evening meal had ended, and Mamaeth told her there was a small supper waiting in the bedchamber. Roanna hurried up the stairs.

She wanted to wash away all traces of Cynric's touch, telling herself that she couldn't believe his lies. She should have listened to Emryss instead of being so determined to do the correct thing. Trusted his judgment rather than worry about giving anyone reason to cast aspersions on them.

She could only hope she would never see Cynric again.

She opened the door, walked in and stopped. Emryss, apparently asleep, lay soaking in the huge tub. The tang of herbs filled the air, and braziers warmed the room. His clothes lay in a heap on the floor, the patch on the top.

This was the first time she had seen him so still.

She closed the door softly and leaned against it, studying him. The scar on his face was wrinkled and reddened by the heat. The space where his right eye had been was a sunken hole. She stared at him, trying to picture him as he had been before the wound, but it was impossible. To her, the scar was as much a part of his face as his lips, his straight nose, the strong chin.

She took a step closer. His broad shoulders lay against the wet wood, droplets of water shimmering on the muscles. She wanted to reach out and brush them away. No, she wanted to lick them away.

Abashed at the brazen shape of her thoughts, she looked away, but only for a moment. His nakedness tempted her beyond modesty. She took another step closer.

The water was cloudy from the herbs, and deep. She closed her eyes and breathed in the lovely aroma.

"What are you doing?"

His words startled her, and she stepped back quickly.

"I...I was coming to...wash," she finished lamely.

"Give me that cloth there."

Roanna bent to a pile of linen and picked up the top one.

"No. The big one."

She found the largest and held it out to him. He stared at her for a moment, then grinned derisively. Slowly he began to rise.

Roanna quickly turned her back to him and held the towel out. He snatched it from her hands with a low chuckle.

She felt the blush creeping up to her face and fastened her gaze on the wall. She heard the splashes as he got out of the tub.

"You can turn around now. I'm presentable."

She glanced sideways as he moved past her. His idea of presentable was the cloth wrapped around his waist, so she kept looking at the wall.

Suddenly he stumbled, his left leg seeming to go weak.

"Do you need help?" Roanna asked in a subdued voice.

"No," he barked in response, running his hand through his tangled curls. He rubbed his leg a little.

"Where's my damn patch?" he muttered as he limped toward the chest.

Roanna walked to the pile of clothes and picked it up. "Here."

He took it with a rueful smile. "Not a pretty sight, my face, is it?"

Why didn't he put some clothes on? "It doesn't disturb me," she said quietly.

He limped to the pitcher of wine sitting on the table and poured a drink.

"What happened to your leg?" she asked.

"An old wound and a long story, so I won't tell it now. I'm too tired." He looked toward her, and she didn't breathe. "Take off that damn wimple."

"Yes, my lord." She reached up and undid the veil. As she did so, her hair fell around her shoulders.

He stared at her. "God's blood, you are beautiful," he whispered.

Slowly she walked toward him. "Emryss," she said softly.

His strong arms encircled her and drew her against his naked chest. Gently yet insistently his lips met hers. Desire burst into flames inside her, pushing her willing body closer to his. She felt his hands undo the laces of her gown, then his hands moved inside, warm against her back.

She moaned softly as her knees grew weak, and she clung to him. His hot moist skin excited her almost beyond belief. His tongue pressed open her lips.

Then she was in his arms, weightless, suspended as he carried her and laid her on the bed without breaking the kiss. His hands moved through her hair, down her neck and into her bodice, his fingers cupping her breasts. Exquisite agony blossomed, and she thrust upward to his touch.

As his lips followed the path his hands had taken, she wanted to return the delicious pleasure. Her hands moved slowly around his sides to move to his chest. His nipples were hard, and she rubbed her fingers lightly across them.

Emryss groaned and began licking her nipples lightly. Roanna threw back her head, her hands caressing every inch of his chest. She felt his knee move between her legs and opened them wider.

This was so right, so good, so wonderful.

"Oh, God," Emryss groaned. He rolled off her and lay beside her, staring at the ceiling.

"What, what is it?"

"I...I can't."

Roanna sat up, ignoring the bodice that fell around her waist.

"Please, Roanna, don't look at me like that." He turned away. "I never should have married you."

"You said I was beautiful," she said in a tiny voice.

He turned to her and reached out to touch her face, but withdrew his hand. "You are. Too beautiful." He stood up, holding the cloth around his waist.

"Then why won't you love me, Emryss?"

He walked around the bed until he stood beside her. "Because I am only half a man." He let the cloth fall, and she gasped at the gash that began below his left nipple and ran down to his knee. It was red and deep below his waist. Another scar crossed this one, and reached almost to his manhood.

"A Saracen almost made me a eunuch," he said grimly as he picked up the cloth. "He might as well have done the complete job, between his sword and the infection."

Roanna looked at his sorrowful face.

"Oh, most the parts are there, and God knows they seem to work. But only for a short time." He walked over and took another gulp of wine, swaying slightly.

"Can you be sure?" Her voice was low, and she desperately wanted him to be wrong.

He grinned ruefully. "Oh, I've tried, Roanna. A complete failure. So you see, my wife, I should never have proposed this marriage. It's unfair."

Roanna pulled up her bodice and climbed out of the bed. "Why did you?"

He stared at his cup of wine. "Because you looked at me as a woman looks at a man. Not as a freak, to be scorned or pitied. But with respect and—" his voice grew very quiet "—desire."

He sighed, and his voice grew stronger. "That's why I've been riding myself to exhaustion. You are much too tempting."

He picked up his chausses from the floor and pulled them on. His leather jerkin followed. Without another word he left the room.

Roanna stared at the door, then sat down dejectedly on the bed. She wanted to be at least a little relieved that the problem was not with her, but instead felt shocked and overwhelmed.

Two large tears began to roll down her cheeks.

Suddenly a woman screamed. Roanna ran to the door and pulled it open. There was a great commotion in the hall, and she ran down the stairs.

Emryss lay sprawled on the ground, unconscious. Roanna's heart seemed to drop into the pit of her stomach as she hurried toward him.

"What happened?" she cried, just as Mamaeth knelt by his side.

"I was talking to him," Gwilym said softly, "and then he…just fell over." There was some kind of accusation in his face as he looked at her, but she paid no heed when Emryss groaned loudly.

"What is it?" she asked Mamaeth anxiously.

"Fever and what else I don't know," the old woman said tersely. "Riding out all day in all weather, what was the lad thinking of? Here, Gwil, help me take him to his bed."

Gwilym brushed past Roanna and helped Mamaeth get Emryss to his feet. Roanna went forward to help, too.

"We'll manage, my lady," Gwilym said coldly as he put Emryss's arm over his shoulder. Roanna followed behind, leaving the people in the hall hushed and solemn.

In the bedchamber, Gwilym helped Mamaeth lay Emryss on the bed. "Go now, and fetch my bag," Mamaeth said brusquely as Gwilym stood in the door. Roanna waited for him to go by, then entered the room.

"Help me get his clothes off," Mamaeth barked. They pulled off his shirt.

"Jesus, Mary and Joseph!" Mamaeth exclaimed. "He's burning. Come on, off with his chausses now, while I get the brazier lighted."

Roanna gingerly put her hands on the waist of the garment and tugged lightly. It didn't move. Emryss moaned softly.

Dear Lord, help him, she prayed silently. He looked so ill, and she, stupid fool, had been too selfish to notice.

Mamaeth clucked loudly and came to the bed. "I said get his chausses off, girl." She grabbed the leather leggings at the top and yanked.

Mamaeth gasped. "By the Lord…" She looked at Roanna, who wouldn't meet her gaze. "Is this why you're still a virgin?" she asked bluntly.

Roanna flushed and said nothing.

"Men!" Mamaeth said under her breath. "Letting himself get this sick, and not saying a word about this other, too. Just wait till I get him better!" She tugged a sheet over him.

Roanna took hold of Mamaeth's arm. "He will get better, won't he?"

"Of course, my girl. It's a fever, but I've nursed sicker men than this. Time should do the trick. If only the fools will learn that!"

Roanna wished she felt as confident as Mamaeth apparently did.

There was a rap at the door, and Bronwyn came in with Mamaeth's bag of herbs. "About time you got here," Mamaeth snapped. "Hot water and quick, and no making eyes at Gwilym till you've brought it."

Bronwyn ran from the room.

"Now you just sit and rest, my dear," Mamaeth said, not unkindly.

For the next few days Emryss lay in bed feverish and delirious. Roanna stayed by his side as much as Mamaeth would allow, awaiting any improvement.

Several times he spoke out loud, snatches of words and songs and sometimes even shouting. He tossed and turned fitfully, and Mamaeth had to force her medicine down his throat.

Often he cried out as if in pain, and spoke of thirst, but no drink seemed to alleviate his agony. He muttered of eating the flesh of horses, of freezing, continuous rain, of pestilence. On and on the litany went at times, until his voice was hoarse. Only then would he fall silent.

His suffering filled her with such torment that she wouldn't leave him. Sometimes she took his hand in hers and held it without speaking, as if by doing so she could infuse him with her own life.

Once she dared to bend forward to kiss his parched lips.

She didn't want to lose him. She couldn't imagine a life now without his smile, his jokes, his songs. Things would be incomplete without him.

Finally, one night, when she was beginning to fear that he would never recover, Mamaeth came in, stared at him for a moment and felt his forehead.

"Jesus, Mary and all the saints be praised! The fever's broke!"

Roanna felt nothing except a great weariness that came crashing over her like a wave against the shore.

"He'll do now, my dear," Mamaeth said softly. "And now you must have some rest. He'll sleep sound for a long time, so best you do, too."

Roanna nodded and got to her feet.

"Mamaeth, how can I ever thank you?" she asked softly.

"Have a baby," the old woman snapped and marched from the room.

Roanna looked at Emryss. Clearly he hadn't told his old nurse that he had already tried and failed. She sighed softly and touched his lips with her fingertips.

She walked to the window and looked out at the night sky.

How could she begin again with him?

She let her gaze rove over the land he loved so much, down to the river. The mill wheel turned slowly, leisurely. It would be harvest time soon, she thought as she watched the moon hanging in the dark blue sky, and the mill would be bustling with activity.

Gratitude filled her as she looked out upon the beauty of the land. "Thank you, God," she whispered, and the stars seemed to wink knowingly at her.

Clouds were scudding low across the sky as she took deep breaths of the cleansing air. Oh, how tired she was!

She filled her lungs again, taking a last look at the sleeping countryside.

Something was not right. She sniffed again, then again deeply, her eyes searching for anything amiss.

She stared at the mill.

"Fire," she gasped. She dashed to the door. "Fire!" she shouted. "Fire at the mill!"

Her panic grew as she raced down the stairs. If the mill was destroyed now, it would take months to repair it. Months without flour or any ground grain.

She ran into the courtyard, still sounding the alarm. People ran past her, heading pell-mell down the road to the mill.

Great flames leapt from the roof of the stone building and out of the upper windows. The huge wheel lay motionless, the bottom of it on fire.

To her dismay, Roanna realized the fire had progressed far. She stopped and looked around. The mill was stone and could probably be repaired. If they could save most of the waterwheel, they could have the mill working soon.

People seemed to be running about pointlessly, unsure of what to do. She looked over her shoulder, wishing Emryss was there to direct them. What she saw filled her with panic.

Smoke billowed from a corner of Craig Fawr. The weapons store.

Roanna called out for Mamaeth and in a moment her familiar face appeared through the smoky haze.

"Thank God," Roanna said. "Keep the women here, and ask if anyone saw anything or anybody. I'm taking the men back to Craig Fawr. The weapons store is aflame."

Mamaeth stared at her, and Roanna realized a crowd had gathered around them. "You women stay here and get this out. We must go back. The fortress is on fire."

The crowd gasped and the men began running up the hill. Roanna didn't waste any more time, but followed behind as fast as her long skirts would allow.

By the time she reached the courtyard, it was in chaos. Men were running helter-skelter with buckets of water, bumping into each other in their haste to reach the weapons store. Smaller fires, started by blowing embers, added to the smoke-filled air. A man ran past her carrying spears and arrows, dropping them in his haste.

A gust of wind cleared the air for a moment, and she was grateful until she realized with a shaft of fear deep in her stomach that it would carry the embers to the stable and the straw.

Roanna shouted, but no one paid her any more than passing heed.

Quickly she went to the nearest scaffold and began climbing. When she was above the heads of all below, she suddenly screamed in the loudest voice she could summon.

Everyone stopped and stared. Only the sound of the flames continued.

"Rhys. Where is Rhys?" she called out.

"Here." A figure covered in soot stepped forward.

"Line up the men from the well to the tower to pass the buckets. Get the boys to put out the small fires at once, and the oldest lads should wet down the roof of the stable before it goes, too. Everyone else should be out of here, and all the horses, too. Don't send anyone into the tower for more weapons. Put out the fire before it spreads first!"

The men stared at her, dumbfounded.

Suddenly Roanna saw a figure standing in the doorway of the hall.

"Do as she says," Emryss called out. "What are you waiting for? The lady's giving orders, not asking you."

Then came the crash of a floor caving in from within the tower, and the people moved again. Roanna climbed down from a scaffold and went toward him.

"Thank you," she said.

His face softened. "They would have done it anyway. You look like the avenging angel."

Roanna smiled into his still-pale face.

"Come on," he said. "We've a fire to fight."

"But your leg…"

"I'll go up on the stable roof and help the boys."

She would have protested, but he was already gone, disappearing into the smoke.

Roanna helped Rhys organize the line to pass the buckets

of water, only to discover that there were not enough vessels to make a line from the well to the tower. Frantically she ran to the kitchen and grabbed any dish that would hold water, even Jacques' favorite mixing bowl, and passed them out among the men.

The oldest lads, delighted at having a responsibility of such import as saving the stables, fought over who would be on the roof, but she heard Emryss's calm voice and turned her attention to the storehouse.

She was too busy to notice the burning ember that landed on the hem of her dress.

Chapter Fourteen

With the dawn came welcome rain, which put out the last of the glowing embers.

Emryss looked out from the hayloft window. He would have preferred to be outside, up on the roof with the boys, but common sense had prevailed, and he had directed their efforts from inside the barn. The courtyard was a mess, with scattered puddles of water and pieces of blackened wood and stone. Most of the tenants had gone home, but a few men remained talking quietly beside the weapons store. Though the stones of the storehouse were black with soot, Emryss saw with relief that there were no cracks in the walls. It might have been worse, much worse, if Roanna hadn't given the alarm when she did. He scanned the yard, but couldn't see her anywhere. "Damn my blind eye," he muttered, then caught one of the lads staring at him from behind a bale of hay. "All out?" he asked.

"Aye, it is," the boy said, moving closer to his idol. Emryss reached out and ruffled his hair. "You lads all did a fine job. I'm proud of you."

A gaggle of smoke-blackened youths came climbing down the ladder from the roof, their faces broken by wide, white grins. Emryss stood up gingerly and went slowly to the wooden ladder that led down to the floor of the stable. He had climbed the ladder quickly, when the need was great, but he took much more time getting down.

Gwilym greeted him with a yell and ran toward him. "Not much damage, thank God," he said.

"And the mill?"

"Mamaeth made the women move right smart. The wheel's a little scorched, but workable."

Emryss nodded and felt exhaustion creeping over him. "Where's Roanna?"

A strange expression crossed Gwilym's face. "Inside the hall."

Emryss began to walk slowly across the ward until he spied a garment, torn and black, on the stones. A dress. *Her* dress. He broke into a run and burst into the hall, now crowded with sooty tenants.

Oh, dear God, if she was hurt…

"Roanna!" he shouted.

Rhys—at least he thought it was Rhys—stepped forward. "She's in your room, my lord."

"What happened?"

"Her dress caught fire…"

Emryss didn't wait to hear any more, but hurried to the bedchamber. His leg began to throb, the pain searing, but he ignored it and took the stairs two at a time. As he reached the corridor, he saw Mamaeth coming out of their room. She saw him and put her fingers to her lips.

"Sleeping now, she is, so quiet."

"Is she badly hurt?" he asked urgently.

"No, the poor lamb's just weary, is all, and no wonder. Why, Emryss, what's the matter?"

"Nothing now, Mamaeth," he said, leaning against the wall and feeling the full extent of his pain for the first time.

"Except that leg, eh? Come with me to the barracks, and I'll put a poultice on it."

"No, never mind…"

"I said, come to the barracks and I'll help."

Emryss knew there was no way Mamaeth would take a refusal when she spoke in such a tone.

Once inside the barracks, Mamaeth began mixing the poultice, all the while glancing at him out of the corner of her eye. "Praise to God for the rain," she said, frowning. "And your wife's sharp eyes. Take off your chausses."

With his back to her, Emryss peeled off his leggings and covered his lap with a sheet from one of the beds.

"You look like a sick dog." Mamaeth carried a bowl over and Emryss wrinkled his nose with distaste.

"No making faces at me, Emryss. This will help. And would have sooner, if you'd not kept secrets from me." Then she grabbed the edge of the sheet and threw it back.

"God's blood!" Emryss cried, reaching for the sheet.

"No swearing, boy, or I'll not help."

Emryss resigned himself to the inevitable but didn't care to look at Mamaeth's face as she spread the noxious poultice.

"So your wife's still a virgin."

Emryss got to his feet unsteadily and pulled on his chausses.

"You might have come to me, Emryss."

"And have my shame known?"

"What's to be ashamed of?"

"That I can't…" He shrugged his shoulders. "That I can't give her children."

"Of course you can't, if you never love her, you fool."

"Mamaeth," he said, trying to keep his voice firm, "I *can't* love her."

"Why not, for the sake of the saints? Because you're missing one?" Mamaeth sat on the bed in exasperation. "Heaven preserve me, think your brains was there, sometimes. Men!"

She saw her boy's distress, and her voice softened. "Lost one eye, haven't you, Emryss, and you're not blind."

"Nor am I whole."

Mamaeth looked at him. "Lucky you are then, because what you've lost makes no difference at all."

"What?"

"Knowing what he was doing, God was, when he made Adam. He gave you two, and losing one makes no change in the way things work."

Emryss sat down beside her on the bed. "That's what Abram said, Mamaeth, the one who saved my life. But…" He sighed softly. "I tried on the way back. I seemed to be healed, but then, when…"

"Ah." Mamaeth shook her head. "Worried you was, and fearful, and with a women you didn't know, or care to know beyond a tumble? Of course things will go wrong, in that state. But it will all be different now."

"How can you be so sure?"

"Because this woman wants you for her husband. Such a look in her eyes! And you're married to her. Be taking your time at first is all—better that way any time. And not tonight. Give yourself a chance to heal."

Emryss felt curiously light, as if he could fly around the room if he wanted to. "How long?"

"Ah, that's more like my Emryss. Impatient. Well, give it about a week." She put her arms around the man she had known all his days and loved fiercely, and let him lay his head on her shoulder as he had done a hundred times.

"Thank you, Mamaeth, little mother," he whispered softly.

She cuffed him playfully on the side of his head as she sniffled loudly. "Tch! Just like a man, you are! Not saying a word, even to me. Thought you'd never get like that, boy. No good at keeping secrets, you. But you fooled me this time." She stood up. "Expecting some babies, now I am.

Your wife's made for children and she wants them, too, or I'm in my dotage and might as well sit in the yard all day."

Emryss grinned, feeling as if he could shout and run and dance and sing, just as soon as his heart came down from the sky. "Tell me, Mamaeth, my oldest love, how did you know Roanna was a virgin?"

"Knew by the walk, boy. No looseness in the limbs."

He looked at her doubtfully.

"Go to her, fool—but only looking for now!" she barked, then winked and went out, banging the door behind her.

Emryss jumped to his feet, but the queasy feeling in the pit of his stomach warned him to slow down. He began to sing little snatches of his favorite songs as he went out of the barracks.

He looked about at the fortress, happy that so little had been damaged. They had until December to work on the walls before they would have to stop. The cold weather would crack wet mortar, so they would cover the top of the walls with straw mixed with dung. The walls were progressing better than he had even dared to hope back in the spring, when he had first begun the work of rebuilding.

Craig Fawr would be impregnable, except for the most sophisticated siege machines. And who would bother, for his estate was too small to warrant the expense such machines would represent.

He walked jauntily into the hall, greeting and thanking everyone. He spotted Gwilym huddled in the corner with Bronwyn and sauntered over. "Bronwyn, tell Jacques to make a good meal for this evening. We all deserve it."

Bronwyn dipped a curtsy and smiled prettily. "Aye, my lord." With another, broader smile at Gwilym, she hurried away.

"*Brawdmaeth,*" Gwilym said, "I have to speak with you."

Emryss grinned. "Later, Gwil. Right now I have something important to do."

Gwilym looked about to speak but only nodded.

When he reached the door to the bedchamber, Emryss knocked softly. He heard no reply, so he pushed the door open gently.

Roanna lay sleeping on the bed, a soft fur covering pulled up to her chin. Her long dark hair was spread out on the pillow, and he could see traces of soot in the corners of her eyes and lips. He glanced at his own hands, and realized he was still black from the fire.

As quietly as possible he began to wash away the soot, although he was hard-pressed to keep from touching his slumbering wife.

"Emryss?"

He turned to find her looking at him. "Yes, wife," he said, knowing he was grinning like a simpleton, but too happy to care. He went and sat on the bed beside her, allowing himself to touch her face. Her eyes widened. "Thank you for saving the mill, and the storehouse," he said softly.

"I only gave the alarm," Roanna said, her delectable brow furrowing a little. "I hope you're well?"

"Never been better, Roanna." He bent down and brushed his lips across hers. She began to tremble, and he resisted the urge to gather her into his arms. "Mamaeth and I had a little chat," he said. "Apparently I've been very stupid."

He was rewarded by a charming look of astonishment.

"Mamaeth says if I don't…rush anything, we may yet have children."

Roanna's smile began in the depths of her green eyes, moving down to the tips of her mouth.

Then her lips were on his. She clung to him, demanding

a response that he was only too willing to give. After a long moment, he pulled away, breathless.

"God's teeth! And *I'm* supposed to be impatient!" He grinned. "A week, Mamaeth says, so I think I'd better sleep in the barracks till then." He stood up. "That will be about harvest time." With a roguish wink he said, "I think I'll have more to celebrate than a fine crop."

Roanna smiled, feeling the warmth of his smile right down to her toes.

There was a knock at the door. "What's going on in there?" Mamaeth called out. "Better be following my advice, Emryss!"

He pulled open the door to find Mamaeth almost invisible behind the wooden tub she carried. "Well, you nit, help me before I drop it and you lose something else!"

He chuckled and carried the tub into the room. Mamaeth looked from one happy face to the other.

"I'll have the water as soon as Lardgut gets the fire going in the kitchen. Lazy thing he is, too busy claiming he put the fire out single-handed to get on with his work."

"We only need enough for one tub full," Emryss said solemnly.

Mamaeth stopped frowning and cackled delightedly. "Of course, my lord," she said, winking broadly. "Mind, now, a week—or doing serious harm perhaps."

"I won't forget," Emryss said as Mamaeth went out.

"Think of all that time wasted!" they heard her mutter as she closed the door.

Emryss began to laugh until he looked at Roanna. "Roanna," he said, his voice ominously low and soft, "what have you on under those covers?"

She suddenly felt very shy.

"I asked you a question, oh wife," he said, walking deliberately toward the bed.

"Nothing," she said in a little voice. His approach was

sending delightful thrills of anticipation to every particle of her body.

He sat on the bed and brushed his fingers along the fur, close to her naked breasts. "You know, wife, it strikes me that there are other ways to enjoy ourselves in the next week."

His fingers left the fur and began to caress her soft skin. Roanna sighed and closed her eyes as he began to nibble gently on her earlobe. Her hands moved slowly up his arms to clasp his neck.

His touch became more firm, and he pushed the cover from her body. Arching against the strong hand, she turned her face to kiss him.

"That's more like it."

They sprung apart as Mamaeth charged into the room. Roanna scrambled to cover herself as Emryss, blushing furiously, got to his feet.

"Water for your bath, my lord," Mamaeth said, grinning devilishly, "and yours, my lady."

A troop of maids came in, each bearing a ewer of water.

"Just set them down and leave," Emryss said jauntily. They did, giggling under their breath, and went out like a flock of chickens.

Emryss ignored Roanna for the moment and began emptying the ewers into the tub.

"Do you wish to wash first?" she ventured when he still said nothing.

He straightened and turned to her. "First?" He shook his head. "No. We're washing together."

Before she could say anything, he picked her up and, ignoring her squeals of protest, plopped her in the water.

In another moment he had thrown off his sooty clothes. With a lascivious leer, he climbed in beside her.

He made a few halfhearted attempts to splash water on

his chest, then reached out to touch her white shoulder. She shuddered with the pleasure and moved closer.

"Oh, no," he said, waggling his finger. "I'm beginning to think this was not one of my better ideas. After this, I'd better keep to the barracks, or I'll forget every word Mamaeth said."

Roanna blushed and looked down at the water, all too aware of their nakedness. She was very warm, and she knew it wasn't from the water.

"Still, this is very nice," Emryss said with a chuckle. "Now, suppose you tell me why your dress is lying ruined in the courtyard?"

Roanna cleared her throat. "It caught on fire. Just the skirt, from an ember, I suppose." She didn't dare look at his face as she went on. "It began to burn so I...took it off."

It took a few moments for Emryss to understand the full import of her words. "You took it off? Where?"

"Well, Emryss, there. In the courtyard."

He began to laugh. "You mean my modest wife tore her gown off in the middle of the courtyard? Oh, the indignity of it all. Oh, how will I live with the shame!"

Roanna said nothing, but her face burned. "There wasn't time to do anything else."

Emryss fished under the water until he captured her slender hand. "Roanna, look at me. That's better. I don't give a damn if you stood naked in front of all my tenants." He paused and grinned again. "Well, that's not exactly true." His face became serious. "Nevertheless, you worry too much about what the people think. The important thing is, you saved the weapons and the mill. Without them we'd be as helpless here as a newborn lamb, and starving, to boot."

Roanna's heart filled with happiness.

"That's better." He let go of her hand and rubbed his

chin thoughtfully. "Still, beginning to think you should have a priest about to show you the error of your ways."

Roanna lunged forward to grasp his shoulders, sending water sloshing over the sides of the tub. "Oh, Emryss, really?"

"If I'd known letting you have a priest about would make you act like this, I would have done it sooner." He smiled at her. "Yes, have your priest." His face hardened for an instant. "Just don't think I'm going to have anything to do with him. I hate the hypocrites."

"I won't, Emryss."

"I wish I knew what makes you set to have one about."

Roanna sat back on her side of the tub. "When I lived with my uncle, the only times I truly felt safe were when I was in the church. It was almost like being at home."

"Well, this is your home now," he said, smiling warmly. He splashed water over his head. "God, I stink of smoke."

Roanna crept closer again. "So do I."

"Get away, woman. I'm not that patient."

She sat back.

He grunted skeptically. "Well, let's get back to your priest. I suppose he should be having something better than that leaking bucket for a chapel. In the spring, *if* the wool's good, we'll think about building one of stone."

Roanna smiled. "Thank you, Emryss."

He groaned. "Don't look at me like that. I'm only a mortal man, you know." He stood and glanced down ruefully as he stepped out of the tub. "God's wounds, how the hell am I supposed to wait a week?"

"I don't wish to wait, either."

Emryss glanced at Roanna, her skin glistening with moisture, her full lips parted, her eyes shining at him. He pulled on his clothes.

"Going to see the damage," he said. "And stick my head in the stable trough," he muttered as he left the room.

Roanna got out of the tub and began to rub her skin briskly with a towel. Her whole body was tingling, and she couldn't keep the smile from her face, although a week seemed like a very long time.

Emryss stepped over a large puddle outside the entrance to the hall. Rhys and Gwilym, holding a charred piece of wood, stood outside the entrance to the weapons store, talking in hushed voices.

As he crossed the courtyard, Rhys nodded in his direction. Their faces were grim as he drew closer.

"Emryss, I must talk with you," Gwilym said.

"Right. How many weapons lost?"

"A few. Rounding the rest up now," Rhys said.

"Let me know the final tally," Emryss replied. Rhys nodded and entered the building. "Now, what's so important, Gwil?"

"The fires were set. We found pitch and torches at the mill and even inside here."

Emryss felt a surge of anger. "The mill I can see, but how could anyone get inside here?"

"The mill was torched first, and like fools we all went there. It must have been then that someone got in and set the store alight."

Emryss rubbed his jaw. "Did anybody see anything?"

"Not here." Gwilym's expression hardened. "But something I did see, and that I must tell you. At the monastery." Emryss stared at the ground as his foster brother continued. "Cynric was kissing your wife's hand. He had her off in a corner, and she let him."

"How do you know this?"

"I got eyes, Emryss."

"And you think this has something to do with the fires?"

"Well, it was her gave the first alarm that sent everyone down to the mill."

"Who saw the fire here?"

Gwilym shrugged. "Her."

"So she sent you all down there and then led everyone back here to put out a fire she helped cause? Not making sense, Gwil."

"I hope I'm wrong, for your sake, *brawdmaeth.*"

"You're seeing plots that don't exist, Gwil. She wouldn't do it. I'm sure of it. We'll post double watches. For now, come on with me and we'll ask her."

Roanna stopped brushing her hair and smiled as Emryss came into the bedchamber.

"Gwilym tells me Cynric spoke with you at the church," he said bluntly. Gwilym came in, looking at her with barely disguised loathing.

"Yes, he did."

She looked puzzled as Emryss went on, determined to set Gwilym's fears at rest. "What did he want?"

"He wants to end the fighting between you," she said quietly.

Gwilym guffawed. "What a liar!"

Roanna frowned. "At least he's made an overture of reconciliation."

"Oh, he can make all the overtures he wants, but I wouldn't believe the snake for a moment," Emryss said, seeing honesty in her frank eyes. "Anything else?"

"He took my hand and kissed it. He said something else, but I thought I was being spied upon and didn't hear it."

Emryss let his breath out slowly as relief flooded through him. "There, Gwil, see? Cynric up to his old tricks is all."

"Well, then, no more to be said, is there?" Gwilym said. He turned on his heel and left the room.

Roanna went close to him. "I don't like being spied upon, not even by your friend."

Emryss went to her and took her hands in his. "He's

worried, is all. Like an old nursemaid he can be, but he means well. Still," he frowned as he looked into her up-turned face. "I don't like the idea of Cynric touching my wife."

Roanna's lips curved up beguilingly. "I only want one man to touch me."

Emryss took her face in his hands and kissed her lightly. "God's wounds, woman, beginning to think I've got more than I bargained for when I married you."

Below in the kitchen Gwilym pulled Bronwyn into the pantry. "I want you to stay close to Lady Roanna."

"Something wrong?" She kissed his serious face lightly.

"Maybe nothing, but maybe everything."

Three days later Father Robelard sat perched on the edge of the abbot's hard wooden chair as his trembling fingers toyed with his cassock. Every sound that penetrated the abbot's stark chamber made him jump. The waiting was becoming unbearable, his sense of foreboding growing with every moment since the abbot had waylaid him after yet another special Mass for Baron DeLanyea and told him to wait in his chamber.

Father Robelard doubted that any number of prayers or masses would see that soul into heaven, but at least, he thought with a relieved sigh, he was spared from any further contact with the great sinner.

He shivered as he remembered the last time he had seen the baron alive. The once proud man had been wasted by the fit that struck him down like the hand of God. Little more than a corpse already, every breath had been a painful struggle. Still the baron managed to speak, sending all from his room except his son, Fitzroy and his priest.

Father Robelard frowned. He had known he was not there to offer solace or comfort, but he had not expected to hear a tale of such monstrous malice and cruelty that it had been hard to believe, even of the baron. Then he, too, had been ordered from the room, leaving only Cynric and his friend, if one could call a mercenary a friend, to witness his father's last moments. The baron had probably given his son orders to be obeyed even after his body was in the tomb.

The door of the abbot's sparsely furnished room opened, and Father Robelard rose. Cynric DeLanyea, now baron and a lord of the March, walked into the room, his shoulders bent.

Father Robelard's jaw dropped in surprise. He had expected the new baron to behave with even more pride and arrogance now that he was no longer held in check by a domineering father, but Cynric's countenance was humble and apologetic. He motioned to the priest to sit, then sat in the abbot's chair.

"You must understand that this is a most difficult time for me now," Cynric said. "However, I must put aside my own feelings and deal with the task of running my estate." He paused, the shrewd expression that crept into his eyes more in keeping with the Cynric DeLanyea Father Robelard knew. "As I'm sure you've realized, my father has no further need of your services."

Father Robelard nodded. "Yes, my lord, and a blessed thing…" He halted confusedly. "That is…"

Cynric steepled his slender fingers thoughtfully. "I won't pretend before a man of such obvious intelligence and discernment that there was any great love between my father and me."

Unsure if he was expected to reply to this announcement, Father Robelard pursued the course of neutral silence and waited for the next revelation.

"I need some assistance in a very delicate matter, and it has occurred to me that you are the very person to help me.

After all, my father felt sure enough of you that he allowed you to hear the rather unpleasant details of the exact relationship between Emryss DeLanyea and our family.''

The priest shifted in the chair, uneasy in spite of Cynric's confidential manner.

"I do not think it's necessary to divulge those details to anyone. Don't you agree, Father?"

"Yes, my lord."

"Good. After all, that happened in the past and cannot be altered."

"Very true, my lord."

"However—" Cynric smiled wistfully "—I wish to make amends, to better the relations between Emryss and myself."

"A most Christian attitude, my lord, if I may say so."

"Well, be that as it may, I am certain Emryss will make no response to any overture sent to him. He ignored my request to attend the memorial Mass for my father."

Father Robelard shook his head sadly.

"But if a man of discretion, sent to attend the chapel near Craig Fawr, were perhaps to speak to his wife…"

"Of course, my lord, but he is most hostile to the church."

"It appears, Father, that his wife has managed to persuade him to allow a priest in the town, if not in the fortress."

"Bless her!"

"Yes, well, Father, I have spoken to the abbot, and he agrees with me that you are the most suitable candidate."

Father Robelard coughed nervously. Did the abbot really think so, or had he somehow heard of Father Robelard's recent fall from grace and wish to be rid of him?

"The abbot understands that this requires an intelligent, sensitive priest, so naturally you came to mind."

"I am most flattered, my lord…"

Cynric rose from the chair and straightened his dark wool tunic. "Think nothing of it, Father."

He began to walk to the door, then turned back. "Oh, and Father Robelard, I'm certain I can rely on your silence as to what my father said before he died. No need to cause Emryss and his charming wife any embarrassment. These things can be so corrupted in the mouths of ordinary folk."

"A sad fact, my lord. Rumors are…"

"Yes. Exactly." Cynric's face suddenly twisted with mocking scorn. "Oh, I shall give your *love* to Lynette, Father. I'm sure she'll be most upset that you must leave."

Sickening fear made the priest look at the other man in horror. Cynric knew, obviously knew, that he, a priest of God, had broken a holy vow and been with a woman.

"But I'm certain you'll find reason to return to the monastery from time to time. I shall look forward to your news of my cousin and his wife." Cynric smiled cruelly at the trembling little man, his face like the face of a demon who has captured a soul.

Chapter Fifteen

In the days following the fire, Roanna discovered how delightful it was to be courted. Emryss was as charming as any woman could wish.

There were no more attacks on shepherds or sheep. This was some comfort to Emryss, for Mamaeth decreed that he mustn't ride for the next week, either. Roanna was happy to have him so close by, although several times she found him looking at her in such a way that she could barely remember her own name, let alone the task she was supposed to be engaged in. Confined to Craig Fawr, Emryss supervised the rebuilding. Roanna enjoyed watching him with the workmen, laughing and helping as much as the ever-watchful Mamaeth would allow.

Once he stood arguing with a mason, and she was amazed that a lord, even one such as Emryss, would allow any man to speak to him in such a familiar manner. The two men faced each other over a huge block of stone, gesturing wildly, until Emryss had apparently given in. The mason then completely ignored Emryss. Caressing the stone, he crooned to it in a low voice before placing his chisel carefully and tapping it once with his hammer. The massive block neatly split into two nearly perfect halves.

Another time she heard Emryss speak of the fortifications at Acre and some of the other fortresses in the East. Later, at the evening meal, when he was particularly jovial, she ventured to ask him about the Crusade.

She almost wished she hadn't, for his happiness seemed to disintegrate before her eyes. Nevertheless, he told her something of the troubles the Crusaders had faced—the incessant rain that soaked their food and made it rot, as well as causing their coats of mail to rust; the sickness, the fevers, the coughing and choking, the disease that made the teeth fall from the gums; and the starvation, which made a horse more valuable as a source of meat than a mount, even if it, too, was diseased. "And for what?" he finished bitterly. "So some pope gains a measure of glory conquering a land no sane man would want?"

"But to leave Jerusalem in the hands of the infidel…" she began, horrified that such a noble cause should be the source of so much suffering.

The look on his face as he turned to her! For the first time he let her see all his pain, and she knew that he was sparing her from many other terrible stories.

"Emryss," she said gently, "I will never be able to understand what you have suffered, but please let me try to help you forget."

"You are the only one I've ever told even these things to, Roanna. I think I knew, from the moment you looked at me, that you would be good for my soul."

The moment passed as Rhys called for a song and Emryss willingly obliged. Yet Roanna had known that something had changed, become somehow deeper between them, and gloried in the knowledge.

But all her time was not spent in the fortress. Emryss had a long talk with Mamaeth, who agreed to let Roanna assume some of the duties. "Only waiting for you to tell me, boy," she had said as if it was none of her fault at all.

Emryss had winked at Roanna and grinned his delightfully boyish grin.

She began taking small journeys around the estate, accompanied by a helpful Bronwyn and watchful Gwilym, who seemed convinced that the outlaws had not left their territory. Roanna met more of the tenants and began learning some Welsh. She had been especially happy to meet little Hu's mother, a quiet, tiny young woman who wove the most exquisite woolen cloth Roanna had ever seen. She had bought a lovely piece dyed dark blue with blackberries and later had told Emryss of the woman's skill.

It had thrilled her when he had listened carefully and agreed when she suggested Hu's mother teach others, for not only was her weaving very fine, but she was fast and efficient, too.

Nevertheless, the week passed very slowly and the nights were lonely as she lay in the huge bed. She tried not to imagine Emryss beside her, near her, touching her, but that only seemed to increase her passionate dreams, dreams so lustful that, if they had been of a man other than her husband, she would surely have been condemned to eternal flames.

Then Father Robelard arrived to take his place as the parish priest, and she began to feel as if Wales could truly become her home.

The final day of the grain harvest, and the last day of that long, long week, Roanna awakened to the sounds of bustling activity in the courtyard. Many voices shouted and called with suppressed excitement. She sat up and looked at the sun streaming through the open window.

Old Daffyd, a toothless shepherd whose age she couldn't begin to guess, had been right after all. It would be a fine, warm day with no sign of rain.

She arose and went to the window. The yard was filled with people of all ages milling about. At once she caught

sight of a familiar pair of broad shoulders and heard
Emryss's booming laugh.

Roanna went to the chest and took out the dark blue
gown she had completed the night before. She drew it on
over a new embroidered shift. It fit to perfection. With a
guilty smile, she hoped she wouldn't have so much time to
sew in the days ahead.

She began to brush her hair and discovered she was singing Emryss's favorite song. Glancing at the wimple on the
table, she stifled a sigh. She didn't want to wear it on a
warm day, but married women should cover their hair. Reluctantly, she picked it up and put it on.

Mamaeth's familiar rapping sounded on the door, and
she bustled in. "Hurry up, my lady," she said. "Not waiting, them. They want to finish today."

Roanna nodded, then turned so that Mamaeth would tie
her gown. Mamaeth tugged on the laces, ignoring Roanna's
squeak of protest at the constricting tightness.

"Loosen them a little, please."

"No need, my lady. Looks lovely."

Roanna glanced down. Her breasts were much too exposed. "I can't wear it like this."

"You'll have to. No time for fussing this morning."
Mamaeth chuckled softly, but then loosened the knot a little. "Not needing any encouragement, him. See you like
that, he'll drag you behind the nearest tree."

The courtyard was filled with people and snorting horses.
Apparently every farmer and family on Emryss's land had
congregated in the yard. Rhys, his round face bright red
from shouting, stood on a cart in the middle, calling out
orders directing people to various parts of the courtyard.

A hand touched Roanna gently on the shoulder, and she
turned. Emryss smiled at her, and she was at once uncomfortably aware that his light shirt, loosely tightened by his

sword belt, was unlaced at the neck, exposing the dark skin
of his chest.

"A fine dress that is. But I hate your hair hidden under
that disgusting thing."

Roanna said nothing, flushing hotly as he gazed at her.
She looked at the ground, encountering the sight of the
tight, rough linen chausses on his muscular legs before
coming to stare at his worn old boots.

Gwilym's voice sounded across the courtyard. "Emryss,
are you cutting today?"

Everyone turned toward Emryss expectantly. Mamaeth
came charging out of the kitchen like a horse in a tourna-
ment. "Of course not! Want the lad crippled, you *costog?*"

Emryss shrugged his shoulders and shook his head.

"Well, what's everybody standing about here for?"
Mamaeth bellowed. "Rhys!"

"We're ready," he shouted back.

"Off to the fields. There's a wagon for you somewhere,"
Emryss said, smiling at Roanna. She knew Mamaeth had
told him he could ride today, provided he didn't "go gal-
loping off like a mad fool," and that he could hardly wait.
"I'll see you at the field."

Roanna moved off to the side of the yard, out of the way
of the moving mass of people. Jacques appeared in the door
of the kitchen, wiping his hands on his apron. He scanned
the crowd, caught sight of her and waved.

She heard Bronwyn calling and turned as the maid
dashed across the yard. When she reached Roanna, she
pointed to a small cart near the stables, with a donkey in
the harness.

Roanna recognized it at once. It was the same cart she
had hidden in when she had escaped her uncle. Hardly an
appropriate vehicle for the lady of the manor, but it was
likely all the other wagons were needed for the work.

The crowd surged through the gate, and Bronwyn and

Roanna quickly got in the cart and joined the boisterous mob.

"Oh, going to have a grand time, we are," Bronwyn said with a laugh as she slapped the reins against the donkey's back. Roanna held on tightly as the donkey moved ahead, jerking the cart roughly.

They followed the laughing crowd of people to the waving fields of grain. Instead of drawing the cart up near the others, however, Bronwyn went to the farthest field, jumped down and pulled on the bridle of the donkey until he stood under a tree.

"There now, this is grand."

Roanna raised one eyebrow questioningly. "But everyone else is at the other field."

"Don't worry, my lady, this is the best place. Cutting this field last, they'll be, and you'll want to be able to see that. For now, we can walk to the other fields if you'd like."

Roanna nodded her agreement and climbed down. Bronwyn raced ahead, around the edges of the three fields, until she was lost in the crowd.

For a brief moment Roanna saw Emryss on his horse with his hand raised. A shout went up from the crowd the same instant she felt a stabbing pain in her foot. She bent down and removed her slipper.

A pebble dropped out. She rubbed the sore spot on her foot tenderly. Another cheer went up from the assembled people. With an exasperated sigh, Roanna replaced her shoe and tried to walk again, but the bruise on her heel made her limp. The wimple began to chafe her neck, and perspiration trickled down her back. She stopped and tried to draw a deep breath, but Mamaeth had pulled the laces too tight.

"Roanna!" She heard Emryss call her name, and she

raised her head. He rode toward her. "I've been looking for you." He dismounted. "What's wrong? Are you ill?"

"I had a stone in my slipper and Mamaeth's laced me too tight."

Emryss grinned wickedly. "I like the way Mamaeth's laced you."

"Well, I cannot walk and breathe at the same time like this," she replied, trying to keep her treacherous mind on her body and not his.

"Let me help." He dropped Wolf's reins and came behind her. With agonizing slowness he untied the knot of the laces. Then she felt his hands, warm against the skin of her back. "I thought this week would never end," he said softly into her ear.

"I felt the same." She leaned back against his hard chest.

His hands moved under her gown, around to her breasts. Her breath caught in her throat as he caressed her, pushing against her willing body.

A cheer brought her attention back.

"Emryss!" she said and he quickly withdrew his hands.

"Right," he said with a low laugh as he tied another, looser knot. "Mustn't get carried away. At least—" he laughed again "—not yet."

The sound of the crowd grew closer, and she looked up to see a line of men moving slowly down the nearest field. She straightened her dress as Emryss went to Wolf and picked up the reins. "Come, wife, give me your hand," he said merrily, and walked with her to the edge of the field.

The cutters' scythes moved rhythmically as they crouched over the grain. As they drew near, she watched as they gathered, cut and bound the stalks in rapid, fluid motions.

Their movements were slow compared to the rapid beating of her heart, with Emryss standing close beside her, his hand holding hers lightly.

When that field was finished, there was a frenzy of talk and drinking as the men rested for a moment. Women spread blankets on the grassy verge and got out bread and ale and cheese. Bronwyn appeared again, followed by Gwilym, and brought a huge basket from the cart.

Emryss eyed the basket, trying to appear shocked. "All that for my dainty wife and me?"

"And us, and Mamaeth, too, *brawdmaeth*," Gwilym said. "Even then, I think that Jacques put in enough for everyone here."

Roanna helped Bronwyn spread a blanket, and the four of them sat down. Jacques had outdone himself. There was fine white bread, several cheeses, a huge jug of ale (which Emryss and Gwilym made short work of), several sweetmeats and even a small flask of wine.

Roanna looked around at all the happy people enjoying the outdoor meal. Children tumbled and played under the watchful eyes of their parents. The women laughed and gossiped, while several of the men slept soundly nearby. When she turned back, she realized Bronwyn and Gwilym had gone.

Emryss, laying on his side with a piece of hay protruding from his mouth, smiled lazily. "What are you looking at, Roanna?"

"The happiest tenants I've ever seen," she replied. Her limbs seemed to have turned to dough suddenly. "Where is Bronwyn?"

"With Gwilym."

He was still looking at her in that unnerving way, and with all the people around, too. She cleared her throat. "That is the last field?" She nodded at the one close by.

He ignored her question and nodded at her wimple. "Are you going to wear that hideous thing all day?"

"I'm a married woman. I have to."

"Your hair is too beautiful to keep hidden." His voice was soft, low, intimate.

She stood up quickly. "Perhaps I should find Bronwyn."

"Yes." He nodded, looking serious. "It's time to start the last field, and where she is, I'm sure Gwilym will be."

"Which way did she go?"

"I think that way," he said, gesturing toward the willow trees at the edge of the river.

Roanna walked off, trying to maintain some semblance of dignity, although she felt warm and soft and light all at the same time.

She called Bronwyn's name several times, but the girl didn't answer. When she reached the river's edge, she looked up and down the banks but could see nothing of anyone.

It was hopeless to try to find her here. She should go back and gather the things herself. Perhaps Bronwyn was already at the field.

As she turned, a hand reached out and yanked the veil on her head. It gave way and her hair tumbled about her shoulders.

"That's much better," Emryss said, stepping from behind a tree, holding the veil in his hand.

"Emryss," Roanna said with a touch of anger. "Please give me my veil. And look...you've torn the chinband."

He stepped close to her. "Oh, I'm sorry," he said, but his face was full of laughter. "I suppose you'll have to go without it now?"

"Emryss, you are impossible."

"So Mamaeth's been telling me all my life." He looked around. "Well, well, well, wife, we seem to be all by ourselves at last. Maybe we don't need to wait for tonight..."

Just then they heard Mamaeth shouting for Emryss.

He looked as if he'd like to gag his old nurse, and it was

Roanna's turn to smile. She put her hands on his shoulders and stood on her tiptoes to give him a light kiss.

"Tonight," she said.

"God's wounds," he said as he wrenched himself away. "For once I wish I wasn't the lord!"

He stalked away, and Roanna stooped to pick up her ruined wimple, but this time she didn't put it on. She did feel much cooler without it.

Bending down, she dipped the veil into the cool water of the river and wiped the back of her neck.

A movement in the bushes nearby caught her attention. "Bronwyn?" she called out softly.

"Aye, my lady," Bronwyn said, appearing behind her.

"Oh, I thought you were there," Roanna said, pointing a little farther downriver.

"Oh, likely that was Gwilym," Bronwyn said, blushing furiously. Roanna could only smile, since she knew exactly how Bronwyn felt. If it hadn't been for Mamaeth's interruption, she and Emryss would have been rattling the bushes, too.

Emryss, tall and commanding on his horse, rode to the edge of the last field. The cutters stood ready along the edge, and this time Roanna saw Gwilym among them.

"Why is Gwilym cutting?" she asked Bronwyn.

"Because it's the last field," she replied matter-of-factly. "Emryss used to help with the cutting, and good he was, too, but Gwilym's taking his place today."

Emryss raised his hand, and all became silent.

Then his hand came down, and the men, their faces filled with grim determination, began cutting. The way they glanced around, keeping track of the other cutters, soon made it obvious that this was some kind of competition.

Mamaeth stood at the side, screaming what were either curses or exhortations, and soon Bronwyn was jumping up and down with excitement. Roanna told herself it would be beneath her dignity to shout, but she did move around to get the best view.

Then Gwilym stumbled, and when he tried to stand, his face twisted in pain. Instantly Emryss was there, dismounting and bending low over his friend. The cutters ceased. Emryss spoke softly to Gwilym, then helped him stand and mount his horse.

"Fine time to turn an ankle," Gwilym said loudly as he rode slowly off the field.

Roanna looked around at the disappointed faces of the crowd. Clearly Gwilym had been expected to make it a good contest.

Then Emryss drew off his shirt.

Roanna's heart seemed to miss a beat. Surely he didn't intend to cut grain. Not today. Not when he had so recently been ill. Not when the last thing she wanted was an exhausted husband.

A great cheer rose up as Emryss picked up Gwilym's discarded scythe. He faced the crowd and bowed low, then made a great show of checking the sharpness of the blade.

"Emryss," Mamaeth admonished, but he raised his hand for silence.

"My honor is at stake," he said.

Roanna held her breath as Gwilym, clearly enjoying his new role as substitute lord, raised his hand, squinting one eye in an impersonation of Emryss that drew laughter from the crowd. Emryss made a great frown and said something, obviously condemning Gwilym for the liberty he was taking. Then Emryss bent low, ready to cut, and his face became intent.

Gwilym lowered his hand, and instantly the cutting began afresh. Roanna watched the steady progress of the men, Emryss moving forward quickly. She was amazed at the speed with which he cut the grain and worried to death that he would suffer for his folly.

A grizzled old farmer kept the lead, his scythe moving through the grain like a hot knife through butter.

Emryss began to drop behind, going more and more slowly until he finally stopped. Roanna realized, as he glanced at her with a secret smile, that he had purposely refrained from pushing himself.

She hurried up to him. ''Are you all right?'' she asked urgently.

''I'm not *that* proud.''

Gwilym, waiting at the end of the field, rode up and down the side restlessly. The old farmer reached the last sheaf and threw down his scythe. His hands deftly moved through the straw, plaiting it into a beautiful shape.

A roar went up from the crowd as Emryss walked over and congratulated the old man, who beamed with pride. Exhausted, the other cutters collapsed on the edge of the field.

After a short rest, Emryss called to the men again. At once the other cutters rose and walked to the plaited stalk. They stood gathered around it, speaking quietly.

Roanna looked at Bronwyn, who had come to stand beside her.

''That's the *caseg fedi*,'' Bronwyn explained. ''Meaning the harvest mare. Watch now.''

All around the women and children sat on the grass, chattering and pointing, as the men, holding their scythes, lined up in the middle of the field facing the stalk. A hush fell over the crowd as the man on the left edge bent low, then sent his scythe whizzing down the field. It missed the stalk.

Every man took a turn, until only Emryss and Gwilym were left to try to cut the stalk. Emryss went next, and as he bent to throw, he looked up at Roanna, then let his scythe fly.

The stalk fell, sliced neatly through the bottom. The men charged forward, and at the same time the women all leaped to their feet.

"Come on!" Bronwyn cried as she raced to the cart and quickly climbed on the seat. "Hurry!"

Roanna did as Bronwyn said, although she was mystified by the people rushing around. "What is it? What's happening?" she asked as she got into the cart. She glanced at the men, scrambling to pick up their scythes as Bronwyn whipped the donkey into a trot. The men began running after the fleeing women.

"Oh, saints above!" Bronwyn cried looking over her shoulder. "They'll beat us yet!"

"A race? This is a race?" Roanna asked, shouting to be heard above the rumbling wheels of the cart and the shouts of the people.

Bronwyn didn't answer, but continued to urge the donkey forward. Roanna clutched the sides of the cart and looked back. Gwilym led the pack of men, while Emryss rode around like a shepherd whose flock had gone astray.

As they drew near Craig Fawr the women began shouting. As if in response, the gate began to rise slowly. Roanna could make out Mamaeth in the first cart, standing up like some ancient female chieftain at the head of a column of warriors. The women rushed through the gate, up the road, through the second gate and the third.

By the time Roanna and Bronwyn reached the courtyard, it was crowded with carts, now empty of people. Women were rushing about with buckets and anything else that would hold water, going from the well to the kitchen and back again. For a moment Roanna was afraid there was another fire until she realized that the women were all giggling hysterically. She heard Jacques' bellows of rage, followed by a string of curses.

He must be furious, she thought as she climbed down and hurried to the kitchen.

"Roanna!" he shouted when he saw her enter. "What are these barbarians doing?"

Roanna quickly surveyed the kitchen. Every vessel was filled with water except the stew pot and the pans containing bread. Women crowded into the room, laughing and joking, while Mamaeth peered out the door like a sentry.

Roanna saw Bronwyn and made her way through the mob of women. "What is it now?" she asked loudly.

Bronwyn turned, smiling. "They're bringing the harvest mare. We've got to get it wet before it's up." She nodded toward the hearth, and Roanna saw the hook above Jacques' head.

Mamaeth shouted something that sounded like a battle cry, and all eyes turned expectantly toward the door, which Mamaeth slammed shut.

"Pen medi bach mi ces!" Gwilym shouted on the other side. Bronwyn, no doubt reading Roanna's confused expression, sang out, "Here comes a little harvest mare!"

Mamaeth, apparently satisfied that everyone was prepared, threw open the door. A figure loomed in the frame for a moment, then Gwilym dashed into the room. At once he was drenched by a barrage of water and surrounded by a gang of the women. Roanna, standing beside Jacques, who had armed himself with a ladle, watched in shock as they pulled at his clothes.

"Not him!" Mamaeth cried. The women rushed to other buckets as a group of men burst through the door. Water flew about the room as the women proceeded to half strip the men, who, to judge by their faces, were quite enjoying this strange search.

Roanna began to relax. Then Emryss sidled in the door,

his usual grin lighting his face. His gaze met hers for an instant, and he winked roguishly.

She noticed several wisps of straw sticking out of the bottom of his shirt. Quickly she grabbed Jacques' ladle.

"*Mon Dieu,* what now?" Jacques cried, but she ignored him. Instead she went to the nearest full bucket. Dipping the ladle in, she watched Emryss as he moved slowly around the side of the room. He seemed vastly amused by the antics of the men and women, but he got slowly closer to the hearth.

Roanna inched toward him, holding the ladle carefully behind her back. She waited until Emryss was looking at the sharp-eyed Mamaeth.

With better aim than she would have thought possible, she flung the contents of the ladle at Emryss. The water hit him full in the face. He let out an angry roar, but she ran up and reached under his shirt, her fingers clutching at the plaited straw.

His strong fingers closed on her arm and prevented her from drawing out the harvest mare.

She looked at his dripping face. He seemed so surprised and angry and…and wet! A great bubble of laughter grew and burst from her throat.

He let go, looking more surprised than ever. Then he gathered her into his arms. "Worth a drenching, to finally hear you laugh," he whispered in her ear.

Flushed with her triumph, Roanna twisted in his arms and held up the straw harvest mare.

The women cheered, and the men stared.

Suddenly Emryss grabbed the straw from her hands and let go of her. Roanna, after almost falling to her knees, stood gaping as he made a dash to the hearth and hung the *caseg fedi* on the hook.

The men cheered heartily as Emryss stood smugly on the

hearth with his arms crossed. In fact, he looked so pleased with himself that Roanna couldn't help what she did next.

She picked up a bucket of water, walked toward him and dumped it on his head.

He gave a yelp like a startled hound, and she ran out of the kitchen, followed by the other women.

How could she have done that, she wondered incredulously as she stood panting in the courtyard. How could she be so bold and so brazen in front of the tenants?

Bronwyn, laughing, embraced her, and she found herself surrounded by women congratulating her for her daring. As she looked at them all, her face broke into a wide smile. *This* was belonging.

In the next moment a torrent of freezing water descended on her. Sputtering and gasping, Roanna wheeled to see Emryss standing in the door, holding an empty bucket. He grinned malevolently.

"Emryss, my dress…" she began indignantly, only to be interrupted by Mamaeth's irate voice.

"Oh, you *man!* Hours of time that took to make and look what you've done!"

The women all nodded sympathetically and some offered their aprons to Roanna to dry her dripping face.

"Come here, wife," Emryss said in a tone that made her heart race.

She didn't move. Couldn't, with all her limbs as liquid as the water on the ground.

"Get out of the way, you. Got to change now, and the feast almost ready!" Mamaeth took Roanna's hand and began pulling her toward the hall. Bronwyn and the others made a wall around her, trying to push past Emryss and the men.

"Yes, it's time to celebrate," Emryss said loudly. "But I'm going early to bed."

Chapter Sixteen

The women bustled Roanna into the hall. "Go on, my lady," Mamaeth said, "we've work to do."

Roanna hurried up the stairs to the bedchamber. Shivering from the freezing water Emryss had dumped on her, she took her dress off, carefully draping it across a chair. The gown was damp, to be sure, but far from ruined.

She began to sing softly as she opened the lid of the chest. Inside she saw the white silk garment. Holding it up for a moment, she caressed its delightful smoothness, then made a bold decision. Off came the shift. On, over her bare skin, went the silken fabric.

The very touch of it on her flesh was sinfully luxurious, hinting at every forbidden pleasure she had ever heard about or imagined. Soon, so soon, his lean strong hands would move along this fragile barrier.

She picked up her brush and began to run it through her hair, delaying the moment when the heavier garment would have to go on.

Would he take her garments off, or watch as she did? As she imagined the night to come, her nipples hardened and pressed against the delicate fabric. Would he kiss her…everywhere? She closed her eyes, almost sensing his lips traveling softly over her.

"Time for the feast," Emryss called from the other side of the door.

Roanna jumped up and got her burgundy dress. She pulled it on and fumbled clumsily with the laces until she finally got them tied. Another wimple lay in the chest. Roanna looked at it, then slammed the lid down. Tonight, just tonight, she would wear her hair unbound.

When she opened the door, she caught the flash of pleasure on Emryss's face before he offered her his arm.

He, too, had put on new garments. His black tunic, fastened at the neck with a plain silver pin, reached to his knees. Beneath it he wore a white shirt, and white linen chausses disappeared into the same fine boots he had worn on their wedding day.

When they entered the hall, Roanna was amazed at how quickly it had been transformed. Fresh rushes lay on the floor, and the torches blazed in their sockets. The people all stood expectantly, smiling as Emryss and Roanna walked to the high table.

To her delight, Roanna saw Father Robelard standing nearby. Emryss nodded, and the priest began to bless the feast. When he had finished, Roanna turned to her husband and smiled her thanks as they sat down.

Jacques' cooking was marvelous. Using the most basic of ingredients, he had created masterpieces. And then came the dishes using the more exotic spices that, Roanna knew, the cook would have risked his immortal soul for.

And yet she had no appetite. The only thing that appealed was the delicious wine, which seemed to quiet the pounding blood in her veins. It slowly dawned on Roanna that she would have been wiser to wear her other shift. Every time Emryss looked at her, she squirmed with embarrassment, only to have the soft fabric brush against her skin like an illicit caress.

She didn't even notice that she had finished her chalice for the third time. As she reached for another sip, Emryss put his hand over the top.

"That's enough," he whispered in her ear. Startled, she turned to look at him. "I don't want you to be senseless." The import of his words was unmistakable, making her burn brighter with the desire she was trying to keep under some kind of control.

When the last course was cleared away, Emryss got to his feet. He held up his chalice and spoke quickly in Welsh. Roanna recognized some of the words and knew he was thanking them for making a good harvest. As she raised her chalice again, she caught sight of Mamaeth, whose wrinkled face burst into a beatific smile.

When Emryss sat down, Roanna asked, "What did you say at the end, to make Mamaeth smile like that?"

"I said I hoped next year would be fruitful. Why?" His look of innocence slowly changed as they continued to gaze at each other, making her forget that they were sitting in the midst of a hall full of people.

He reached for her hand under the table. "I've waited long enough," he whispered.

A very drunken Rhys stumbled to his feet.

"My lord," he said, weaving back and forth, "a song, if you will."

Emryss frowned. Roanna let go of his hand. "Just one, Emryss. It would be unseemly to leave now."

"Very well," he muttered under his breath. "Just one." He got up and called out, "What's it to be?"

Several people answered as he went for his harp. Picking it up, he glanced at Roanna.

He began to sing a mournful tune, ending each line with a huge sigh and a long yearning look at Roanna. The people

started to laugh. As each successive verse began to go faster
and faster and the sigh became more like a gasp, they guffawed and chortled, swaying on the benches, slapping their
knees and stamping their feet. At last the song finished with
a great flourish and sigh, and Emryss put down his instru-
ment.

"I am greatly fatigued," he announced rather too loudly
as he stood up. Roanna didn't know where to hide her
blushing face. "Come, wife, to bed!"

Keeping her gaze firmly on the ground, and trying desperately to look as if nothing exceptional was about to take
place, Roanna put her hand in his. His fingers closed around
it and gently he pulled her up.

"Good night!" he called out, then led her from the hall.

Alone on the dark stairs with him, Roanna felt suddenly
abashed and shy, as if he were a stranger. Her knees began
to quiver and her heart to race. Emryss said nothing, and
when she glanced at his face, she saw no smile there.

He opened the door of the bedchamber and let her enter
first. Turning, she watched as he closed the door quietly.
The heavy wood muffled the sounds of the merriment below, almost as if the hall had disappeared and they were
the only two left in Craig Fawr. Roanna clasped her hands
together and waited.

Emryss walked to the small table and poured a goblet of
wine. She saw that his hands trembled as much as hers.

"God, nervous as a lad," he mumbled, then took a long
drink.

Roanna was nervous and frightened, too, but the time
had come. Deep in her heart, she knew she had waited for
this night for too long. For him too long. Timidity dissipated like mist in the sun.

"Emryss," she said, walking toward him. "Husband."
She put her palms on his chest and looked up into his face.

He put down the goblet. Slowly she moved her hands up

the hard muscles and tenderly touched him. He bent his head and kissed her gently, tentatively.

Desire, heated, feverish wanton desire blossomed in her breast. Stepping back, she pulled at the knot of her laces until it came undone. The dress fell unheeded to the floor, and she stood dressed only in the white silk garment, trembling, but not with fear.

With a ragged sigh, Emryss gathered her into his arms and pressed his lips to hers. Soft pleasure, sure firmness, met in the passion of his kiss.

Every touch of his hands on her back penetrated the thin sheath of silk.

A kiss was not enough.

Her hands found the neck of his tunic. Without taking her lips from his, she undid the pin. He groaned as her hand slipped inside to feel the hot, hard flesh beneath. He pulled away for a moment, but only to pick her up and lay her on the bed. She watched him pull off the long tunic, leaving only his full shirt and chausses.

Then he was there beside her. His lips crushing hers insistently, possessively, tasting of mulled wine and cinnamon. Her tongue pushed hungrily inside his mouth. She craved more of him as the wondrous rapture became a frenzied heat, growing upward from her loins to fill her. Her hands sought his bare flesh without her guidance. Her lips left his to travel to his neck.

"Oh, dear God, yes," he groaned as she pulled the shirt from him. He rolled onto his back and pulled her onto his heaving chest.

Another deep kiss. And another. Hard chest against soft breasts, fingers stroking her as if she were his harp.

Then her lips were upon his chest, her tongue moving in slow circles around his nipples. Ignoring the silk, his kiss wet her tender white breasts. Igniting her. Melting her.

On her back. Arching toward his touch. Flesh pressed

against flesh. Aching for his lips. Panting breath, soft words murmured against nakedness.

Calling his name at the sweet sudden pain.

Flooding, filling, pulsing, flowing, wave after wave after wave.

Triumphant cry.

A shudder. A low moan. Her own rapid breathing as the throbbing slowly ceased. She was filled. Complete.

"Beloved," he whispered as she clung to him.

"Roanna, come back to bed."

Roanna stopped gazing at the slight pink and gold flush that tinged the edge of the eastern clouds and turned toward the bed. The rough woolen blanket, pulled about her like a cloud, scratched her naked skin. Sometime in the night the silken tunic had become that pile of white on the floor at the foot of the bed.

Tawny curls and one long, muscular leg were the only parts of Emryss she could see clearly in the tumble of bed-clothes.

"Roanna?" His muffled voice called sleepily.

She smiled and took a final glance at the sun rising on this new day.

Then she was beside him, letting him enfold her in his warmth. His lips nuzzled her neck as he held her tightly.

"Shouldn't you rest, Emryss?" she asked after a long moment.

"In bed, aren't I?" he mumbled, his lips against her breast.

"But not resting," she insisted, laughing softly.

He rolled onto his back and looked at her. "Wanting to make you laugh again, is all," he said, trying to look serious.

"Thank you, my lord," she responded, equally seriously. "But now *some* of us have duties to attend to."

"As the lord of Craig Fawr, I think your most important duty right now is to kiss me."

Roanna willingly complied. More than once.

She pulled away. "Mamaeth will be pounding on the door any minute."

His grin was devilment incarnate. "She'll be happy to see us in bed together. She's been after me to get a wife since before I went on the Crusade." He drew her close. "I'm glad I waited."

Several minutes later, Roanna climbed out of the bed and picked up the silken garment. Opening the lid of the chest, she glanced at the bed. Emryss lay with his head cushioned on his hands, staring at her.

Suddenly he laughed out loud.

"What is it?" Roanna asked as she pulled her shift over her head.

"Nothing. Everything. I feel...wonderful!" He kicked off the sheets. "I feel completely rested."

The look on his face made no secret of his intentions. Roanna shook her head and tried not to smile.

"Emryss, it's too late in the day."

"It's never too late, little wife of mine."

He came toward her slowly, wearing only a roguish grin.

"Emryss, you'll get sick again."

"Worth it, I'm thinking."

Roanna backed into the chest as he crept toward her.

He reached out for her, but she stepped sideways. "Really, my lord, there are better things to do than stay in bed all day."

"Like what?"

"I...I promised Jacques I'd help with the bread. And Father Robelard and I were going to visit some of the tenants, and *you* should be checking the mill..."

"I had other work in mind."

"Now, Emryss, stop this."

He sprung at her like a cat after a mouse, taking her in his arms. She smiled, closed her eyes and tilted her face up for the expected kiss.

Instead, she felt his fingers moving along the side of her ribs. Giggles burst from her lips as she tried to push his hand away, but he held her tightly, smiling all the while.

"Stop, Emryss, please," she gasped. He complied, and she crossed her arms against her chest.

"Do you intend to attend to your duties as naked as the day you were born, my lord?"

Her mischievous tone obviously delighted him. He stood back, chuckling softly. "Maybe I will…if you'll stay with me." He ran one finger up her arm, sending delicious thrills along her spine.

"Well, perhaps I needn't go just yet…"

A loud pounding on the door sent Emryss rushing to the chest, where he managed to pull on his shirt before Bronwyn entered, carrying hot water. She halted in mid-step, took one look at the blushing Roanna, clad only in her shift although the sun had been up for a long time, glanced at the scowling and equally undressed Emryss, set the pitcher on the floor and hurried out the door.

Roanna didn't even try to suppress her laughter. Emryss pulled on his chausses as if nothing untoward had happened, but his shaking shoulders told her he, too, was vastly amused by Bronwyn's startled expression.

She tiptoed toward him as he bent to pull on his boots. Her fingers darted out, seeking the spot on his side that would make him helpless with laughter. His iron fist caught her fingers as he turned to her. Slowly he lifted her hand to his lips.

A cry from the battlements made him pause, unmoving. Then instantly he dropped her hand and bolted to the window, peering into the courtyard below. Without another word he grabbed his jerkin and sword belt and stormed from the room.

Roanna quickly took his place at the window but could see nothing except an excited crowd of people. Pulling on the dark blue gown, she followed Emryss outside.

"Who done it?"

"Are you hurt, Ianto?"

"Did you see them?"

"Killing sheep, were they?"

The questioning group of masons gathered around the big shepherd who stood in the middle of the yard, cradling the lifeless body of his dog to his breast. Ianto stared straight ahead, saying nothing. Dried blood coated Mott's side, and a dagger protruded from a deep wound.

As Emryss approached, the crowd parted to let him near. His gaze locked onto Ianto's face until the man blinked and looked at him. Emryss spoke quietly but firmly. "Ianto, who did this?"

Ianto shook his head. "Don't know who done it," he said, his voice drained of any emotion.

"When?"

"In the night they come." The shepherd's voice was a dry whisper. "Heard Mott barking, I did, so I come running. Hit me on the head, someone. I saw nor heard nothing till I woke and found my poor Mott."

"Where's Hu?"

A look of anguish crossed Ianto's face. "Couldn't find him. I looked and looked, then come for you."

Emryss glanced at the sun. It must have taken Ianto hours to walk from his pasturing place to Craig Fawr. The knaves who had done this would be far away by now. Nevertheless, he spoke in a determined voice. "Ianto, we will find the men who did this, and they'll be punished."

"Aye, my lord." The big man's voice was weary and

heartsick. Emryss moved forward and held out his hands to take the dog's body, but Ianto clutched Mott tighter.

"Begging pardon, my lord, but no one touches Mott but me."

Emryss nodded as Gwilym pushed his way into the midst of the crowd and stared.

"I need to see the dagger," Emryss said softly. Ianto nodded, and Gwilym gently pulled out the ugly weapon. He looked at it for a moment, then offered it to Emryss. With a shrug of his shoulders Emryss returned it to Gwilym. "Norman, maybe, or Saxon. Hard to tell. Mount a patrol." He turned toward the stable.

Roanna ran to him and clutched his arm. "Emryss, take care."

He frowned bitterly. "I should have been more careful. Kept a better watch. This is my fault," he said. Pulling away, he stalked off to the stable.

Roanna watched him go, unaware that her hands were balled into fists. The men stood silently for another moment, then Gwilym began shouting names. Men ran to the barracks to fetch their weapons.

"Where's Mamaeth?" Roanna asked, desperate to do something. Anything.

"Down to the mill," Bronwyn answered. "I'll fetch her." She ran toward the gate.

Ianto began swaying. Still holding Mott, the big shepherd crumpled to the ground. "Hurry!" Roanna screamed, then fell to her knees in the mud.

She gently took the dog's body from Ianto's limp arms and held it to her chest as Emryss came from the stable. Quickly he peeled off the shepherd's tunic. The inner fleece was stained with blood from a gaping wound. Fresh blood escaped around an arrowhead. The shaft had been broken, leaving the iron point in the flesh.

It seemed hours before Mamaeth rushed up, panting

heavily. She knelt and peered into the man's face, then laid her wrinkled cheek against his chest. "Dead," she said softly.

Her single word hung in the air as Roanna's hands tightened on her burden. Emryss remained perfectly still for a long moment, staring down at the big man. It was as if he had been turned to stone.

Then he leapt to his feet and ran to his waiting horse. "I will find them, and by God's wounds, they will suffer!" he cried. He mounted and wheeled his steed to join the group of men waiting at the gate.

"Bled to death." Mamaeth's voice drew Roanna's attention. "If only he laid still, and not come all this way, he might yet be living." She wiped the hair from his forehead as the tears began to fall down her wrinkled cheeks. "Stupid oaf," she whispered tenderly, like a benediction.

Roanna stood up awkwardly, Mott still in her arms. Then she bent and gently laid the dog's small body on Ianto's chest.

"Anything?"

"No. Careful they was." Gwilym's response from the bank of the stream came laden with disappointment.

"Any sign of Hu?"

"Not yet." Emryss pressed his lips together, clutching at the hope that Hu had been able to escape the marauders. He looked around at the few scattered sheep on the rocky hill. They munched the underbrush, seemingly unaware of the men's presence.

Emryss checked the clouds piling in the sky. Not long before rain. With a growing sense of frustration, he dismounted as Gwilym scrambled up the bank to join him.

"Now what?" Gwilym asked, equally frustrated.

Emryss walked to the bank and peered at the rows of

willow bushes, seeking anything that might point out the way a group of men could have come.

He straightened and slapped his thigh with a fist. "God's wounds, they can't have vanished without leaving something."

He grabbed the reins of his horse and began heading to the blood-stained grass, still scanning the ground.

Damn his blind eye. He moved slowly toward the north. Then he spotted the small, barely discernible trail of flattened grass. And some small toes peeking out from under a bush.

"Hu? Is that you, Hu?" he called softly, making his way closer and trying to sound calm.

"Aye." The boy's head popped out of the bush, his face stained with tears.

In the next moment Emryss had gathered him into his arms, holding him tightly. "Are you all right, Hu? They didn't see you?"

"No, but I seen them. A bunch of men there was, Emryss. And they gone that way." Hu pointed toward a narrow path leading away from Craig Fawr.

After assuring himself that Hu was indeed unharmed, Emryss ordered his men to follow the trail. They crashed through the underbrush, Gwilym leading the way. His keen eyesight soon found a piece of torn fabric on a low-hanging branch, and more blood.

"Making for Beaufort," Gwilym said, his voice both triumphant and wary as he turned toward Emryss and the little shepherd boy following behind.

"Then so are we."

Chapter Seventeen

"They're on to us!"

The outlaw turned his panic-stricken face to his leader as the sounds of the approaching men grew louder outside their hiding place.

Dolf shifted forward and peered from the cave's mouth. Sure enough, a sizable group of men was drawing near. "Damn them all to hell," he muttered as he unsheathed his sword. The others hiding in the cave also gathered their weapons, even the man whose leg had been badly bitten by the shepherd's dog.

"How could they know so soon?" one whispered to a companion.

"Quiet!" Dolf's voice was harsh. "All that matters now is that they do know."

The smell of fear tainted the musty air as they waited. Dolf peered out again. "They're close by. This is our chance. Now, for it!" He signaled the charge, and the thieves crashed past him onto the path, screaming oaths at Emryss's men.

The wounded man clutched his dagger as Dolf turned to him and spoke. "Wait here."

When the wounded man relaxed his grip on the dagger,

Dolf jumped toward him and plunged his knife into the man's chest. As his companion gasped and stared at him, Dolf twisted his knife deeper. "Can't leave someone to tell. Part of the bargain, ain't it?" When the man was dead, Dolf withdrew his knife and crept out of the cave.

Silently skirting the fighting, he crept away. His men would never beat the soldiers from Craig Fawr, not if that one-eyed bastard who fought like he had the hounds of hell nipping his heels was among them.

The sounds of the fighting grew fainter when he had gone over the top of the hill and made his way through the underbrush.

"Well met."

Dolf halted in mid-step at the sound of Cynric De-Lanyea's voice.

Dolf drew himself up. Cynric DeLanyea leaned against a tree, smiling in his own evil way. His lackey, Urien Fitzroy, stood silently a little way off, his hand on the hilt of his sword.

"Well met, indeed, my lord," Dolf said slowly.

"Out taking in the fine summer day?" Cynric asked scornfully.

"Lads and I got a bit of trouble over yonder. Them ones from Craig Fawr."

Cynric stopped leaning, and now it was Dolf's turn to grin.

"How did they find you?"

"Don't know, but they have."

"Did your men escape?"

Dolf shrugged his shoulder. "Don't think they will. Didn't hang about to see."

Cynric walked slowly toward him. "They'd better not say anything."

Dolf's hand moved toward his dagger. "Most of 'em dead by now, I should think."

Cynric stopped. His lips twisted upward. "Is that so?"

He lunged. Dolf gasped at the pain as Cynric's dagger struck and his own weapon fell to the ground.

"You bastard!" Dolf clutched his stomach. "You bloody bastard! After all the risks we took for you! The women we got you!"

Cynric nonchalantly wiped his knife on the grass. "One less to talk, eh, Dolf?"

The man slumped to the ground.

Cynric paused as he walked past Urien. "Finish this dog and then go over the hill. I want to know how many got away."

Urien didn't move. "What did he mean, the women we got you?"

Cynric smiled mockingly. "Never taken a woman against her will, Urien?"

He saw the flicker of guilt in the other man's eyes.

"I thought so. Now finish him. Do it, or don't bother coming back to Beaufort," he barked as he mounted his waiting horse.

Urien obeyed.

The man's mouth twisted into a toothless grimace of hate and fear and desperation as he aimed for Emryss's chest. Emryss jumped out of reach, landing hard on his aching leg. His sword had been twisted from his hands minutes ago. Swiftly he drew out his dagger and advanced on his enemy. He neither saw not heard the commotion around him as he put all his attention on his attacker.

The man licked his lips, and the gesture brought Emryss hope. He was afraid! Emryss felt the surge of blood in his veins, the prick of triumph. With a wild cry, he tore the leather patch from his eye.

The man's eyes widened, and he paused long enough for Emryss to reach down and grab his sword again.

"Stayed too long on my land, stupid ass," Emryss hissed as he smiled and began to advance. "Know how I lost this eye? Plucked it out and threw it at a Saracen."

The man blanched as Emryss began circling closer and closer, waiting for the right moment.

His foe glanced around, but the way afforded no escape except up into the trees.

Inexorably, Emryss came closer. "Going to kill you for what you done," he said slowly. "But not too quickly."

He lunged forward, aiming for the hand that held the dagger. He missed, but he tried again and this time his opponent's weapon fell to the ground.

The outlaw's foot lashed out desperately, striking Emryss on his weak leg. He gasped at the sudden pain but held on to his sword. The man moved away as Emryss continued to press forward until his back was to a huge rock and he could go no farther.

"For Ianto," Emryss said, driving his weapon to its mark. The man fell to the ground.

"Thought you needed some help, *brawdmaeth*," Gwilym said as Emryss stood panting heavily. "See I was wrong."

Emryss became aware of the silence. Looking around, he realized the fighting had stopped. Seven corpses, none of them his soldiers, lay in various positions on the ground.

Emryss smiled grimly. "Not ready to take to my bed yet," he said, the wild throbbing of battle still pounding through his veins.

Gwilym didn't smile back. "A pity they're all dead."

"A better death than they deserved, I'll grant you," Emryss replied as he began to wipe his bloodied sword on the grass.

"Don't you see, brother? They might have told us something, but now they're all dead."

A branch rustled in the trees above. Emryss glanced up

but saw nothing. He turned to Gwilym. "What's to tell? They killed Ianto and my sheep, and now they're dead. That's the end of it."

"Wanting to know *why* they done it, Emryss. Maybe they was paid to do it. And what about the fire?"

Emryss sighed heavily and flexed his leg. "Who'd pay to slaughter sheep and leave the carcasses laying about? Cynric's too cheap, and nobody else that mean-spirited around. As for the fires, these louts don't look clever enough to get inside my defenses."

"Maybe they had help."

Emryss stared at Gwilym. "Are you saying someone inside Craig Fawr betrayed us?"

"I'm saying it's damn suspicious, is all, and maybe these men might have told us something."

Emryss swung his blade and cut off long pieces of grass. "Well, it's done now." He sheathed his sword. "I'm going up there," he said, pointing into the trees above, "thought I heard something. You get these ready to take back to Craig Fawr. Maybe someone will recognize them."

He climbed up the narrow path. He could see no one, and the air was still.

He paused and looked around. There was something familiar about this place. They were close to the river that divided his property from Beaufort land.

He remembered coming here with Ianto sometimes, to cut willow switches to guide the sheep. There was a cave.

He found it quickly. Pulling out his sword, he went slowly inside the dark hole in the rocks.

A man! Emryss prepared to fight, but quickly realized he was staring at a lifeless corpse, the teeth bared in a diabolical smile.

Emryss could find nothing else of any significance, so he climbed down, biting his lip to keep from crying out as pain surged through his leg.

At the bottom of the path, the soldiers cleaned their swords and glanced with disgust at the thieves.

Emryss joined Gwilym. "There's another body up in a cave. Didn't see anything else."

Two soldiers were sent to fetch the corpse as the others hefted the rest of the dead outlaws onto horses they found tethered a short distance away.

The patrol arrived at Craig Fawr after sunset. Weary and in pain, Emryss dismounted slowly. He gave orders for the bodies to be laid out in the stables, and for the people of the village as well as the castle to look on them.

"It doesn't make sense, *brawdmaeth*," Gwilym insisted as he followed Emryss to the hall. "Thieves not stealing, just killing."

"Outlaws not known for their minds, are they?" Emryss replied. "And the dolts hadn't counted on Ianto."

Ianto. For a while he had been able to forget about Ianto.

"I'm hoping you're right," Gwilym said. "Because if you're not, Emryss…"

"Let it rest, Gwil." He could hardly think for the pain. "Finish for me, will you? The leg's starting to ache." He tried not to grimace as he walked, although his leg felt as if a dagger of heated metal was embedded in the flesh.

When he pushed open the door, Roanna came forward, a smile of happy relief brightening her features for an instant.

He limped over to his chair and sat down with a low groan. Roanna gasped.

"Blood!" she whispered. "Are you hurt?"

"Not mine," he said heavily.

"And Hu?"

"Safe."

She sighed with relief and went to the table to pour him

some wine. He was thankful she didn't ply him with questions as he gulped down the cool liquid.

All he wanted to do was rest and try to put the fight from him. He had fought and killed too many times to find anything but relief in his survival.

He had known men who gloried in fighting, as he had in his youth, but they were usually the ones who used their skills only in tournaments, where the field was not littered with the wounded and dying. Where people cheered their champions, not waited out of sight to strip the corpses. And they were noblemen, men whose lives in battle were rarely at risk because they were more valuable as hostages.

And he was ashamed, because, for a moment, he had felt the blood sing in his veins and the ecstasy of victory when the other man had died.

After a while, he sat up and realized Roanna was standing nearby, looking at him. Looking at him with love.

The memory of last night took away the last of his pain. "Wife, come here," he said softly.

She came to him.

"Thank God I married a woman who knows when to keep quiet," he murmured as he reached up to take her hands.

She bent down and kissed him. "Was it so terrible?"

"At least none of my men were hurt and all of those vultures are dead."

She pulled away. "You killed them *all?*"

He sat up and swung his feet to the floor. "Yes, all. They didn't give us much choice."

"But Emryss," she said, clasping her hands together, "now we won't know why they did it, or if Cynric's involved."

He stood up abruptly and began to limp around the room. "It appears that everyone seems to think I've made an enormous blunder. Perhaps I should have let that toothless oaf kill me. At least then you could all have your precious answers!''

"Emryss," she said softly. He stopped and turned to her. "Emryss."

He took her in his arms and held her tightly. "Forgive me," he mumbled, his lips against her hair. "I know you're right, but there's not time to think when a man is about to kill you."

"I'm sorry, Emryss," she whispered. Her lips brushed his cheek. "If anything had happened to you, I..."

He stopped her words with a long, deep kiss. Afterward, she drew back and smiled into his face.

"Emryss!" she gasped. "Sit down at once. You look horrible."

"I haven't looked good since that infidel got my eye," he said, trying to smile.

"Don't joke. I'm getting Mamaeth. *Please* sit down."

Mamaeth met Roanna at the top of the stairs. "How is he?" she asked urgently.

"Tired, and his leg pains him more than he cares to admit."

"Always like that. Thinks I can read his mind when he's hurt. But don't worry. I'll see he doesn't do any more foolishness." Her face became serious. "They've laid the bodies out in the courtyard. Emryss said everyone is to look at them and say if they know them."

"Of course," Roanna said.

She went into the courtyard. Torches blazed in the dusk, held by a few of the soldiers. People filed slowly past the bodies. She joined the line, scanning each face. She recognized them all from that terrible day when they had attacked her and Jacques.

When she reached the end, fear crept up her spine. The leader. The one with the huge black beard and rotten, stinking teeth. He was not there. But Emryss didn't think any had escaped.

Jacques saw her from the kitchen door and hurried out to her. "Come, little kitten. It is a bad business, this looking at corpses of rotten scoundrels. Come sit by the fire and warm yourself."

"No, Jacques. I have to tell Emryss."

"What?" Jacques called, but she was already running to the hall.

She bumped into Mamaeth as she reached the door of the bedchamber.

"Go slow, my girl," Mamaeth said, holding her by the arms. "He's fine. I've given the lad something to make him sleep."

"But…"

"He'd wear a grove in the stones otherwise, pacing like a caged thing. And no telling what his leg feels like." She looked into Roanna's eyes and spoke sympathetically. "Not serious, not yet, but he's got to stay off that leg for a while."

Roanna hesitated. If she woke him, he would want to pursue the missing man.

What harm could it do to let her news wait? Surely the leader of the outlaws would flee, now that his band was dead.

"That's better, girl. Calm yourself. Come get a bite for him when he wakes."

"Where's Hu?" Roanna asked as she followed Mamaeth down the stairs.

"In the kitchen. Bronwyn's taking care of him for now."

Roanna nodded.

Mamaeth shook her head. "Poor little man. He'll be *gwylio'r corff.*"

She saw Roanna's puzzlement. "Watching the body. In the chapel. Emryss'll be there later, and all the men."

242 A Warrior's Heart

Roanna stopped as they went out the door. "To watch Ianto's body? Why?"

Mamaeth faced her. "It wouldn't be right to leave Ianto alone. I made Emryss sleep because Hu can watch now. But it's Emryss's place, with Ianto. Almost like his father, Ianto was. Taught him everything about sheep, and dogs, and about men, too."

"I see."

"Do you?" Mamaeth asked bluntly.

"Yes, I do," Roanna replied firmly. "It's his duty, and I won't stand in his way. But—" she began walking toward the kitchen "—I won't let him get sick again either."

Emryss slept through the evening meal and into the early night. Roanna sat beside the bed watching him sleep, until at last he groaned groggily.

"Oh, God," he moaned. "What was in that drink?"

"Mamaeth wanted you to sleep," she answered softly.

"Is it night?"

"Yes."

He struggled to sit up, and she moved to assist him. "Where's Ianto?"

"In the chapel."

He rubbed his head. "I have to go."

Roanna nodded and went to get his clothing. When she turned back, he was sitting on the bed, his feet apart on the floor, his head in his hands.

"Emryss, are you all right?"

He looked at her. "Well enough."

She clasped her hands in front of her as he slowly dressed. "Mamaeth told me about…this. I know you have to go and be there, but please, Emryss, promise me you'll come back if you're in pain."

His face filled her with sadness. "Pain? It's my fault he's dead, and you don't expect me to feel pain?"

She reached out and touched his cheek as he pulled on his boots. "I know how it feels to lose someone you love. And it's not your fault."

He grabbed her hand tightly, his face grim. "*Not my fault?* I laid around here thinking only of myself, and now Ianto's dead." He dropped her hand and walked to the window. "What kind of lord am I?"

Roanna walked toward him. "You're the best kind," she said fervently. "Generous and honorable. How were you to know this would happen?" She reached up and put her arms around him as he continued to stare out the window. "Would it have helped if you had ridden out every day and killed yourself?" She laid her head against his chest, holding him tight.

He sighed deeply. "Oh, Roanna, I want to believe your words."

She leaned back and took his face in her hands. "If you must blame someone, blame me. Or Mamaeth. We made you stay here, to get well."

"Do you think I'd let a woman take my burden? No. It's my duty to keep my people safe." His chest rose with another sigh. "At least we got the devils."

A lump of stone seemed to settle in her stomach.

"Is that for me?" he asked, looking at the meat and bread set out on the small table.

"Yes," she said, trying to keep her voice light. How could she tell him one of the devils had gotten away?

He took a couple of mouthfuls. "God, I can't eat. I'm going to the chapel."

Roanna nodded. "I'll wait for you."

"No point. I'll be there all night. Go to sleep."

"I'll wait."

He turned to her with a wistful smile. "Are you always so stubborn, woman? And never arguing, just say a thing and keep repeating till I give in?"

"Yes."

Opening the door, she heard him speak again in a quiet voice. "Ianto was the same."

She went to the window and soon saw him limping slowly toward the gate. His shoulders slumped, and his greeting to the guards was quiet and subdued.

She peered over the village to the chapel. Light glowed from the small windows, and she thought she could hear the sound of singing.

Turning away, she wrung her hands slowly. He mustn't sit up all night, not yet. If he fell sick again, he might not get over it. Mamaeth had tried to sound unconcerned, but Roanna knew the old woman well enough to see past her outward good spirit.

Roanna thought she would go mad with worry as the long minutes passed. At last, glancing at the tray of food, she decided to take it to the kitchen.

When she reached the kitchen corridor, it was obvious Mamaeth and Jacques were in the middle of another argument, although even their usual fiery tempers seemed suppressed. When Jacques caught sight of Roanna, he rushed to her, taking the tray from her hands. "Here, kitten, sit. You look ill."

"I'm fine, Jacques," she said, taking the offered stool. "I'm just worried a little."

"Humph! No wonder, when we must live with such incredible imbeciles as that woman! Imagine, telling me what to look for in milled flour!"

Roanna smiled slightly. Jacques' problems were always refreshingly simple.

He bustled about the room, placing a roll and a cup of ale in front of her. "Eat," he ordered.

She nibbled at the roll, and he watched her out of the corner of his eye as he mixed some dough for the morning.

"Lady Roanna, what is it?" he said finally, wiping his

huge hands on his floury apron. "He is well, your husband. And I think all is…as it should be between you? At least so that witch has said. I agree this business with the outlaws is sad, but you look so lost…"

"I'm just tired, Jacques," she said, making a decision. The missing thief could be dealt with later, if necessary. For now, Emryss's health must come first. She smiled a little.

"Ah." He beamed at her. "That is good. You look more like yourself now. Of course, my food always does that to people." He chuckled richly. "Why don't you stay and help for a little? I have hardly seen my kitten, she is such a lady now."

Roanna lingered a long time with her old friend. He told her all the gossip, including a warning that she should insist Gwilym and Bronwyn wed.

At last she had to leave. It was late, and Jacques always rose early to prepare the first meal. Craig Fawr was silent and still. In the sky, clouds drifted past the moon. Shadows shifted on the walls, making eerie shapes.

Roanna hugged herself, looking up at the stars and trying to listen for that elusive sound of singing. All was quiet.

She walked to the gate. A guard immediately called out, and she answered quickly. "I'm going to the chapel," she told him, ignoring the surprised expression on his face.

Once there, she paused outside the darkened building. Muted voices spoke inside, and she quietly pushed open the door.

Ianto lay on a bier in front of the altar. He wore a fine tunic, and his hands had been crossed on his breast. Mott lay at his side, curled up as if asleep. Candles had been placed at each end of the bier, casting a pale light about the chapel.

Emryss sat on a bench beside Gwilym. Some soldiers she recognized sat on the nearby benches, joined by others who must be shepherds. A pitcher of wine passed from hand to hand.

She slipped inside and closed the door, keeping in the shadows. She had no place here, she knew, but she didn't want to be alone. She wanted to be near Emryss.

Swaying slightly, Gwilym stood up and began to speak. His words were a slurred mixture of Welsh and Norman. Listening carefully, Roanna was surprised at how much she could understand.

"The time it was Emryss was learning to shear." He grinned lopsidedly. "Almost sliced off his own fingers, the *ffwl,* but our Ianto said not a word. Always treated him like a lord."

"Waiting for me to nick myself, he was!" Emryss said sullenly. "Always taught the hard way, him. Treated me like a lord, indeed. Don't you mind the time he slapped my face?"

Gwilym's confused expression made the other men laugh. "Well, so he did, and right he was, too. You were playing with one of his dogs."

"A fine one he was to train a good dog," one of the old shepherds said.

"Aye, Dewey," another responded, "or a good man, for that. We won't see his like for a long, long time."

The men gathered in the dark chapel all nodded and drank deeply.

"Hoping I can do as much for Hu as he did for me," Emryss said softly.

The men nodded again. Silence stretched between them as each sat wrapped in memory. Finally Roanna dared to peer out from her shadowy hiding place. The men leaned back against the walls, their eyes closed and their chests moving slowly.

Emryss had moved. He knelt in front of the bier, one arm around Ianto's chest.

Roanna stepped out slowly. He mustn't sleep like that, in this chill place. Tiptoeing, she moved slowly up to the altar.

Then she stopped. Emryss was singing, his voice so low that she could only hear when she drew near.

She began to go back when the song ceased. Turning, she saw Emryss's broad shoulders begin to shake as a great sob burst from his throat.

Without thinking, she ran up to the bier and knelt beside him. "Emryss," she said softly, wanting to touch him but afraid he would be angry that she had dared to intrude.

He lifted his tormented, tear-stained face. "Oh, God help me, Roanna. I might as well have held the blade myself!"

She took his damp cheeks in her hands. "No, Emryss," she said firmly.

He bowed his head, saying nothing, but he lifted his arms and enfolded her in his strong embrace. She held him to her, rocking gently, and stroked his curls as he wept.

As the days passed, Roanna became convinced that her worries were groundless. Emryss sent patrols out every day, and they found no sign of other outlaws.

He grew stronger, and seemingly less racked with guilt. More like the Emryss she had first known. Each night he took her in his arms and loved her until she thought the passion she felt was heaven on earth. As he aroused her in new ways, each more exciting than the last, she began to understand why lust was a sin, for he couldn't even look at her without driving all thoughts from her except those of their rapture. Roanna even began to hope that their troubles with Cynric were finished.

But at Beaufort, Cynric DeLanyea had decided the time for action had come.

Chapter Eighteen

Father Robelard knelt in the cathedral of the monastery, oblivious to the pain in his knees. The afternoon sun could not penetrate the heavy fog in the valley, so the huge space was as gloomy as a tomb.

"Dear God," he prayed fervently, "deliver me. Help me in my hour of need. Show me the way to put Satan behind me." He crushed the note he had received that morning into a ball in his sweaty hand. His voice rose in supplication. "For your servant has sinned, and begs your divine forgiveness and mercy."

"A touching plea."

Father Robelard felt his stomach heave at the familiar voice. He rose and turned.

The light from the altar candles threw bizarre shadows in the church. Cynric loomed like some demonic shape against the closed door, and his face was a mask of light and darkness. He approached the altar.

"Feeling a little guilty, Father?" he said, a mocking smile on his handsome face.

"You sent for me, my lord. What do you want?"

"Want? What do I want? Not a very gracious greeting, Father. Perhaps I come to confess."

Father Robelard's hands began to twist the belt of his robe. Cynric walked forward until the priest was forced to step out of his way.

He glanced at the little man. "But perhaps not." He continued until he stood right in front the altar. He leaned against the huge carved block of wood. Too shocked to speak, Father Robelard mouthed a prayer for assistance.

"Tell me, Father, how does my noble cousin?"

"He's quite well, my lord," Father Robelard said after a short cough.

"I'm delighted to hear that. I trust Emryss thinks he has seen the end of all his troubles, now that he's slaughtered those thieves?"

"I believe they hope so."

"Dear me, it seems a pity that it is not so."

Father Robelard's mind darted about like a trapped bird's as he tried to see what Cynric was leading up to.

"It has come to my attention that certain—shall we say, malcontents?—wish to cause more trouble for Emryss," Cynric continued. "He is, after all, Norman, though he tries to pretend otherwise. I suppose he believes the local upstarts will leave him alone.

"But however much he'd like to believe it, he isn't immune to the hatred these Welshmen have for Normans." Cynric sighed. "I'd like to warn Emryss, but he'll have nothing to do with me."

Father Robelard's cassock was becoming a wrinkled mess.

"I don't suppose he'd listen to you?" Cynric pushed away from the altar as the priest shook his head. "No, I didn't think so, since it's no secret that he hates priests."

He waited until Father Robelard nodded before going on. "So who will he believe?"

He walked slowly toward the priest. "Perhaps the charming Lady Roanna? If I were to provide evidence to back up her warning, I think we can safely assume he would believe her.''

"Yes, my lord. He listens to her counsel."

Cynric smiled. It was like seeing a snake grin. "Just so. So you see, I have a predicament. How shall I deliver this evidence to the Lady Roanna?

"I can't have it falling into the wrong hands, and I dare not take the risk of setting foot on Emryss's land again. Nevertheless, I wish to give it to the lady myself. I want to show her I meant what I said about mending the rift between her husband and myself."

"Lord DeLanyea will not permit her to go onto your land, my lord."

"I know that," Cynric snapped, then smiled again. "I had a more neutral place in mind. Say, the riverbank that divides our lands. The bushes will afford us suitable cover, and if something should go amiss, it will be simple enough to get back onto my own land, where Emryss also dare not go."

The priest twisted his belt with sweaty fingers. He didn't want to trust this man, and yet Cynric might have knowledge that would be valuable to Emryss DeLanyea.

"Naturally, Father, you may accompany the lady, at least to the top of the bank."

Father Robelard cleared his throat and tried to control his shaking knees. "What if she won't go with me? And how can I be sure you mean to leave her in peace?"

Cynric's mouth twisted into a scornful smile. "Ah, becoming a hero, are we? Well, Father, you may set your fears to rest. I give you my solemn word before God that I will not harm her. Or you, if you bring her to me."

The priest wiped his sweaty palms on his robe. "Very well, my lord."

"I'm delighted we understand one another. Say, on the morrow, in the morning."

Cynric turned to leave, then paused. "Oh, and I should tell you, Father, that if Lady Roanna is not at the river, I shall be forced to reveal Lynette's shame."

Father Robelard felt sick. "Shame?"

"She's with child. And you know what will happen if that becomes common knowledge."

Father Robelard knew all to well what Cynric DeLanyea would do. He would have the poor girl stripped and driven from the village.

In panic, he grasped at Lynette's one chance. "The child, my lord. It might be yours."

Cynric grabbed the little man by the collar of his cassock. "Listen, *priest,* if I say she bears your child, that is what people will have to believe. So make sure Roanna is at the river."

He let go. Father Robelard fell to the floor as Cynric strode from the church.

The next morning Roanna arrived at the chapel early. Emryss was still asleep, and she wanted to be back before he woke.

"Lady Roanna!" Father Robelard said, looking at her as if she were some supernatural being. Then he seemed to almost wilt with relief.

"God must have sent you at this opportune hour." He raised his eyes heavenward. "Surely this is a sign to his humble servant. I must speak to you of a matter of great importance."

Roanna subdued her surprise at his unusual behavior.

"It has been brought to my attention that someone intends more harassment against Norman lords."

"None of the Welsh will do anything against Craig Fawr, Father."

"So we would all like to believe, my lady. But I think this person may very well have something to listen to. I have arranged to speak to someone who knows the details. Perhaps if you would accompany me…''

''Surely it would be better if my husband were to go with you.''

''I'm sorry, my lady. He said he would tell only you. He has given me his word that you will be safe.''

Roanna clasped her hands together. Father Robelard's words had a ring of truth. Emryss was one of the hated Normans, no matter what he preferred to believe. It was just possible that the outlaws had also been discontented Welshmen. And if that were so…

''Where are we to go?''

''Not off your husband's land, my lady, but you should ride a horse.''

''Very well.''

''After Mass, then, my lady?''

''As you wish.''

A short while later, Roanna sat swaying on the back of her placid mare, following Father Robelard's donkey. When she had gone to the stables, no one had questioned her. Usually Emryss insisted Gwilym or another soldier escort her when she went on errands with Father Robelard, but Father Robelard had been adamant that they go alone.

As they went down the narrow road, the sun shone feebly through thick clouds. Water from yesterday's heavy rain lay in muddy puddles. Each step of the horse's hooves made loud sucking noises as she lifted her feet from the ooze.

Roanna kept her eyes on the road, trying to guide her horse around the largest of the puddles. After a while, Father Robelard halted, and she looked up.

They were almost to the river, on the road that led to Beaufort.

''Father,'' she asked, ''is this the place?''

He dismounted from his donkey and peered nervously at the trees. "Yes, my lady."

Roanna caught a flash of metal in the trees. Suddenly Cynric DeLanyea and Urien Fitzroy stepped out from behind the willow bushes.

Cynric stared at the woman before him. He could scarcely believe that this was the same girl he had hated at first sight. Her skin seemed to glow in the dim light of the forest. And it was amazing how a little flesh added to her slender form could render her so appealing. Indeed, he felt a familiar, pleasing tightening in his groin as he looked at her rounded breasts.

Roanna gasped and grabbed her reins tighter as he walked toward her. Her gaze flicked to the priest.

"Have no fear, my lady," the little man said quickly. "He has given his word before God he will not harm you."

"Quite right, my lady." Cynric smiled in his most charming manner. "I only want to warn you."

Roanna eyed him suspiciously. "Is that true?"

He stepped forward and held out a hand. "Please, Lady Roanna, listen to me. I give you my word that I come in peace and goodwill."

He saw the flash of doubt in her eyes. "You must forgive me for this little ruse, my lady. Emryss would close his mind if I were to try to warn him about anything, so I had to speak with you."

Roanna made no move to dismount.

"Father, stay here with Fitzroy. Lady Roanna and I should discuss this matter in privacy." He went to her and held out his hand. She hesitated a moment, then allowed him to help her dismount.

"Come, my lady," he said, pulling her gently toward the cover of the trees. "It is best discussed alone. Please, my lady," he pleaded softly.

He led her away from the road, to the shelter of the hazel trees along the banks of the river.

"Who is planning to attack us? When?" she asked when they stopped in a small clearing.

"Roanna," he said softly, "I knew you wouldn't want to listen to me unless it concerned danger to your husband. That's why I had to convince Father Robelard to bring you."

"Then there is not going to be any..."

"Trouble from the Welsh?" he finished for her. "No. At least, not that I know of. Forgive me for that little deception." He smiled appealingly, holding her hand lightly in his own.

"I realize, Roanna, that I behaved terribly to you. And I've tried to forget you. You are married to my cousin, and that must be the end of it. Nevertheless, I am tortured with guilt for the way I treated you. I have come to beg your forgiveness."

He moved toward her, and she took a step back. He stopped with a mournful smile. "I see that you still don't trust me. Well, perhaps it was foolish of me to think otherwise."

Suddenly he lifted her hand and pressed his lips against her palm. Her flesh was soft, warm, lightly scented. Desirable.

Roanna stepped back. "What are you doing?" she asked, her luminous green eyes wide.

"Roanna," he said, "I love you. I need you."

She stared at him. "You are mad!"

He knelt down in the mud and lifted his hands in a pleading gesture. "Yes, I am. Mad with love for you."

The words had the ring of sincerity. He heard it, and tried to put it down to his cleverness. "Oh, I know you won't believe me." He looked at her, determined to carry out his plan. Only his plan. "I could scarcely believe it myself. And I tried to deny it, too. After all, I had lost you. Forever.

"But I can no longer keep silent. Oh, Roanna!" He buried his face in his hands.

"I'm sorry, Cynric," she said softly. He looked up, up into her pale face with those rich, red lips.

The hell with his plan. He jumped to his feet and took her in his arms, pressing his heated lips against hers. Miraculously, she made no struggle, but hung limp in his arms. He moved his lips across her down-soft cheeks, toward her neck.

"Cynric," she said softly, her chest rising delectably. "Stop, please!"

For the first time in his life, he listened to a woman's protest.

She made no move away. "Why are you doing this, Cynric? There are so many women more beautiful than me."

Cynric stepped back as if she'd struck him. Confused, he couldn't look at her. What had happened to his plan, his delightful, perfect plan to rape Emryss's wife and send her back disgraced?

What had happened to him?

He straightened his shoulders. He was Baron Cynric DeLanyea, and he would have his revenge on Emryss, the man who had been the thorn in his side from the day he was born. "You see, Roanna, you and I have been secret lovers."

She gasped, and he let the feeling of power dominate everything else.

"Surprising? Who will not believe that a woman would choose my face over his ruined one? But let me tell you how this came to pass." He began to pace, not looking at her.

"You fell in love with me the first time we met, and

were delighted that we were to be wed. Unfortunately, I made a little error, and in your anger, you wed another. Your husband was not very loving, and soon you were consumed by thoughts of me.

"Even when Emryss made love with you, you thought only of me." He had rehearsed this story a hundred times, but this time, this time, the thought of Emryss making love to her filled him with anger. His voice grew hard. "You begged and pleaded with Father Robelard to arrange a meeting with me. He was reluctant, but he agreed. We met. You told me of your feelings."

He stopped and turned to her. His feet moved slowly toward her. "I have fallen in love with you, too." He couldn't stop looking at her face. "You are torn by your feelings. I try to convince you to leave your husband. You are loath to do anything dishonorable."

He touched a lock of her hair, rubbing it between his fingers, staring into her eyes. "You see how the story goes, Roanna?" It fell to her shoulder as he forced himself to turn away.

"We agree, against your better judgment, to meet again. We become lovers. Unfortunately, your husband is about to learn of your treachery.

"Emryss will challenge me to combat, and I will kill him."

"Do you think he'll believe you?"

Cynric looked at her. "Does it matter? He will still demand to fight me. You can understand how one feels when honor is insulted. I will have no recourse but to defend my honor, too. And I will kill him."

His voice rang with triumph, the thought that his vengeance was so nearly in his grasp overpowering the spell of her eyes. "I have known that cursed bastard all my life. I've watched him fight a hundred times. I know every move, every feint, every trick. I know every weakness. And

he is weak now. So he will be dead, his land will be mine."
He stopped and looked at her. "Unfortunately, your only
choice will be to retire to some secluded convent to con-
template your sins."

"Cynric," Roanna said softly, "how did you guess?"
She walked toward him. "How did you guess that it was
you I loved? That in my foolish womanly way I had taken
revenge by marrying Emryss, only to harm myself?"

His eyes narrowed. "What is this you're saying?"

She came toward him slowly. "That you are right. I love
you. Only you. I yearn to be with you, to feel *your* arms
around me. But I was afraid. Afraid you would scorn me.
Afraid of what Emryss might do." She reached up and
caressed his arm. "But now I know what I must do. I will
leave him, gladly. He will be dishonored, as you wish. I
will tell people whatever you want me to. That he is vicious
and cruel. That he beat me. Even that he prefers men."

The blood coursed through Cynric's veins as she ran her
fingers up his arm. Her full lips smiled. "Or no one but
ourselves need know. We can be secret lovers. That would
be exciting, wouldn't it?"

He thought his vessels would burst as he grabbed her
arms and kissed her, plundering her warm, sweet mouth.

"What of Emryss?" he mumbled as his lips sought the
tender white skin of her breasts above the gown. Her
breathing was as fast as his own, and her fingers clutched
his hair.

"He will leave us alone. Look how he hides in his tower,
even now. And as for his loving, he does not...please me."

"I will," Cynric whispered, pulling her close. He rubbed
against her, moaning with the ecstasy of the moment.

"I have learned some marvelous things, Eastern things,
from Emryss," she gasped.

As if he needed more to inflame him! Slowly he pushed

her to the ground. His breathing quickened as he plunged his hand into her gown.

"Please, Cynric, not here, not now," she protested, pushing away. "Not like servants."

He rose and stared into her heated face.

The words penetrated through the fog of his lust, but he didn't want to stop. "No, now," he panted.

Roanna suddenly looked frightened. "What was that?" She twisted her head and looked toward the trees. "I heard someone."

Cynric glanced over. "Urien?"

No one answered.

"Cynric, please. Not here. It's too dangerous." She reached beneath her back and pulled out a sharp rock. "And uncomfortable." She leaned toward him and whispered, "And some things are better with a bed."

He rolled off her. "Very well. When?"

"Soon. I'll send word and find a place, a safe place." She kissed his cheek and stood up shakily. "Soon. Now I must go."

He rose to his feet and grabbed her arm, staring into her green eyes. "First give me your word that you will come to me."

She nodded slowly, and triumph flowed through his body. "I give you my word."

He straightened his tunic. "Farewell for now, my love." Dread crept into his heart and moved him to speak. "If you don't come, I will do as I have said."

He wheeled around and went back along the path while Roanna leaned against a tree, too weak to move.

But she couldn't stay here. Mustering her strength, she pushed herself away from the tree, wanting nothing more than to get away from this place. Grabbing her skirt, she ran to the horses and Father Robelard.

The priest stared at the woman coming toward him, the muddy dress, the disheveled hair, the panic in her face.

Only moments before Cynric had returned and ridden off, clearly quite pleased with whatever had passed between Lady Roanna and himself, bidding him good day in a self-satisfied tone and saying the lady would be with him shortly.

What had that villain done to her? Before he could ask, she clambered clumsily into the saddle without thought of modesty and slapped her heels against the mare's flank. With a whinny, the horse leaped into a gallop along the muddy road.

Father Robelard watched her leave. Obviously whatever had happened had terrified the poor woman. And the priest knew enough about Cynric DeLanyea to surmise the worst.

He knew that raping women was sport to Cynric De-Lanyea.

As he stood in the mud, the weight of his culpability bore down on him. *His* lack of rectitude had made it possible for Cynric to compel him to bring Lady Roanna here; it was his fault she suffered.

The little man drew himself up and straightened his shoulders. It was too late to make amends with the lady, but he would go after Cynric DeLanyea and tell the evil man that he would no longer assist him in his vile machinations. Then he would go to the abbot and confess his sins. All of them.

Chapter Nineteen

She had to get back to Emryss. Safe in his arms.

The mud splashed her bare legs and skirt, but it didn't matter. She needed a bath, a hot, steaming bath to cleanse her skin from Cynric's evil touch.

Sickness rose in her stomach, and she clutched at the mare's reins, willing the nausea away.

Oh, dear God, she prayed frantically as the mare almost ran into a low tree branch, let me get home safely.

At last the village came into sight. She never slowed, but rode headlong past the quiet houses and through the gates. She pulled the horse to a stop and climbed down. Her disheveled hair hung in her face and her muddy skirts clung to her legs as she swayed dizzily.

The courtyard came into focus.

A silent crowd stood there, young and old staring at her as if she were a stranger to them. Slowly she looked around for Emryss.

He stood, still as a stone, his legs wide apart, in front of the hall. Gwilym waited to his left, and on the ground in front of them she saw a shape. A blood-stained shape of a man.

She ran toward Emryss, but he lifted his hand.

"Do you know him?" He pointed at the corpse.

She followed his finger to look at the dirt-covered bearded face. The lips were drawn back as if in a scream, exposing rotten teeth.

"Yes." She took a step toward him. Oh, God, she knew the man. Emryss's face was hard. No love shone from it as he stared at her. "When his body wasn't with the others, I thought he had fled," she said hurriedly. "And when nothing else happened, I was sure of it. I thought there was no need to alarm you."

"Were you with Cynric?" Hard cold words from hard cold lips.

There was no air in the yard, no air in her lungs. How could he know? She nodded.

"Why?" His accusation, and the pained look, loosened her tongue.

"He tricked me into meeting him. And what else he had to say is for you alone to hear, Emryss."

"I will hear it now."

"Emryss," she pleaded, aware of the watching eyes. "Please, let me tell you alone."

"I will hear it now."

Roanna clasped her hands together and paused, collecting her scattered thoughts. Drawing her dignity about her like a mantle, she began. "Father Robelard told me that someone had information about more planned attacks on our people, but that this person would speak only to me. So I went with him. But when we got to the place, Cynric and Fitzroy were waiting."

There was not a sound as she spoke, not a whisper or cough. Not even the children moved.

"Cynric took me away from the others and told me he had wanted to see me because he wants to be friends."

Gwilym folded his arms across his chest.

"But he lied. In a while I discovered why he wanted to

speak to me." She took a deep breath. "He wants me to be the excuse he needs to fight you."

Gwilym glanced at Emryss, who still stared at her.

"How?" Emryss's voice was like the tip of the outlaw's dagger at her throat.

She twisted her hands, the knuckles white. "He would say that we are lovers," she whispered.

The crowd gasped, and Gwilym's look was triumphant. Emryss raised one eyebrow. "Are you?"

She looked at him boldly and spoke strongly. "Since I have been spied on, you will have heard what happened. But I feigned affection for him only to get away, to come to you."

"And that is also why you let him kiss you, let him run his hands all over you like a common whore?" Gwilym demanded.

"No!" she shouted, agonized. She took a step toward Emryss. "What else could I do? He could have taken me at any time, with his strength. And I thought I was alone, except for Father Robelard, so screaming would have been useless. I let him think I agreed, let him think I care for him, but only so that I could get away. You must believe me. I swear that is the truth."

Emryss said nothing.

Suddenly a voice rang out. "Lady Roanna does not lie."

A murmur stirred through the crowd as Jacques strode out of the kitchen door and came to stand beside Roanna. She reached out and clutched his arm.

"Then when she told Cynric she would do anything he wanted, she did not lie," Gwilym said harshly. "And when she gave her word to come to him, she did not lie." He turned to Emryss. "*Brawdmaeth*, I heard her say these things with my own ears. I saw them together. She didn't look frightened."

"Then why didn't you let your presence be known? Why didn't you help me?" Roanna demanded.

"Why should I help a traitor?" Gwilym said hotly.

Emryss remained stock-still, watching her.

"I believe her." The piercing voice of Mamaeth came from the back of the crowd. The thin old woman pushed her way past a group of soldiers. She came and stood next to Jacques. "You men can't know how it feels to be a woman caught in a trap like that. What was she to do? Get herself killed? Or use the brains God gave her to outwit that devil? And didn't she do just that?"

"Aye!" Bronwyn came forward, and stood beside Roanna. Gwilym's eyes flashed with anger, but Bronwyn straightened her shoulders defiantly. "Thankful we should be she was fast at the thinking. Why would she ride like the wind to get back here, unless it was as she said?"

"Maybe she knew I seen her!" Gwilym shouted. "And who was it gave the alarm the night of the fires, and got us all to the mill so someone could sneak in here and fire the weapons? Maybe she lit the fire herself, eh?"

Emryss turned and strode toward the stables. Roanna waited, but he ignored her, and she couldn't seem to move.

Gwilym cast a quick glance at the women in the middle of the yard, then hurried after him.

Emryss was saddling his horse.

"I'm going into the hills," Emryss said when Gwilym entered. "I've got to think."

"I'll go with you."

"No, Gwil, stay here and watch Craig Fawr, and her. I'll be back come morning, and I'll know what to do."

Roanna sat beside the small brazier in the bedchamber and tried not to sink any lower into despair.

Beside her, Bronwyn stared into the shifting flames. "Gone into the hills to think, he has, my lady," she said quietly. "A good sign, is that. His da used to say Emryss would be a fine leader, if he'd learn to think more. Looks to me like he has. After all, Gwilym surprised everybody coming into the village with the body slung over the saddle. No time to be thinking and asking questions. Let Emryss rest on the rocks a bit, and he'll come to see you're not betraying him."

"I *was* with Cynric." Roanna sighed. "But it was as I said. I did the only thing I could think of, to get away."

"There's not a woman here wouldn't understand how it was. He'll see it." Bronwyn took her hand and held it tight. "He loves you. He'll believe you."

"If only Father Robelard were here! He would tell them the truth." Roanna wrung her hands slowly. "Perhaps something has happened to him. Why hasn't he come back?"

For the rest of the afternoon, from the time Roanna had ridden away from him in the woods until now, when the sun had been down for some time, no one had seen any sign of the little priest.

"Are you sure he's blameless in this?" Roanna heard the halting hesitation in Bronwyn's voice as she said what Roanna had dreaded to believe.

"He must be," Roanna said after a long moment. "He's a priest."

"Rumors I've heard, we've all heard. About him and a girl in Beaufort."

Roanna stared at her. "A girl?"

"Woman. Lynette's her name. Always a vain thing she was." She saw Roanna's surprise. "Oh, yes, born in this village. But gone to work in Beaufort, although it seems her notion of work is different from yours and mine." She sighed. "I hope nothing's happened to the priest. Maybe he's gone back to the monastery, and we can find out soon what he was about. It could be Cynric tricked him, too, for he never struck nobody as a clever man, learned though he was.''

"I must convince Emryss I spoke the truth. *I must*," Roanna said, watching the yellow and red flames of the fire intertwine and move apart. "How else can I mend the rifts this has caused?"

"It will be all right, my lady," Bronwyn said softly. "He loves you."

He loves me. Roanna twisted the ring on her left hand. Did he still? The way he had looked at her, that was not the look of a man who loved.

If only Father Robelard would come. If only she could go to the monastery and speak with him. She would convince him to tell her the truth.

Roanna waited until Bronwyn's head slumped forward in slumber, then slowly crept to the door. Opening it cautiously, she peered out.

At the top of the stairs a lone guard stood. Gwilym's orders, no doubt, so that she couldn't escape. Silently she went toward the steps leading to the roof.

Hiking her skirt up and tying the fabric around her waist, she slowly began climbing down the scaffold on the inner walls. Then she crept in the shadows to the gate and waited until the guard's back was turned to slip outside.

By now she had remembered every frightened gesture, every nervous word the little priest had said, and she believed that he had known Cynric would be there.

No doubt he had fled back to the safety of the monastery, at least for the present.

She would go there and make him come with her to Craig Fawr, to tell Emryss how they had tricked her, even if it meant rousing the whole monastery.

She would prove her innocence.

* * *

Urien Fitzroy scowled at Lynette. "Girl, take this money and go, I say, before you're thrown out of Beaufort with nothing."

Lynette's pale eyes gleamed in the flickering candlelight as she fingered the heavy pouch. "Just like that? You're giving me this, and not wanting anything in exchange?" She glanced at the bed in the corner of Urien's small room.

He pressed his lips together. "Yes, just like that. And if you're smart, you'll take it and get out."

Lynette walked toward him, swaying her hips. "You're a nice fellow. A pity you want to be rid of me."

His strong hand reached out and pulled her close.

"That's better, but what will your master say?" She laughed softly.

Urien's dark eyes seemed to burn into hers. "Cynric DeLanyea is not my master, not after tomorrow. Do you know, you little fool, what he's planning? He's going to take his cousin's *wife* for his lover." She gasped, but he went on mercilessly. "And where will that leave you? Do you think he'll want you then?"

"But I've got his baby!"

He let go. "God, you are a fool! He wouldn't care. All he thinks about is cuckolding his cousin. Once I thought he would be a great man, the noble lord of a huge estate. Instead he has become obsessed with revenge—and that woman. He makes me sick!"

Lynette rubbed her wrist where he had held her, but held her head up defiantly. "I'll go to Father Robelard then. He'll help."

"How? With what?" Urien looked at the girl's face and narrowed his eyes. "Why him?"

"Because he...because he..."

In that moment, Urien saw everything. "Because he's been used, hasn't he? Because you seduced him. For Cynric. And now you expect Father Robelard to help you?"

Urien laughed harshly. "My God, girl, you are simple! Take the money and get out. The priest is dead. Cynric killed him."

Lynette's eyes widened and she shook her head silently.

"You can believe it. The fool followed us, after the tryst that Cynric had arranged, and refused to be part of his plans any more. The priest said he would tell the abbot everything.

"He never knew what happened, the poor dolt. Cynric killed him as easily as if he'd planned to do it all along. And who knows, maybe he had." Urien gazed at her thoughtfully. "*I* know enough that he'll probably try to kill me someday, and so do you. It's time we both left while we still can."

"Why are you giving me this money?" Lynette asked softly, her voice tiny in the stone-walled room. "Don't you need it?"

Urien's lips curled up in a tired smile. "You'll need it more than I will."

Lynette clutched the purse to her ample bosom. "You're a strange man, Urien Fitzroy."

He shrugged his broad shoulders.

Lynette leaned forward and put her slender forefinger to her lips. "How can I thank you?"

"Get out of here. Tonight."

She went close to him, letting her breasts brush against his arm. "In the morning."

Urien pushed her away gently. "If someone is willing to pay you to leave, take the money and go."

Lynette nodded wistfully and slowly walked to the door. "Farewell, Urien."

He watched her go. Tomorrow. Tomorrow he would ride to Craig Fawr, tell Emryss DeLanyea what he knew, and then he'd leave this horrible country forever.

He was a mercenary who fought for pay, but he wasn't

so desperate that he'd fight for a dishonorable blackguard like Cynric DeLanyea.

The embers from the small fire glowed in the darkness of the night. Emryss hugged himself tighter in the pitiful shelter of rocks, trying to keep warm as he waited for the dawn to come.

At first light he would ride back to Craig Fawr, certain in his heart that Roanna had spoken the truth.

Laying his head on his knees, he remembered another woman with dark skin and dark hair. Young and frightened beyond speech, beyond screams. The look in her eyes! He had let her go untouched, sickened that other Crusaders could ignore the faces of the women whose bodies they used so cruelly. He could readily believe that Roanna would use any means to get away.

A sharp rock poked into Emryss's back, and he shifted to a more comfortable position.

He thought of Gwilym's sudden arrival with the corpse that had caught him by surprise. He had listened as Gwilym told his story of finding the body hidden in a pile of old wood and leaves, picking it up and bringing it home by the river. There he had come upon Roanna and Cynric, enjoying an adulterous tryst.

He had not believed Gwilym, at first. Oh, he couldn't deny the body, of course, but he had been certain Gwilym had been mistaken about the other. But before he had time to think beyond Gwilym's angry words, Roanna herself had come riding into the courtyard. To face the accusations.

How closely he had watched her pale face as she spoke. Not wishing to appear weak and uncertain before his people, he had said nothing. He had needed the peace of the hills to think, and to remember the look in her eyes. The look of honest truthfulness.

It was also the truth that he loved her, as much as his life. As much as his land.

He believed her, and Gwilym would have to take that as proof. Now it was time to go back to her and keep her safe. Time to tell her that he trusted and loved her.

All would be well again.

"We must do something," Jacques said as he pounded the bread dough furiously. His huge fingers warmed slowly with the work. It was not yet dawn, the kitchen chill as the first fires struggled to heat the room.

Mamaeth looked up from the potion she was preparing in the corner. Pots and jars crowded a small table, and each of her fast movements threatened to topple the whole lot. "Aye. She's telling the truth in this, or I'm in my dotage." She began shaking a small bottle, her arm a blur, and sat down on the narrow bench along the wall. "Gwilym can't see it, because he's a fighter, not a thinker. The women all do. Easy for them to imagine how she'd feel, trapped in the woods with that wolf."

Jacques nodded, shaping the dough expertly into round loaves. "If only the priest had come back."

Mamaeth snorted. "Seen the back of him, that I'm sure of. Little sneak of a man, always bowing and smiling. I never trust a man that smiles too much."

Jacques stopped and looked at her. "You never trust any man."

"Never been proven wrong yet, have I?" she shot back as he began working another batch of brown dough. "Look you. Here's Emryss so in love with his wife he can't hardly take his gaze from her, and she so in love with him she doesn't know night from day, it seems, and now this. By the saints, I'd like to get you all in such a predicament as she was in, and see what you ninnies would do. Probably start bawling like babies, every one, or do something stupid and wind up dead.''

"Perhaps her husband believes it is better if a woman die fighting for her honor," Jacques said slowly.

Mamaeth sat down heavily. "If that were so, Emryss himself would never have been born."

"What is this you say?" Jacques wiped his hands on his apron and stepped toward Mamaeth. The wiry, energetic woman suddenly looked every one of her fifty years.

"It's no secret to a some of us hereabouts, but it is to him, poor lad." She sighed softly. Jacques sat down on the bench beside her and took her work-worn hand in his.

She didn't seem to have the energy to pull it away.

"I always meant to tell Emryss, but never finding the right time, me." She looked sideways at Jacques, her sharp eyes measuring. "He is Cynric's elder brother."

Jacques' eyes widened and his fingers tightened on Mamaeth's hand.

"Aye. That *da i ddim* Ulfrid DeLanyea raped his own brother's wife."

Jacques exhaled loudly, his breath a hiss in the quiet. "And Emryss, he does not know Cynric is his half-brother?"

Mamaeth shook her head. "No. He knows the baron attacked his mother and beat her when his father was away on the king's business. That was all his mother wanted him to know, and his da agreed to keep it quiet. The baron was a good fighter, whatever else he became later, and Emryss's mother was terrified Ulfrid would kill her husband, brother or no.

"William loved him like his own—" she sighed "—and treated him well, but still there was a place in his heart that Emryss couldn't reach." Mamaeth pulled her hand free and jumped to her feet. "I should have told him, long ago."

"It is not always easy to know when the child is ready to become a man," Jacques said gently.

Mamaeth brusquely rubbed her eyes and turned away.

"But if Emryss DeLanyea is a bastard," he said resolutely, "under Norman law, he has no rights to Beaufort. How does he threaten Cynric?"

The spark had returned to Mamaeth's dark eyes. "You nit, the Welsh don't give that—" she snapped her fingers "—whether a child is of the brake and brush or no. Always traced our line through the mothers. The sensible thing to do, after all. And Cynric knows the people hereabouts would fight to have Emryss lord before him."

"So Cynric knows of this...business?"

"I'm not certain. Emryss looks more like that devil Ulfrid than Cynric does, and maybe the old toad told him. Cynric would want Emryss dead so no one can challenge his right to Beaufort. But firstly, Cynric hates the very air Emryss breathes. Always has. Always will."

Jacques got to his feet slowly. "Why, unless he knows the truth?"

"Having to know Cynric, to understand. A sly, sullen boy. A good fighter, too, but never good enough to beat Emryss. A man to hold a grudge is Cynric.

"And then there was his father. Ulfrid DeLanyea wasn't fit to raise a pig, let alone a man."

"*O'r annwyl!*" Jacques cried in unconscious imitation of Mamaeth, "and if he found out the one person he could never beat was his father's bastard?"

Mamaeth's lips turned up into a grim smile. "Aye, *o'r annwyl!* That's why I can believe he'd find a way to bring disgrace to Emryss. That would be that snake's way. Not to challenge him outright to a clean fight, but to use a woman's shame."

Suddenly the door flew open and a frantic, rain-soaked Bronwyn ran into the room. "It's the Lady Roanna. She's gone!'' She halted and stared wildly at Mamaeth and Jacques.

Both looked at her in astonishment, as if they couldn't understand her words.

"I only feel asleep for a moment, I'm sure, but when I woke up, she was gone.''

At once Mamaeth and Jacques stood up. "Fetch Gwilym. He will have to find her," Jacques said grimly.

"Where do you think she's gone?'' Mamaeth asked quietly, fear in her voice. "Not to…''

"She would not dishonor herself. Perhaps she has gone to find her husband, to make him see reason.'' He turned to Bronwyn. "Where is Gwilym?''

"In the barracks." With that, she ran out into the rain again.

Mamaeth turned to Jacques, her eyes wide with concern. "We'll have to find her soon. She shouldn't be out in this weather, not when she's going to have a baby.''

Chapter Twenty

"**G**wilym!" Bronwyn's voice sounded like a trumpet of alarm in the chill downpour.

The barracks door opened and Gwilym stuck his head out. "What? What is it?"

"It's Lady Roanna. She's gone."

Gwilym stayed still for a moment, then he opened the door wider, although he remained on the dry threshold. "So?"

Bronwyn halted, unmindful of the falling rain. "You've got to go after her, you *ffwl!*" she shouted.

"No. If she's gone to her lover, let him have her."

Her jaw dropped. "Are you mad, Gwilym? He's not her lover! Something terrible is going to happen to her, out there alone."

"Let it."

"I'll find her myself, then," she said with fierce determination. Not about to let a stubborn man cause more trouble, she ran to the kitchen.

"He won't help." She looked from Jacques to Mamaeth. "We'll have to find her ourselves."

"Where would Emryss be?" Mamaeth said, almost to herself. "Which way should we go?"

Suddenly Bronwyn recalled the last words she had shared with Roanna. "She's gone to the monastery, to find the priest!" she said. "We were talking. She was worried and upset about what Emryss would think, since she had no one to vouch for her words. I told her the rumors we'd heard about the priest and the girl. We talked a little more, and then I fell asleep." Tears began to fall down Bronwyn's cheeks. "I should have stayed awake. Now what's to become of her?"

"There's no time to be lost," Mamaeth said. "Bronwyn, fetch the women on her side, and if I'm not mistaken, that's most of them. *We'll* go out after her. And ask Old Daffyd for his dogs, although they might not be much help in the rain."

Jacques reached for his cloak by the door. "I go, too, to find her."

Mamaeth frowned. "We'll be more like to lose you, too, you big oaf. Stay here and mind the babes. I'll have the women bring them here." She saw Jacques' stricken face. "I'll send Cathwg and Kyna to help. Make some stew. We'll all be needing it. And it's a good one you make."

Jacques looked shocked but nodded and reached for his biggest pot.

A short while later, Gwilym stomped down the corridor toward the kitchen. His men were all sitting in the hall, awaiting their food, and there was no sign of any of the women.

"God's blood!" he muttered when he reached the kitchen. "What's this about?" he shouted above the din.

Cathwg and Kyna, two old women, sat on a bench by the fire, watching the children who were just beginning to take steps. Hu and some of the other lads were in another corner, playing with Old Daffyd's latest batch of puppies. Jacques was engulfed in a cloud of steam, but Gwilym knew he was cooking by the muttered oaths. Bronwyn was not there. Nor Mamaeth. Nor any of the other women who worked in the kitchen. In fact, except for Cathwg, Kyna and Jacques, there were only children.

He shouted again for an explanation in his loudest voice.

"No need for bellowing," Cathwg shouted back.

Jacques appeared. "They are looking for Lady Roanna."

Gwilym's face darkened. "Why?"

"Because you would not."

In the sudden quiet, Gwilym heard the sound of a horse's hooves clattering on the stones outside. He hurried out the door.

Emryss dismounted slowly as Gwilym walked toward him and saw at once that something was very wrong. "What?" he demanded, twisting the reins in his hand.

"Your wife is missing, and the women are gone to look for her."

Emryss's hands froze. "What?"

"Gone to her lover, probably."

Emryss bunched his hands into fists. "Gwilym, never say that or anything like that again to me. My wife has no lover but me."

Gwilym smirked, and in the next instant he was lying on his back in a puddle, the rain hitting his bleeding cheek. He spit out hot, salty blood as he rose to his feet. "She's gone! Run off to be with him, man! Where else would she go?" Gwilym got up, swaying. "Like a thief in the night."

"How long?" Emryss stared at him as if he were a stranger.

"Long enough."

With two long strides Emryss was close to him. He grabbed Gwilym's shirt. "How long has she been gone?"

"She went sometime in the night," Gwilym said sullenly.

"Gwilym," Emryss said softly, looking into his friend's

face, "*Brawdmaeth,* listen to me. I believe her. I trust her. *I love her.*"

Gwilym nodded, but Emryss knew he had not convinced his foster brother. Maybe he never would. But now Roanna was alone and unprotected in the woods because he had not trusted her completely, either.

"How many men have you got out searching?"

"None."

Emryss's hand gripped his shirt even tighter. "None?"

Gwilym struck his hand away. "Aye, none," he shouted angrily. "Not wasting men looking for a traitor." Emryss looked about to strike him again, but Gwilym didn't care. "The women are out, much good might it do! If you want to know more, ask her friend. She left him behind this time."

Despair soaked into Gwilym. Emryss was blind to her. She would be his death.

Roanna watched the path carefully, trying to see through the heavy mist that cloaked the valley. The way was rocky and uneven, and a fall would be dangerous.

Somewhere ahead, if she kept to the river, lay Beaufort and the monastery, and Father Robelard. And, she fervently hoped, the truth.

She glanced down the rocky bank at the swirling mists that covered the rushing, babbling river. She tried to tighten her grip on the skirt hoisted around her shoulders, but her fingers were too frigid. The mud clung to her shift and wet legs and caked her shoes. Inside them, her cold, numb feet felt like two rocks.

The drip of the rain from the trees made a perpetual patter as Roanna trudged along the narrow path. Soon she could barely hear it above the sound of her chattering teeth.

A rustle in the bushes made her look up quickly, but it was only a squirrel. The small animal, dry in the shelter of the willows, watched her for a moment before scampering off.

As the mist grew even thicker, she kept her gaze fastened to the path. She must be almost to the bridge by now, and once on Cynric's land she would have to be even more careful.

She could no longer hear anything but the chattering of her teeth and couldn't think beyond forcing one foot in front of the other.

A brown shape blocked the path. A fallen tree, perhaps, or a mound of earth washed down by the rain, she thought dully.

She saw a blue-tinged, mottled hand.

She gasped and hurried forward as quickly as she could. The brown-cloaked body lay facedown in the mud. Quickly she knelt and rolled it over. A cry of anguish and pain broke from her lips.

She had found Father Robelard.

With her numbed hands she lifted his shoulders. His head slumped back unnaturally, showing her the dark bruises on his neck.

She laid him back down, made the sign of the cross and whispered a benediction. His lifeless eyes stared at her, looking as timid and surprised as they so often had in life. After a moment's hesitation, she reached out and closed his eyelids. Then she covered her face with her hands as wave after wave of sorrow and hopelessness washed over her.

There was another sound in the stillness. A faint jingle of harness and hoofbeats. A voice called out. "My lady?"

She raised her eyes. Cynric DeLanyea, wrapped in a long dark cloak and with a troop of men behind him, pulled his horse to a halt.

"This is a most unexpected meeting," he said, his lips curling into a slow smile.

"He's dead." Roanna's voice sounded small and far away even to her own ears.

"A pity." Cynric glanced down at the cold body as he walked toward her. "We'll see to the body." He gave brisk orders to the soldiers behind him, while Roanna tried to move away into the cover of the trees.

"Why do I find you here, like this?" Cynric stood beside her. His gaze traveled over her soaked, muddy form. "And where is Fitzroy?"

She stared at him, not understanding. All she could think about was getting away.

"Did you come to meet him?" He grabbed her arm and yanked her away from the soldiers, who were putting Father Robelard's body on a horse. "What games have you been playing? Are all men fish in your pond?"

"I don't understand," she said truthfully, trying not to show her revulsion.

"Don't you? Yesterday you play me for a fool, and this morning I find that Fitzroy is gone. Have you told him what you told me, that it was only him you loved?"

"No, I know nothing of him." There was only one thing to do, and that was to fall back on the ruse she had used before. She moved back, pulling him into the cover of the trees, her eyes downcast. She hoped he would take that for coyness, while she searched the ground for a stick or rock or anything she could use to hit him. "I was coming to you, Cynric. Emryss knows about us. I have been cast out."

He took her face roughly in his hands, forcing her to look at him. "Is this the truth?"

"Yes."

He pulled her full against him. His arm tightened around her waist. She struggled to keep her breathing steady as Cynric whispered in her ear, "I don't care if you're telling me the truth or not. Either way, I shall have you. Now I know of an adequate place nearby, where we shouldn't be disturbed.''

With that, he picked her up and carried her to his horse, turning to his men. "Go back to Beaufort." He set her in front of the saddle and wrapped her in the prison of his damp cloak. His arms reached around her to take the reins.

Roanna sat as still as she could. As long as they were near Cynric's men, there was little hope of escape. But perhaps, if they were alone, she would find a way.

Somehow, she would find a way.

A short distance down the road Cynric stopped at what appeared to be an abandoned hut. Made of stone and earth, it nestled in the hillside, barely discernible in the gray mist. Dismounting, he led his horse to the shelter of a nearby tree.

Roanna looked down at him warily. The scent of wet leaves and muddy earth was all around her, almost as if she were buried. She felt worse than dead, her pulse throbbing in her ears, fear filling every part of her.

She should have stayed at Craig Fawr. She should have *made* Emryss believe her.

Cynric looked at her, his lascivious thoughts written on his face. She made no sound of protest as he reached to help her down from the horse. She knew if she did not go on at least feigning willingness, he would probably rape her anyway. And she knew he was quite capable of killing her.

Nevertheless, a pretence of love might give her time. She forced herself to smile at him as her feet touched the ground. Bending his head low, his full lips found hers, forcing them apart in a hard kiss. His tongue pushed inside the soft inner chamber of her mouth.

She submitted to his plundering for a brief, endless moment. Turning her head, she began to cough.

"Forgive me, Cynric," she whispered hoarsely, "I think I am ill."

Cynric's hands lingered on her waist, then moved slowly up her body. Her breath caught as he touched her breasts. "Come, then, inside."

He took her cold hand and led her toward the rude building. They had to duck low to go through the small door. Inside, there was wood, and clean straw. Cynric saw her expression.

"I use this place sometimes." His eyes raked over her body, and she knew what he used the hut for. He let go of her hand and bent to build a fire.

"Are we on your land?" she asked. If they were on Beaufort land, there was little chance anyone from Craig Fawr might find her. Her whole body weakened at the terrible thought.

"Close enough. But you're soaked through, my dear. Why don't you take off your gown?"

Roanna's chest tightened. She hesitated until she saw his eyes narrow. "Of course."

Still wrapped in Cynric's cloak, she pulled it tighter around her shoulders. Turning her back to Cynric, she wriggled free of her sodden dress. She would not remove her shift. Not here. Not even if she caught a chill that would kill her.

When she faced him again, his eyes gleamed in the light of the flame.

"That's better." His tongue moved slowly over his lips. "How fortunate that we happened to be nearby."

The wood caught slowly, filling the small hut with smoke as it traveled to the small hole in the thatched roof. In the haze, Roanna moved as close to the door as she dared. Keeping her gaze on him, she began to spread her gown on some straw. He watched her, then patted the earth floor beside him. Coughing again, she pretended that she didn't see his gesture and sat instead on the far side of the fire, nearest the door.

Even in the smoke-filled room, lust shone in Cynric's eyes so plainly that Roanna drew the cloak more tightly around her. She was chilled far more by that look than she had been by the rain.

"So, who told Emryss about us?" he said, his voice low.

Roanna coughed as her mind worked quickly. "I did. I...I couldn't bear his touch, not after yours. Cynric, I feel ill." She put her hand to her head.

"Perhaps you should like down a while," he said.

Fighting panic, Roanna realized she had little choice. "Yes, I think that would be wise." She moved toward the straw and lay down.

Cynric watched her like a hungry wolf stalking a lamb.

"Damn country." Urien Fitzroy swore softly as he worked the stone out of his horse's shoe. He'd be glad to be gone.

He had been a hired soldier since his youth, but there were some things he couldn't stomach. It was one thing to attack a man outright; it was another to get at him through his wife.

Somehow Cynric had a hold over her, something that would make her commit adultery eventually, judging by Cynric's triumph after the meeting by the river yesterday.

From what he had seen of the woman, he knew she deserved better than to be some pawn in Cynric's game.

They were both fools, these DeLanyeas. Fighting over land he could understand. Or money. Or power. But a woman? There were plenty of women.

To be sure, she had a certain beauty of face and form, and a shrewdness that he admired, but women were useful only for a man's needs, and bearing children.

Urien dropped the hoof, now free of the pebble. He walked his horse around, and saw that it no longer limped.

Pleased, he mounted. He didn't want to linger any longer than necessary, and he had taken a circuitous route to Craig Fawr, in case Cynric should discover his absence too early. His former employer would not take kindly to his leaving, not with what Urien knew. His heels smacked against the side of his horse.

He slowed when he reached a place where the path divided into two. The small clearing, unsheltered by the trees, was a morass of mud and rock. He leaned over the horse, trying to see the best way to go.

Suddenly he saw a metallic flash in the trees ahead. He reined in tightly and drew his sword.

On the far side of the small clearing, in the mist, he saw a fine horse. And a rider, a one-eyed man.

Emryss stared across the clearing, recognizing the man opposite as Cynric's lackey, Urien Fitzroy. At another time he would have been pleased to encounter one of Cynric's mercenaries, to show him how a real warrior fought. But not now.

Now all he wanted to do was find Roanna.

Gwilym had spoken the truth about Urien Fitzroy. The man was a well-trained, seasoned fighter. Unafraid. Calm. Deadly. Sword drawn, but loosely held. Well-seated on a fine horse. Wet shirt clinging to his arms and chest. Fitzroy raised his arm.

With a loud cry, Emryss pulled out his broadsword and punched his heels into the sides of Wolf. The horse leapt forward. Nostrils flared as man and horse thundered through the mud toward the man who was attacking them.

Fitzroy spurred his horse forward. No time now to tell Emryss DeLanyea he was on his side. No time to warn him about his wife's danger. Fitzroy had seen fighters like this, and knew he must win or die.

He forgot Cynric and the woman and raised his arm to strike.

Swords clashed. The horses, battle-trained, circled as they, too, sought a weakness.

Emryss pushed forward, forcing Fitzroy to defend himself. Again and again he swung his sword, but again and again Fitzroy parried the blow.

Fitzroy's blood sang. This was a warrior! He'd been too long without such a fight.

Once more the horses pressed together, their mouths trying to bite. Emryss felt the exhaustion in his arm as he drew in great rasping breaths. He was tiring, and Fitzroy was as fresh as clean linen.

Gripping Wolf's sides with his knees, Emryss tried to ignore the pain in his lungs, the throbbing ache in his leg, the numbness growing in his arm.

Fitzroy struck again, the forceful blow sending Emryss tumbling into the mud. As he struggled to his feet Fitzroy leapt down from his horse. Emryss gasped at the sharp pain in his arm as he lifted his sword with both hands.

Fitzroy circled slowly, fully aware that the man before him was winded and weakening. But he also knew not to underestimate his opponent at such a time. One blow from those strong arms would still be enough to kill.

If he kept on DeLanyea's blind side, he would win.

Suddenly a woman's scream penetrated the mist.

Emryss lifted his sword, his pain forgotten in the need to dispatch Fitzroy quickly. He struck with all his might. Fitzroy fell to the ground, his sword clutched in his hand, his head striking a rock with a dull thud.

Emryss didn't wait to see if his enemy would rise again. Still gripping his sword, he fought for breath as he limped toward Wolf. He climbed awkwardly into the saddle and turned his horse down the path, then urged Wolf to a gallop that sent jarring pain through his body.

Another cry rent the air. Somewhere ahead in the mist and rain Roanna was screaming his name.

"Oh, God help me!" he whispered, the words torn from the center of his soul.

The faint smell of smoke reached his nostrils. He saw the old stone hut and pulled Wolf to a stop. In one fluid motion he took his feet from the stirrups and slipped off the horse's back.

"Cynric!" he shouted at the top of his voice.

Roanna pulled at the tattered shreds of her shift as Cynric rolled off her and reached for his sword.

"Emryss!" she called, the name a cry of hope and desperation. Another moment and Cynric would have taken her, although she had fought him to the limit of her strength.

Her ragged breathing filled the small room as she lifted her foot and tried to kick the sword from his hand.

"Bitch!" he cursed as he watched the door, crouched like a cat about to spring, fear in his eyes. "You're no better than the rest of them," he croaked hoarsely. "You thought you were fooling me? I knew all along you loathed me. But you've done what I wanted. He's come, and now I'm going to kill him."

Emryss called Cynric's name again. His knuckles whitened as he clutched his weapon, his gaze fastened on the rough wood of the door.

Roanna scrambled to her feet, holding together her torn undergarment.

"Run to him if you like," Cynric said, his voice a whine. "You can't help the bastard."

She ducked under the doorway and ran outside. Emryss, leaning heavily on his right leg, his face and body covered in mud, stood waiting. She splashed through the mud and water and hurled herself at him.

Emryss hugged her tightly for a brief, too brief moment. His chest heaved as he drew in his breath. The rain had not been able to wash away the smell of exertion. He was drained, exhausted, at the end of his strength.

Then Cynric came outside.

"Going to kill you, you *gwrtaith*," Emryss said coldly as he stared at his enemy.

"Are you?" Cynric cried. The feverish, haunted look in his eyes frightened Roanna. Cynric was a desperate man, and there was no way of knowing what he would do to win this fight.

"Please, don't fight him, Emryss. Take me home," she begged. She clung to him tightly, terrified that he would be killed if he tried to fight now.

Emryss looked down at her, love in the depth of his gaze. "No. I should have ended this years ago."

"Come and fight me, you cripple!"

Roanna stared aghast as she saw the effect of Cynric's words on Emryss. His face filled with animal rage.

"No, Emryss..." she protested. He pushed her away gently and prepared to do battle.

"It's time to stop this, Roanna," he said softly, beginning to sway, knees bent, his eye on Cynric. "Time to get our freedom."

"Emryss!" she screamed as Cynric ran straight toward them, his sword held high.

Emryss smiled for an instant and raised his sword. Cynric's blow glanced off with a loud clang. The two men began to move slowly, their feet seeking a sure place in the slippery mud.

"I know you can terrorize women right enough, boy," Emryss said. "Let's see how you do against a man."

Cynric held his sword with two hands just above the wet ground. "I don't see another man here. Only part of one."

"Part's enough to kill you."

Cynric's sword swung through the air. But Emryss was ready once again and threw it off.

"Go, Roanna," Emryss said, keeping his gaze on his opponent. "Go, while I destroy this carrion."

Roanna stood as if turned to stone. She wouldn't run. Not this time.

"Come, Emryss. That's no way to address one's brother, even if you are a bastard."

Cynric laughed in mocking triumph at Emryss's shocked expression. Roanna's mind reeled as all the pieces fell into place. *This* was why Cynric was so determined to shame and kill Emryss. His hatred was as old as the rivalry of Jacob and Esau. *This* was why they were so alike and yet so different. Children of the same father. Sworn enemies.

"You lie!" Emryss spat out.

Cynric smiled cruelly. "You know I don't. You have suspected it all along, haven't you?" The two men circled each other.

"Why else would my father watch you like he did? Cheer for you, and never me?" Cynric's hands began to tremble. "Always you, you damn bastard!" His sword lashed out.

Blood appeared on Emryss's forearm, and he stared at it for an instant. "Beginning to understand now, I am," he whispered.

"Then understand why you have to die!" Cynric charged at Emryss like an enraged bull. The two men grappled, panting in some strange dance of death.

Then Emryss's weak leg crumpled and he fell heavily. Roanna hurried to him as he struggled to his feet.

She didn't reach him. Cynric grabbed her arm, pulling her in front of him like a shield.

His action knocked the breath from her lungs. She twisted in his grasp, but he held her tight.

"Emryss, come for me now, Crusader," he whispered.

Emryss straightened, his face containing immeasurable scorn. "You would have done well in the Holy Land, Cynric, using women as you do. I see I will have to kill you another day, when there are no women about to protect you." He turned and walked away, his back vulnerable.

"I'll kill her!" Cynric screamed.

Emryss froze. Roanna fought for breath as Emryss turned slowly, his expression so strange that even Roanna felt terror as she looked at his face.

"Will you, coward?" he asked softly.

Roanna landed hard on the ground as Cynric cast her from him. "No!" he shouted. "I've waited years for this. I'll fight you now, you bastard, and I'll kill you." He screamed a curse as he ran towards Emryss.

"Run, Roanna!" Emryss shouted as Cynric's sword smashed into his waiting one.

Cynric fought like a man possessed, slashing, lunging, his teeth clenched with fury.

Roanna got to her feet. "Please, dear God, let me help!" Her mind repeated the fervent prayer over and over as she clasped her hands together.

Cynric landed a hard blow on the hilt of Emryss's sword. It flew through the air and landed in the mud at her feet. Emryss fell again, this time his leg twisting under him. There was a sickening snap of breaking bone.

Cynric laughed like a fiend as he placed his sword on Emryss's chest. "Farewell, bastard brother, and die knowing that I have won."

No conscious thought drove Roanna as she picked up the sword on the ground. Primeval instinct made the weapon light in her hand. A strangled cry wrenched itself from the innermost depth of her being.

Cynric turned and stared at the white figure racing toward him, her dark hair flying, both hands hoisting the muddy sword over her head.

Chapter Twenty-One

Cynric gasped as Roanna drove the broadsword through his chest, crashing with him to the ground.

"Roanna?" Emryss's voice reached her, and she rolled off Cynric onto her hands and knees and looked at Emryss. His face was drawn, and he was clearly in great pain, but the corners of his mouth twisted with an effort to grin. "Never knew you could pick up a sword. Should have been training you, all this time!"

Roanna crawled to him and pressed her lips to his. "My love, my love," she murmured softly, clutching him to her. With a low moan, he struggled to sit up and she remembered the terrible snap.

"God, it hurts," he mumbled, laying back down.

She began to feel his leg, hoping the wound was not serious. He jerked when she felt above the knee.

"My God, wife! Can't you wait, or trying to kill me?" he cried. He reached out and pulled her to him. "Leave it for now, Roanna. First I must tell you something." He reached up and cupped her chin in his hand. "I love you."

"And I love you, Emryss," she whispered, leaning toward him. Their lips brushed softly.

Cynric groaned loudly, and Roanna left the warmth of Emryss's arms and crawled toward his prone body.

When he opened his eyes, she drew back, watching him warily. "Frightened of me still, Roanna?" he whispered hoarsely.

She knelt beside him. He could hardly draw a breath. Blood bubbled in his mouth, and his eyes already had the glaze of death on them.

"You have the heart of a warrior, Roanna. What we might have been, together," he whispered.

As Emryss dragged himself toward his brother, Cynric looked toward him. "You win at this, too," he said, trying to make his old, cool smile. "Well, no matter."

Roanna lifted Cynric gently to cradle him in her arms, seeing him now for what he might have been. His long, thin hands, so like his brother's, reached up to touch one lock of her black hair. "I do love you, Roanna. In my own way."

"I'm sorry," she said softly. Now she understood how Emryss felt that day he had killed the outlaw, and why the Crusade was no glorious quest. Hot tears rolled down her face.

"Beaufort will be yours," Cynric whispered to Emryss. His face contorted with a brief spasm of pain when he tried to take a deep breath. "But there is a girl, a servant in my house," he said, his voice almost inaudible. "She bears my child."

Emryss nodded. "I will see to them, brother," he said.

Cynric smiled again, a wistful smile like that of a child who sees a present it knows it can never have. "Thank you. Brother."

There was one last breath, and then he was still.

Roanna laid him down tenderly. She looked at Emryss. He opened his arms and she buried herself in his strong embrace.

* * *

Gwilym pulled his horse to a stop as he saw the figures lying in the path.

"Emryss!" he shouted as he recognized his foster brother, his leg twisted unnaturally, his arms around his wife.

Roanna stood up and Gwilym saw the other body in the mud. He drew his dagger as he approached.

"Saved by a woman," Emryss said with strained joviality. "Won't Mamaeth be pleased?"

Gwilym halted and stared at Roanna. She was barely recognizable. Her torn shift, which she held together, was covered with blood and mud. Her hair hung down, wet and disheveled.

"Saved?"

Emryss pushed himself up on his arms until he could see Gwilym. "Aye. She killed Cynric."

Gwilym looked doubtfully at Cynric's body. The sword had gone into the chest halfway up the blade.

"No woman could strike such a blow," he said, glaring at Roanna.

She didn't move, but her eyes flashed with stubborn fire. "Unless the man she loves is about to die."

Gwilym looked from his foster brother to Roanna and back.

Emryss nodded slowly. "Do you still think she means to betray me, Gwil?"

Gwilym shook his head, then his face broke into a wide grin. "I'm glad I was wrong, Emryss."

Another voice sounded through the mist. "Emryss! Roanna! Fine thing, in this wet!"

"Mamaeth!" Roanna cried as relief swept through her. She would know what to do to help Emryss. The old woman appeared, swathed in a long cloak.

"So, here you are," she said, stopping and putting her hands on her hips. She gasped when she saw Emryss and the body beside him. In an instant, she was kneeling in the mud beside her boy.

"I think his leg's broken," Roanna said, kneeling beside her. "Can we move him?"

"Aye, a bit."

Roanna straightened and looked at Gwilym. She pointed to the hut. "Help me carry him there. And then we'll need some dry wood. And more men to bring him home."

Gwilym looked about to protest her commanding tone until Emryss spoke, pain in every word. "Do as she asks, Gwil." He tried to chuckle. "God's wounds, woman, one fight and you're the leader now, eh?"

Roanna smiled at him, but turned to Gwilym. "Fetch a cart along the road. We'll need more men to help carry him up."

Gwilym nodded. "I'll find Bronwyn, and see about some dry clothes. I want *her* to know I was wrong, too."

Roanna went to Emryss, and he put one arm around her shoulder. As Gwilym took the other, Mamaeth spoke loudly. "No, my lady, not you. You need to rest yourself." She gently pushed Roanna out of the way. Roanna stood back, rather stunned by Mamaeth's insistence. She followed them as they made slow progress to the hut, Emryss groaning with every step.

Panting on the threshold, Emryss looked at her and smiled. "Like the first hut we was ever in together," he whispered, reminding her of that far-off day when he'd held her prisoner.

She smiled back.

"Be quiet and lay down by the fire," Mamaeth said tersely. Emryss pressed his lips together tightly as his leg touched the straw.

"Seeing if there's wood outside, me," Mamaeth said, going to the door. "Don't be moving, boy, or I'll break the other one."

Roanna saw her gown, still in the corner where Cynric had thrown it when he had suddenly attacked her, and went to put it on.

"Not yet."

Emryss's voice startled her, and she turned to him.

"Don't be putting that on just yet. Come here." His voice was low and inviting. She walked toward him and looked down at his pale, drawn face.

"Wanting to thank you, in my own way." Roanna knew just what he had in mind as a way of expressing his thanks.

She smiled but shook her head.

"No, my lord. Not now. When you're…feeling better. After all, you've got a broken leg."

"So I'll keep it still. The rest of me feels fine, Roanna."

"When you're well!"

Emryss lay back and closed his eye. "God's wounds, am I always going to have to put up with bossy women?" he muttered.

Roanna smiled as she pulled on her dress and fed the last of the wood into the fire. Emryss's wet garments should be removed, but she didn't want to risk hurting him any more.

Then Mamaeth came back, carrying some sticks of wood and one large branch. Jumping up, Roanna hurried to help. She took the wood and built as large a fire as the small building would permit while Mamaeth began to examine Emryss's injuries.

"Lay still, now, boy," Mamaeth said softly. "Going to hurt a little." The old woman began to move her hands slowly and gently over Emryss's leg. When she reached a spot near his hip, he bit back a curse.

"No swearing," Mamaeth barked, then looked on him with some pity. "Well, not much."

Roanna knew Mamaeth had set the break when Emryss's face went dead white and there was a sickening sound of grinding bone. Emryss groaned loudly and his face contorted with pain. Roanna wondered if he had slipped from consciousness. She hoped he had.

"Not too bad. Seen worse." Mamaeth sat back and reached for two long straight sticks. She eyed Roanna intensely. "And you?"

"I...I'm well," Roanna replied, a little taken aback.

"Good. Fine thing for a pregnant woman, running out in a rainstorm, fighting with heavy swords..."

"What did you say?" Emryss sat up suddenly, then cried out in pain.

"Your wife's having a baby." Mamaeth's face broke into a wide grin as she pushed Emryss down. "And high time, too. Never thought it'd take this long, you always with the women."

Roanna stared at Mamaeth as she rose to her feet. "But...how...?"

Mamaeth glanced her wickedly. "Don't you know?"

Roanna felt the heat rising in her face as the joy rose in her heart. "But how can you be sure? I wasn't even sure myself..."

"Knew by the look in your eyes. Always shows there first, in a woman's eyes. Now, sit down and rest."

Roanna obeyed, too stunned to protest.

Suddenly Emryss laughed out loud. "A baby!"

Mamaeth snorted with disgust. "Isn't that just like a man? Think you was the only one in the world to father a child!"

Roanna caught a glimpse of Mamaeth's eyes and saw the delight she was trying to hide. Suddenly her happiness and relief bubbled up into a gale of laughter. Mamaeth joined in with her high-pitched cackle, and Emryss's deep chuckle was added to the sounds that filled the small room.

Gwilym entered and stopped, looking at them as if they had all gone completely mad.

"I've got Bronwyn with the cart not too far off. No getting any closer, I'm afraid."

Mamaeth sobered instantly. "Not good, that. But we'll manage."

Roanna nodded and went to Emryss. "Don't worry. We'll get you home."

"You'd better," he muttered. "You need to rest."

"He's right, for once, my lady," Mamaeth said sternly. She turned to Gwilym. "Who else is there?"

"Bronwyn. And some of the men."

"Good!" Mamaeth said. "Send them down." Gwilym nodded and turned to leave. "Ask Bronwyn to marry you while you're about it," Mamaeth said as she turned to Emryss.

Gwilym smiled slowly. "Already have." He ducked out the door.

It took several minutes to get Emryss to the cart, and the ride to Craig Fawr seemed interminable. Every rut made Emryss cry out in pain.

Nevertheless, he was too delighted with the idea of being a father to rest as Mamaeth decreed he should.

"Emryss! With Mamaeth here!" Roanna whispered in exasperation when his hand wandered over her breasts.

"Trying to feel my son, is all," he said, attempting to look serious.

"It may be a girl," she chided softly, bending to kiss him.

"We'll ask Mamaeth." He grimaced as the cart went over a stone, then rocked as it stopped. "What is it?" he called out.

Roanna peered out from under the covering. "It's Cynric's man. Fitzroy."

Fitzroy, blood oozing from a head wound, swayed in the middle of the road.

"I must speak with Emryss DeLanyea," he said slowly, his words slurred.

Gwilym dismounted and drew his sword. "Why?"

"I must tell him…" Fitzroy mumbled before crumpling to the ground. Mamaeth jumped from the cart.

"Hit on the head, he's been. Put him in the cart. It'll have to be looked to, or he'll die."

Urien opened his eyes slowly.

Where was he? His head throbbed painfully as he sat up slowly. He looked around at the unfamiliar walls.

A shadow moved beside the bed. The woman, Lady Roanna, sat on a stool. She smiled at him.

"How do you feel?" she asked softly.

"Fine," he muttered. "What am I doing here?"

"You were hurt. We brought you to Craig Fawr with us."

"He tried to kill me, your husband."

She smiled again, and her green eyes flickered in the weak flame of the candle. "But you were trying to help me, weren't you?"

He said nothing as he lay down.

"That's why you were riding away from Beaufort. You had left Cynric and were coming here."

Urien turned to look at her. The thought suddenly struck him as she looked down at him that perhaps there were some women worth fighting for.

"Thank you," she said gently.

"I was going to warn him. About Cynric. And to tell him I was sure you were being used, against your will, to hurt your husband."

"Cynric's dead." Pain flashed across her face, surprising him as much as the words.

"Dead?" he repeated. "Your husband killed him?"

"No." She shook her head. "I killed him."

"Good," Urien said. "He wasn't fit to live."

Lady Roanna looked at him curiously. "Why did you want to warn Emryss?"

Urien shrugged his shoulders. "One bastard helping another, perhaps? Who knows. I was leaving anyway."

"Lynette's come home. She told us what you did for her."

Urien felt the heat rising to his face, disturbed at being found out. "She needed the money. I can earn more."

"What will you do now?"

He looked out the narrow window of the stone room, then turned his face to her. "Leave this cursed country," he said harshly.

"Craig Fawr can use good men like you," she said.

He smiled, a brief flash of laughter in his face. "Thank you, my lady. But I've seen enough of Wales to know it's not the place for me."

Roanna rose and nodded. "This is a hard land, if there is no love to soften it." She smiled at him. "I hope you find love one day, Urien Fitzroy."

She turned and left him, hurrying out of the barracks across the courtyard for the evening meal. The rain had stopped, and over the edge of the nearly finished walls she could see the rosy flush of sunset, tinging the edges of the clouds with gold and purple.

Her footsteps slowed for a moment, then stopped. Roanna gazed at the beauty above, then at the buildings around her. This was truly her home. Here her heart would find peace and happiness.

A burst of laughter came from the hall, and she hurried toward it. Opening the door, she saw the cause of the people's mirth. Emryss was soundly cursing Jacques and Gwilym as they struggled to carry his heavy oak chair, with him sitting on it, onto the dais.

Roanna strode down the hall between the tables where

the people sat. "You'll be hurt!" she called out as the men set the chair down.

Emryss looked at her, his face drawn but flushed with happiness. "No keeping me in bed tonight...at least, not *before* the meal," he said with a comic leer.

Roanna looked slowly around the hall. Mamaeth and Jacques stood together in the door to the kitchen. Bronwyn and Gwilym, their noses almost touching, sat on a far bench oblivious to anyone but themselves.

Roanna laughed as she ran up to the high table and kissed Emryss heartily on the lips.

He stared at her as she sat down beside him. "Going to have to *keep* you with child, if it makes you this happy," he said loudly.

As the meaning of his words dawned on everyone, the hall suddenly erupted with clapping, cheering and cries of congratulation. Roanna took Emryss's strong hand in hers and held it to her lips as he gazed at her, his face filled with love.

He grinned and looked toward the kitchen. "Mamaeth! Another child for you to nag at last!"

The wiry old woman put her hands on her narrow hips. "Begging your pardon, Emryss, my lord, but you'll have to find another nurse. I'm getting married."

Roanna stared as Jacques began to blush furiously. He held up his hands in dismay. "Easier to marry her than to fight with her," he said. His face broke into a wide, happy smile. Mamaeth looked so smug and self-satisfied that Roanna couldn't help joining in the laughter.

Later that night Roanna sat brushing her herb-scented hair as Emryss watched from the bed. The evening meal had been like a feast, with eating and drinking and singing and much laughter. She had enjoyed herself thoroughly, and even now hummed a part of one of the tunes. Candles flickered on the table beside her, casting most of the room in deep shadow.

"Roanna."

She glanced over her shoulder. Emryss lay propped up on several pillows, his leg stiffly before him under the sheets. His naked chest looked dark above the whiteness of the linen.

Putting down the brush, Roanna rose and walked to the bed. "Emryss," she said softly.

He reached up and touched her cheek. "I love you, wife."

"I love you, husband."

She let her shift slip to the floor, then climbed into the bed.

Emryss's breath caught as she kissed his chest, moving closer and closer to the edge of the sheets. He reached out to touch her naked back, running one hand along the soft, smooth flesh. "God's wounds, why did I have to break my leg?" he gasped as her tongue traced the trail of fine dark hairs down his belly.

"You can't move, but I can," Roanna whispered, nuzzling the sheet lower with her chin. "Now, my lord, I shall make you cry mercy."

He stiffened as her lips moved upward, tasting first one taut nipple, then crossing to the other. Her fingers, too, plied his skin, caressing, touching, lingering, before they moved below the sheet.

A low moan escaped his lips as she found what she sought. Rubbing lightly, she heard his breath catch and quicken. Her tongue found his neck, his ear, his half-open lips, his closed eyelid, each touch a flicker of flame and heat.

Again her mouth journeyed slowly down his body as he moaned softly. She delayed until she could no longer wait for her emptiness to be filled. Moving with great care, she straddled his prone body, keeping her weight off him.

His lips sought the firm pleasure of her breasts, and his tongue began a teasing dance of its own upon her white willing flesh.

Slowly she raised herself and felt for his hardness, leading it to her waiting softness. With languid, tantalizing movements, she began.

Ebb and flow, wax and wane, build and release. The movements continued as hands clutched, breathing grew ragged, until their cries echoed off the walls.

Finished, complete, Roanna gently moved to lay beside Emryss.

"Mercy, warrior heart," he whispered. His low, rumbling laugh shook his chest. Roanna smiled up at him, her eyes brimming with love and happiness.

* * * * *

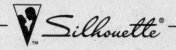

SPECIAL EDITION™

Emotional, compelling stories that capture the intensity of living, loving and creating a family in today's world.

Desire

Modern, passionate reads that are powerful and provocative.

nocturne

Dramatic and sensual tales of paranormal romance.

Romantic SUSPENSE

Romances that are sparked by danger and fueled by passion.

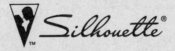

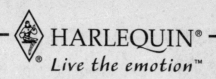

HARLEQUIN®
Live the emotion™

American ROMANCE®

Heart, Home & Happiness

HARLEQUIN®

Blaze™

Red-hot reads.

HARLEQUIN®

EVERLASTING LOVE™

Every great love has a story to tell™

Harlequin® Historical

Historical Romantic Adventure!

HARLEQUIN®

HARLEQUIN ROMANCE®

From the Heart, For the Heart

HARLEQUIN®

INTRIGUE®

Breathtaking Romantic Suspense

Medical Romance™...

love is just a heartbeat away

N*e*xt™

There's the life you planned.
And there's what comes next.

HARLEQUIN®

Presents

Seduction and Passion Guaranteed!

HARLEQUIN®

Super Romance®

Exciting, Emotional, Unexpected

HDIR07

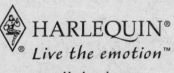

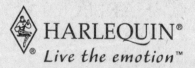